The
West Rand Jive Cats
Boxing Club

The
West Rand Jive Cats Boxing Club

LAUREN LIEBENBERG

virago

VIRAGO

First published in Great Britain in 2011 by Virago Press

Copyright © Lauren Liebenberg 2011

'Lucille' written by Richard Penniman and Albert Collins
published by ATV Music Corp/Universal/MCA Music Ltd

The moral right of the author has been asserted.

A CIP catalogue record for this book
is available from the British Library.

ISBN 978-1-84408-489-0

Typeset in Caslon by M Rules
Printed and bound in Great Britain by
Clays Ltd, St Ives plc

Virago Press
An imprint of
Little, Brown Book Group
100 Victoria Embankment
London EC4Y 0DY

An Hachette UK Company
www.hachette.co.uk

www.virago.co.uk

For Mark, my love, who still makes it possible

Acknowledgements

I owe this story to one night many years ago that I spent sitting in the rough-hewn stands of the Market Theatre in Johannesburg, in the grip of one of South Africa's finest playwrights, Paul Slabolepszy, performing *The Return of Elvis du Pisanie*, which left me sweetly melancholic for something I had never known.

My West Rand Jive Cats were mostly forged from borrowed memories, and so I am deeply indebted to those who so generously allowed me to rummage around theirs: Rod MacRae, Mitch McLean and my father, Ken Liebenberg, who had to spend long hours trawling around the ruins of the mines along Main Reef with me. I am also very grateful to the women, who perhaps lifted the veil on some of the harsher truths, especially Patricia MacRae, Cathy Collins and my mother, Sheelagh.

Few readers will grasp how many dismal drafts of the *Jive Cats* preceded the one they are reading, all brutally rejected by my remorselessly brilliant editor, Lennie Goodings, whose keen instincts and perceptiveness I relied upon utterly.

Trying to choreograph boxing and street fights having

never thrown a punch was somewhat daunting, and I am very grateful to Stephen Castle for his help. While I am certain that I have still made countless technical blunders, it was his passion for the art that brought those scenes to life and infused them with some of the raw energy of the sport.

Finally, an attempt at historical fiction necessitated consulting many tomes, and I am obliged to acknowledge some of the sources I drew on most heavily: Allister Sparks' *The Mind of South Africa*, first published twenty years ago, and still extraordinarily insightful; Frank Welsh's *A History of South Africa* and the concise version by Robert Ross; various of Herman Charles Bosman's still shrewdly comical works; David B. Coplan's *In Township Tonight!*, which was a rich feast, especially for someone as musically illiterate as I; and finally, the profoundly liberating *The God Delusion*, by Richard Dawkins, which inspired Jock's atheism.

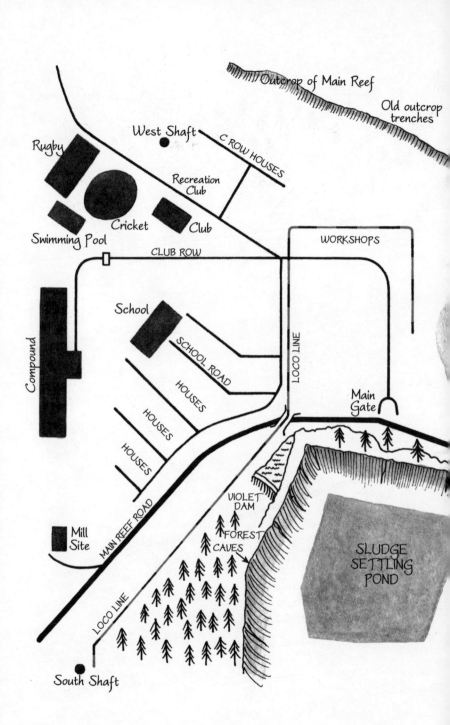

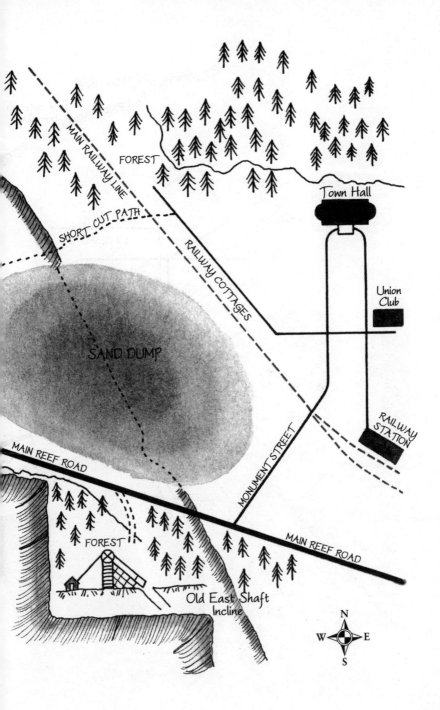

For all of us there comes a fall, a loss of innocence – a time after which we are never again the same. For Tommy and me it was the summer of 1958, the summer we were twelve, the summer we were freed from a kind of bondage most of us don't even see.

PART ONE

1

Elvis

Chris

Elvis hadn't plucked the first chord but, man, I could already
feel the beat, throbbing right down in my groin. A sour fog
billowed eerily in the beams of the projector, softly curing
the maroon velvet that swaddled the walls, the floor, the very
chairs in which we were slouching. I didn't know how I'd
live through the serial and the lousy war flick and all that
crap before we got to it.

We were down in the front row of the Vaudette, Tommy
and me, with Rod and Mitch. Tommy was jogging his knee
up and down next to mine and his lemonade was quivering.
A little had slopped into its saucer. I was itching to tip that
saucer into my mouth and drain it. Tommy got it free with
his ticket, but he told old Mrs Venter behind the counter
that it tasted like they just *gooi*ed some sugar into green
bloody water. He was gripping it now, though, like it was all
he had. Suddenly he wrenched around and hissed at the row
behind us, '*Shht!*'

'Errol's farted again, man,' someone hissed back.

'*Sis!*'

'Did not, man, you lie!'

'Hey! Shut up, you okes! Siddown!'

I knew why Tommy was so nervous. *Dick Tracy*. It was the last episode in the serial today. In the very first episode, the Spider's gang kidnapped Tracy's brother, and the Spider – also known as the Lame One – had had his mad scientist perform a brain operation on him, turning him evil. And every Saturday morning since, for the last fourteen weeks, Tommy had been there, his arse buffing the same seat, yelling and jerking around, firing his tommy-gun at the goons with Dick, '*Rat-tat-tat!*' and every week ended with old Dick unconscious aboard a burning Zeppelin as it crashed to the ground, or falling from a skyscraper after a roof-top chase with his brother, or about to be crushed between two moored ships as they closed in on his motor-boat.

'Hey, what do you okes reckon is going to start next week?'

'Hell, I hope it's *The Lone Ranger*, not the bloody *Zombies from the Stratosphere* again,' said Rod.

'Just shut up, man. I don't want to talk about it,' said Tommy, miserably.

Then he was up there, Dick Tracy, ten feet tall. It was a *lekker* finale. It started with Tracy strapped to the operating-table as that hunchback was wielding his scalpel, but Tracy busted free of the leather straps and there was a *moerse* big fist-fight with the goons. They were coming at him like flies and he was swatting them in time to the beat, his fists making a nice crispy sound – *dish!* – as he hit them. Next

4

thing there was a car chase and Tracy's brother plunged off the cliff. It was Tracy who found him lying next to the burning wreck. As he looked into his brother's eyes, he finally remembered who he was, but it was too late: he died in Tracy's arms.

'*Jisis*, no, man, get up, you *poephol*!' Tommy begged, but it was useless: the oke was a stiff, and it ended right there with Tommy slagging off Dick's mother.

Then the lights went up for the interval before the double feature started. Rod and Mitch were straining round in their seats, trying to get a look at what was going on in the back row. I couldn't help peering over my shoulder through the phlegmy smoke too.

The back row was where the big okes sat and smoked and *vry*ed with the fast girls. Johnny, my brother, was there, of course, slumped low in his chair. Those girls wore gloves and stockings and starched petticoats same as what the other girls wore to the bio-scope, so you couldn't tell them straight away, but if they sat in the back row, then you knew. Me and Tommy and the okes had to sit in J Row down, the cheap seats.

Old Mrs Venter was hobbling up on stage with the lucky dip box. She was always telling me to hold on to my ticket for the lucky dip, young man, and I wanted to say, 'Jeepers, man, lucky dip? Lucky dip?' I wasn't there for the bloody sherbet and packet of pink pellets. Hell, sometimes when Mrs Venter's old man was playing, you scored a ticket to watch Cecil Grimsby and the Serenaders at the Krugersdorp Prison Officers' Club on Friday night instead. That's what I'm telling you, man.

I was there for Vince and his cellmate Hunk. It was the

5

sixth time I'd seen them. One Saturday I watched them three times in a row. Sat there through the matinée, then the lunchtime and afternoon showings. Tommy and the okes all buggered off, and afterwards I marched straight into the town hall and signed up.

I'd spotted the notice on a lamp-post on Market Street – 'Jivers, We Want You!' it said. Entry rules were a piece a piss; two and six to sign up and all you had to do was be under sixteen and present yourself backstage promptly at 7:30pm on the night of the contest to perform for strictly no more than four minutes. The judges' decision was final. It was barely three months away. Then, since I'd spent the tickie for my bus fare, I had to run through town, past the Astoria. We were forbidden to watch flicks in there. They called it the Bug-House.

'Well, you can go,' my dad'd say, 'but you'd want to keep a hand over the hole of your arse, that's what you'd want to be doing.'

I cut across the plantation behind the old mine dump on the north side of Main Reef Road to get home. It rose up like a ghost mountain in the twilight, and, jeepers, that old abandoned shaft by Lancaster East looked spooky.

The mine was littered with shafts, left open as ventilation chambers. There was a chimney over the Lancaster East one, but as it was an old incline shaft, there was a door set into the brick and steps descended into the darkness. The incline shafts were the oldest; the later ones, sunk to greater depths, were sheer, vertical bores.

In 1923, twenty-four men were swept to the bottom of Lancaster East shaft in a ground fall. Only five bodies were recovered, so sacks of quicklime were emptied down the

6

tunnel. The men fell to their deaths still wearing their money belts, so the story went, and a fortune in gold sovereigns lay buried with them. Me and Tommy and the okes planned to find it some day among the bleached skeletons – but, crikey, passing there alone at nightfall gave me the creeps.

Back at the 'scopes, I was getting a bit fidgety, miming Peggy in a breathy, girly voice for the okes: 'Oh, Vince, Vince!' so when Elvis finally got to it, 'Jailhouse Rock', and started movin' and groovin' and going crazy, I practically went crazy myself. Me and Tommy and Rod and Mitch were singing like we were the bloody knocked-out jailbirds. Tommy was sort of gyrating right there in his seat; I was sneering and gyrating beside him. The trick was in the pelvis: you had to shake it like there was an electric cattle prod shoved up your backside. And we weren't the only ones: the okes had gone gaga, dancing in their plush velvet seats, some of them dancing *on* their plush velvet seats – jeepers, there were even okes thrashing about in the aisles. The joint was swinging: the Krugersdorp Vaudette was hot, man!

Afterwards we stood to sing 'God Save the Queen'. I was chafing to get out of there to make it home in time for the Springbok Hit Parade, but we all stayed rooted to the bitter end, staring at the Queen sitting snootily on her horse.

Then, as we left the Vaudette, a bunch of loafers outside flagged us down. 'Hey, you okes, you from West Rand Cons Boxing Club, aren't you?'

'*Ja,*' Tommy said. 'What's the story?'

That was the trouble with always hanging around Tommy.

'These okes from Booysens reckon they can take us on. They'll be here now. We waiting here for them.'

How come it was always okes from the south who reckoned they could take us on? I waited for about five minutes and then said, '*Ja*, no, you see they *poep*ing themselves. Let's go home.'

Tommy reckoned he had to go by his house first to fetch his little sister. It was Saturday afternoon. Black Sabbath at No. 113. I didn't want to go with him, but the Springbok Hit Parade wasn't that much fun without Tommy anyway.

We climbed on our bikes and rode back up through town and across the railway tracks. From the European Bridge, I watched the people over on the Non-European one. An old man in a suit, whose trousers ended halfway up his shins, walked beside a wrinkled old lady with a brightly woven blanket draped about her shoulders and a stack of burnished copper bangles coiled around her throat. An absurdly large pipe dangled from his lips.

We turned west onto the Main Reef Road, the lone strip of tar that ran out of Johannesburg, linking all the mines on the Reef, towards the West Rand Cons gateway. The road traced the line of the main gold seam where it cropped out on the Witwatersrand ridge – 'ridge of white waters', in Afrikaans, so named for the springs galore gushing out of it.

We swung off Main Reef into the mine village, freewheeling past the Rows where I lived and into Club Road at the northern end, where Tommy's house was, though Tommy slowed as we neared his gate. I couldn't help slowing down too. We climbed off our bikes and loitered outside, Tommy vacantly flipping the latch open and closed with his index finger. It whimpered with every flick. We used to

8

cruise the mine village filching latches. Don't know why. We still had a whole pile rusting in our cave in the big dump to the south of Main Reef.

Tommy's road was flanked by huge plane trees that cast deep shadows over the houses on one side and the rec club grounds on the other. The neighbouring gardens were teeming with hollyhocks and those pom-pom things, making No. 113's look all the more barren behind its stark fence – just a severely clipped lawn right up to the red-brick walls.

Jeepers, even Ma, who was always bellyaching about how she didn't have the time to mop the sweat from her brow, what with all of us greedy hogs, loved those dahlias of hers. Maggie, my little sister, picked bunches of them and plonked them into vases all over the house.

Tommy lingered outside the gate, lulled by the monotonous rasping of the hinge. He was always the last one to go home at night, but in the end, the worrying about Cece drove him back. 'No. 113' rusted forlornly on the chicken wire.

Finally Tommy swung the gate open and we walked up the path to his veranda. His house and ours were the same as all the others on the mine; same red brick and painted tin roof, except for the powdery white film coating everything on the gauzed veranda. Whenever the wind blew, great clouds of fine white dust gusted off the dumps and settled on the houses. Ma was always fussing at Beauty to get out there with her feather duster as soon as the wind dropped, but at No. 113 we left a trail of footprints behind us across the polished cement floor.

As we entered through the front door, I could hear the wireless from the front room. It was the cricket, crackling

9

with static. Tommy gently closed the door behind him and crooked his finger at me.

'Hey, Tommy? Is that you, boy?'

The voice had come from the front room. Tommy was forbidden to go in there.

'*Ja*, Dad, it's me. And Chris,' he added, with an edge to his voice.

'Go fetch me more ice, boy.'

Tommy traipsed down the passage, through the kitchen and out the back door to the cold box. It stood against the wall under a frame of matted Catawba grape vines, the water from the dampened sackcloth seeping slowly through the charcoal. It was a relic from before the mine was electrified – ours had been unceremoniously dumped the day the electric frigidaire arrived – but Tommy's dad kept theirs just for his ice. No one else ever had ice either. Mr Michaels ordered it specially from the ice-cream factory in town the last Saturday of every month. It wallowed in the cold box for days, gently melting.

Tommy took the ice pick from the top of the box and reached in to chip ice off the block cloaked back there in sawdust. He left me to wind the chicken mesh closed and walked back to the front room. I followed but lingered outside the doorway.

'Do you think I'm stupid?'

Tommy's old man was sprawled in a mangy armchair bellowing at the wireless cabinet. I could see the outline of his string vest beneath his worn shirt, sweat stains spread under his armpits.

'Do you think I don't know bloody crookery when I see it? It's a bloody bottle of whisky before the game, is what it is.' He grabbed the dripping ice from Tommy's hand, shaking his head disgustedly, and chucked it into his tumbler. This was another thing about Tommy's dad: I didn't know anyone else who sat at home drinking whisky. Sure, Rod's old man spent all afternoon tinkering under the bonnet of his jalopy with Mr Glynn-Jones, the boiler-maker who lived in the semi next door down in R Row, nipping furtively from the bottle of brandy Mrs Wazowski kept for medicinal purposes. Rod kept well away from the garage on Saturday afternoons.

My ma sniffed and called 'those artisans' the dregs, hardly better than the gangers, but I didn't see how drinking all Friday night in the mine club was a lot better. The worst was the last Friday of the month. My old man went down Dorp to cash his cheque at the Majestic Hotel and didn't come out until closing time. Hell, you could hear him crooning 'That's Amore' from three rows away. Dean Martin never sounded so sweet.

Tommy's dad took a swig. 'Happens all the time, man. Where the hell you think that umpire comes from, hey?' he asked Tommy, swallowing. 'He's a bloody Banana Boy. I'm telling you.' He wiped his chin, smacked Tommy across the back of his head and looked up at me, scowling.

'Hello, Mr Michaels.'

'Christopher, I don't know why I subject myself to this. I don't need this *kak* in my life, boy. I mean, Jesus, man, life's hard enough.' He turned back to the wireless. 'Hey, umpire! What'd you do with your six pieces of silver? Bloody Judas! Hope you rot in hell!' He burped. '*Pro-vince!*' He sounded like a cello paying homage to the Cape.

Tommy backed from the room and we scarpered down

11

the passage and out the back door of the kitchen again. 'Whew,' he said.

He was looking at his feet. So was I.

At the bottom of Tommy's back garden, behind the quince tree, was the old outhouse that backed onto the alley. Vilikazi was sitting against the wall with a plate of jam and bread and a copy of *Mining Sun* balanced on his knees. He was the mine boy who came to work in the garden on Saturdays.

'Hey, Vilikazi,' Tommy called. 'Where's Cece?'

Vilikazi jerked his head, 'You open that door,' he said sleepily. Deep grooves had carved a permanent scowl on Vilikazi's face, but underneath it there was a mellowness that we mistook for docility, and Tommy's little sister, who spent just about the whole day long in the back garden anyway, shadowed him when he was there.

Tommy wrenched open the rotted door – the smell of damp earth wafted out – and peered into the gloom. Cece was crouched in the dirt amid the picks and shovels. Her back was to us as she tucked a doll into a tomato crate, her huge bottle-green bloomers peeping out beneath the smocked dress that was rucked up over her bottom. The light fell on the doll's porcelain face, and there was something unnerving about its painted lips. Cece squinted up at Tommy and me haloed in the light. Her brow wrinkled, then she squealed.

'Come on, Cece, we're going to Chris's house.'

'Lulu too?' she asked, beaming at me, pulling down a hem that had obviously been let out over the gusset of her bloomers. Cece was a grubby, pig-tailed six-year-old, and she worshipped Tommy, who was twelve. I was also twelve, but Tommy had half a year on me.

''Bye, Vilikazi.' She waved to him as we headed around

12

the corner of the house. 'I have to go now,' she added, her head tilted apologetically.

'Ssh! You'll wake Ma,' Tommy hissed.

'*Uh-uh*. She's gone to Bible Study,' Cece said gaily, skipping around the house to the front gate, 'but Dad's timing her.'

Vilikazi, staring blearily into his newspaper, lifted two fingers in farewell.

'Hey, Vilikazi,' I called, 'that sweet *gwebu*'s going to kill you, you know.'

'*Gwebu*?' he grunted. 'I'm down to *morara, mfana wam*. I don't know if I'm not already dead.'

'*Ag*, don't make me laugh,' said Tommy. 'Look at my old man – he's been on the *dop* for years, and he keeps breathing, hundred per cent proof.'

Out in the street, I hoisted Cece onto my handlebars and the three of us raced to my house in C Row. By the time we got there, Johnny, my big sister Mona and a load of their mates were already draped over the veranda around the transistor radio. It was Johnny's. No one but Johnny had their own transistor radio. He'd bought his with his winnings – boxing pro – which was even cooler than not having to fight our old man for the airwaves.

We squatted down at the bottom of the steps, and when 'Johnny B. Goode' came blaring out of that thing, we leaped up, twanging our air guitars and bawling at Johnny to be good. Johnny told us to piss off, this wasn't kindergarten, damn it, but we only made a run for it when Ma spotted us trampling on her bloody narcissi bulbs.

She stomped down the steps, slamming the screen door behind her and hollering, 'If I catch either one of you, so help me, I will flay you alive.'

13

Then she spotted Cece, who was running after us, her skinny little legs flailing, and stopped. 'No, not you, Cecelia, sweetheart. I didn't see you there,' she said, much more kindly. 'Why don't you come with me? You can help me with the little ones in the kitchen.'

Ma spent all hours God sent in the kitchen, which stank of great bubbling pots of lumpy Malta Bela, with Maggie and the babies bawling around her ankles. God knows why: what with the wringer Dad got her for her birthday, and Beauty forever scrubbing something to death, I reckon she liked standing in her apron by the deep stone sink, some baby's toes peeping out from under the horrible bits of curtain beneath it, swooning along to Cliff Richard.

I'd told her I'd like to grab him by the pompadour and slap him across the face, but Ma still called him dreamy. It was really Ma I was pissed off with: she shouldn't have been listening to teenagers, not even the drips, and she certainly shouldn't have been saying things like 'dreamy'.

'That's a wedding ring on your finger,' I told her coldly.

She said that might be true, but women still kept a special corner of their hearts for the sins they never committed.

'If I was Cece I'd think twice before going in there with her. There's a bloody good chance she'll never come out,' I muttered.

Tommy, straddled on the low Cherry Pie Lantana hedge, looked relieved, though. 'Um, thanks, Mrs Jameson. Sorry about your flowers, hey.'

'I will wallop your twelve-year-old backside, Thomas Michaels, if I catch you again,' she said darkly, but I could tell the sizzle had gone out of her.

Cece followed Ma back inside, looking helluva pleased

with herself, and Tommy and me headed off to the Violet Dam, jiving down the road, warbling 'Rave On' at the top of our lungs. I was aching to spill my secret, but I didn't have the balls. It was like I was supposed to see that poster. One of its strings had come loose and it was flapping lopsidedly from the lamp-post – even as I read it, the wind tore it free. Hell, when I thought about my name on that entry form, the ink drying before my eyes, I felt like I'd just sucked on an old stompie, my guts lurching with the scrambled brains inside my skull. The thing was, I couldn't dance for shit.

2

The Dare

The blackjack's tiny pincers dug into the soft pad of flesh behind the knob of my ankle. I tugged it off my sock. The shadows were gliding silently across the lawn, the light shrinking back up against the house, but I was too boozy from the sweaty heat of the day to move from the back doorstep. I sat there, dully plucking blackjacks, dark thoughts swooping.

Tommy was changing. It wasn't the dumb fight behind the Luipaardsvlei garage. Hell, Tommy was always in a fight – he went looking for them. That was how we became friends, for Chrissake.

We were five years old, just started school. I was a scrawny little bugger; maybe that was what marked me out. A gang of big boys – hell, they were probably eight – started ambushing me on the way home. They'd lie in wait in the clump of bushes at the end of School Road, pounce on me as I rounded the corner. Cunning, hey? I tried to evade them: I dragged my heels as long as possible leaving the

16

school, hoping they'd get bored and give up, I tried crossing to the far side as I rounded the corner, but I figured out quickly what everyone around here had to sooner or later. They were going to get you anyway, and you could try to get it over with as fast as possible or you could fight back. I chose to fight.

Nah, I'm not a hero. I only fought because I knew that not to would make it worse in the end. I knew they'd get tired of me eventually, scratching and biting like a weasel. There was easier quarry in the ranks of Grade One.

Ag, it wasn't so bad. They'd grab my satchel, tip everything out, shove me against the fence. The worst part was having to get down on my knees afterwards and pick up all my stuff. That was where Tommy found me one day, grovelling on all fours, my chin slick with blood and snot. He didn't say anything, just looked at me. I found out later why Tommy also dawdled so long on the way home. The next day, after the skirmish, I was scuffed, bruised and helluva pleased with the clump of hair I'd ripped from the main oke's straw-blond head when I felt eyes on me. I jerked around and saw Tommy across the road, squatting on the kerb. I scowled at him, but he just gazed at me with his strange blue eyes: dark-rimmed, fading to almost colourless at the centre.

About a week later, I was walking towards the corner, the dread congealing in my stomach, my latest crafty plan to load my satchel with rocks collapsing as they charged me, slamming me against the fence and tearing the satchel from my hands before I could swing it. I heard a bellow, and Tommy dropped from the lowest branch of the plane tree above us, right on top of the mob. He crashed into them, knocking two

17

to the ground, and was kicking and punching before he'd rolled off them. Man, the blood in my veins surged with hope. I started fighting back with him, savagely. I wish I could tell you that we gave them a thrashing.

Eventually they cornered us both. The blond one drew back his fist to punch Tommy right in the face. Tommy didn't even wince, just stared at him straight. Then he kneed Tommy hard in the balls.

'Special punishment,' he said casually, as they strolled off.

Tommy looked up at me from where he knelt on the ground, rumpled and dirty, and grinned. There was something in that smile: it had more throttle than mere happiness. We were still strangers, but I decided in that moment that Tommy was my friend. I didn't know it, but it was one of the best decisions of my life.

We plotted our revenge. We'd get a dog – or a hyena, even better. We'd train him to attack on command: 'Sic 'em, Mambo!'

Sometimes we named him Rumba or ChaCha.

'We'll go round to Standard One's classroom, get Mambo to drag them out onto the playground and kill them in front of all the kids.'

'We'll let Mambo lick the entrails.'

We never did get Mambo, of course, but we stayed tight, and Tommy's smile lived up to its promise. Lately, though, there was an edge to Tommy's recreation; to the fights, the dares. He was hungry for danger, and not just mortal: there was a swagger to his flouting of the rules.

I mean, okay, we all went around stoning the lavvy windows at the rec club and stuff. Rod'd always had killer aim, with any weapon too – catty, BB gun, you name it. Hell, he could flick gobs of paper off his ruler and hit the back of the neck of any girl in the classroom or even one of the thickos who had to sit way down in the front row.

'Bull's-eye!' he'd hiss quietly in the back.

Lately, we'd taken to stoning the driver as the loco ran under the culvert below the Violet Dam, but for Tommy, even that was getting too tame. It was his cock-eyed idea to lay stones on the tracks as they ran out of South Shaft where once we had flattened pennies.

Down in the mine, the locos hauled long trains of coco-pans on the underground rail to the nearest ore pass, where the ore was tipped out to find its way to the bottom. They'd replaced mules back in the twenties. Dad said the poor beasts spent their whole lives down there – they were blinded by the light if they ever came up.

I had a bad feeling when I saw that row of goddamn rocks. I squatted down and grasped the iron rail, held it while it blistered the flesh on my palm. Then I felt the vibrations strum through my fingers.

'Train coming!' I yelped, and we hurtled down the shallow embankment and bunkered in the ditch fifty yards or so away from the site of the booby trap.

Pressed against the cinders, my blood boiling, sick fear mingled with – God forgive me – the buzz, as the noise of the engine grew louder. Just as the loco came into view, I turned to look at Tommy, his blue eyes brilliant with excitement. The little train came jogging on down the track to the crushers, struck Tommy's rocks, and derailed with a shower of sparks and a squeal that spanked the air into a million pieces. The cocopans toppled and ruptured their ore loads.

For a moment after it happened, we lay there completely addled. I found myself kneeling in prayer, my hands clamped over my ears. When I opened my fingers, the air still sang with the aftershock. Then the guard boy's whistle blew. Tommy grabbed me by the shirt and tried to pull me after him. I looked up and saw the others running hell for leather down the tracks. The guard leaped off the back of the last cocopan, which had decoupled from the rest and still stood – somehow obscenely – on the track, and gave chase, but I couldn't run. I staggered and Tommy pulled ahead of me. I felt like I was trying to wade through water with a strong undertow.

'Stop!'

I was reeling from the shrieking whistle, pierced with Tommy's maniacal laughing.

'*Buya lapa!*'

Louder. I was limp, feeble with fear. I struggled to plant one foot in front of the other in the frenzied hullabaloo. Then he caught me. Just hooked me by the back of my pants. I screamed. By now the others had veered off the tracks and were headed for the Randfontein fence and the woods beyond – Rod had almost reached it. At my cry, they looked back but didn't stop. Thank God those *broek*s were practically falling off my arse anyway, because when the guard hooked them, he pulled them right down to my knees. As I stumbled, I realised it was my only chance. I don't know how I did it, still running, but I somehow wriggled out of them, hopping on one foot, then the other, to escape the snarl-up around my ankles. Then I was thundering down the cinders, my flippin' goolies flying in the wind, the guard still after me wielding his truncheon.

By now the others had stopped – they were laughing so hard they couldn't run. Rod was clinging to Mitch for support.

The guard started losing ground. He was a grizzled old geezer and getting wheezy. I kept checking over my shoulder and saw him lagging further and further behind as I streaked off the tracks towards the fence.

'Come on, flatfoot!' Rod screamed happily. 'Don't you want a piece of that skinny arse?'

Tommy fell over then. By the time I caught up, he and Rod were lying weakly on the ground, rolling from side to side, clutching their bellies. Tommy started choking, tears leaking out of his eyes.

'Eat shit and die,' I panted, as I vaulted over the chain-link fence, cupping my dangly bits with my left hand. 'And you know you laugh like a six-year-old girl, Wazowski.'

I hid in those woods, waiting for one of the bastards to fetch me some johns. I had hours to brood on the fact that if those pants hadn't been loose, you could've scraped up what was left of me into a bully-beef can for burial. The thing that got to me was this: Tommy wasn't dumb, he was crazy, but to let him sucker me into his shit, now that was dumb. And it was getting dumber by the day.

I mean, how do you go back to popping lavvy windows after derailing trains? I'll tell you how: you don't. I was drowning in the slimes dump when I knew he'd kill us both in the end.

From the edge, looking out across that vast sallow plane, it struck me how empty it was. No living thing breathed the wind that blew hot and poisonous off its surface.

'Hey, okes, you reckon it's solid?' Tommy probed the

flaking crust with his toe, dug his heel into it. It gave a little, but seemed quite firm.

'Nuh-uh,' Mitch said. 'And if that stuff sucks you under . . .' He was squatting on his lanky haunches after our climb to the top, hacking.

'*Puck! Puck! Puck!*' Tommy clucked quietly.

'Grow up, Michaels.'

'*Ja*, and you make me want to throw up, McAndrews.'

Mitch sniffed and wiped his leaky, red-rimmed eyes.

'Dare you?' Tommy said, looking only at me.

I sighed.

We rushed out onto the scab together, my arms pumping, my heart crouching in the back of my throat, spewing dust behind my soles. I splashed into the film of water still lying in the shallow pan in the middle of the plain and threw myself broadside into the slide. Then I was aquaplaning, just skimming the top of the creamy mud, when suddenly it gave way, and I sank.

Shit, it happened so fast. I was waist deep in sludge and every time I tried to squirm it tugged me deeper. Soon it was up to my chest. My tongue was swollen with fear, thick in my mouth, my saliva gummy. The okes had to crawl out across the mudflat and pull me out, Tommy and Rod lying on their stomachs, Mitch holding onto their ankles from behind. When they finally dragged me out of the gargling muck, Tommy kept saying, 'Sorry, man – hey, Chris? Look, I'm sorry. Honest to God, I didn't know, I swear.'

I staggered to the bank, fell down and lay there with my eyes shut. I felt like I was going to puke. When I opened them again, Tommy's hand was on the back of my neck. 'Tommy,' I said softly, 'you're crazy.'

He got a strange look in his eyes and said, 'Skin it, man.'

I slapped his hand down hard enough to sting. Sometimes you didn't know whether to laugh or to cry.

I mean, I got it too. Cocking the middle finger. That's what rock 'n' roll was. I loved it for that raw, grinding pulse, but even more because my old man hated it – and there wasn't a damn thing he could do about it. Pumping out of the café jukebox, the bio-scope, Johnny's transistor radio, he couldn't shut it off – man, that toy of Johnny's let Elvis and Fats Domino and Chuck Berry right into No. 4 C Row on the sly. Elvis would be caterwauling about some chick hoofing on his blue suede shoes and my old man would start hollering, 'Turn that ruddy junk off right now!'

'But, Dad!'

''Strue's God, I will rock 'n' roll you till you pray for death to take you, my boy.'

I could've sworn he was going to burst a blood vessel one day. But it was the music itself too. Like when I heard the opening bars of 'The Stroll', *jisis*, I got that feeling, same as those holy rollers: the music grazed my ears, then rolled and swooped low and sweet as a peach, my belly flopped and my whole body thrummed. It felt so good, it ached. That's why I had to go for that jive contest. Call it fate or dumb luck or whatever, but chances like that didn't mosey along every day. The chance to do something, like the music itself; that took guts.

So we've all got our thing, right, but Tommy, when he strained against it, he didn't even seem to feel the choke chain biting back. My old man said he was bad news, said he was headed for Spackman House. 'That Tommy Michaels is

23

a smart arse begging to get kicked. He's got a attitude, and it better not rub off, kiddo.'

'I'll remember that.'

I gritted my teeth when he slagged him off like that. He didn't know Tommy, didn't know anything about him. He knew him only from having seen him going in or out of our house, same as the other kids – it was all he knew about me, really. Still, at the arse end of another fight behind Luipaardsvlei garage, it was something Tommy'd said that kept nagging me.

He was crouched against the wall around the back of the workshop when I found him. Davie Rabinowitz was in the middle of a huddle of boys nearby.

'Who you waiting for?' I asked.

'Errol Terblanche.'

I didn't have to ask why.

Boxing promoters. That was what they called them. Davie Rabinowitz was one of the worst. At school they'd corner you at Big Break.

'Hey, Chris, you scared of Errol Terblanche?'

'Errol Terblanche? Do me a favour.'

'Well, he said he'll *donder* you.'

Then he'd go to Errol and tell him the same thing. Next thing you'd be fighting Errol behind the Luipaardsvlei garage and Davie was taking bets.

'Terblanche?' I grimaced, sucking air through my clenched teeth.

I'd squatted down beside him. He had a stick and was drawing lazy circles in the quartz-flecked dirt. A stray mongrel was flopped in the shade nearby, her ribs sticking into her belly, bloated with pups. Flies buzzed drowsily around the rusting carcasses of oil drums and toppled stacks of worn tyres.

'Hey, Chris, remember last time?' Tommy asked me, grinning.

'When I missed and hit the wall?'

'You tried to pretend it didn't hurt,' Tommy was snorting, 'and then you surrendered.'

'Cracked my bloody knuckle,' I said, massaging it tenderly.

'Who was that against?' Tommy asked.

'Rolf.'

I didn't forget fights the way Tommy did.

'Oh, *ja*. The German. I fought the oke.'

Suddenly I heard footsteps on gravel, then Errol and a couple of okes loped round the corner. For a moment, Tommy didn't get up, just sat there slackly, looking down through his elbows resting on his knees. Then he ground his knuckles into his eyeballs.

'Tommy? You all right?' I'd never seen him like that before – it gave me a queer feeling. 'You want me to fight for you, Tommy?'

He turned to me, his head still bowed. 'It's not Errol I'm afraid of, Chris,' he said bleakly. 'It's me.'

That was what he said. I looked at him like he was crazy and he slid his eyes off to one side. 'I'm afraid of my fists, Chris. When I hit someone with them ...' he smiled a terrible smile '... I like it.'

3

The Cheat

'You reckon those bloody gangers will try gyp us again?'

Rod looked impish, perched gingerly on the spiky-legged Formica table we'd scaled from the town dump, his mop of dark, sweat-dampened hair hanging in his glittering eyes.

'I'm buggered if I'm fighting them again,' Mitch said emphatically.

'*Ja*, but you'd like that, wouldn't you, McAndrews?' said Tommy. 'Why don't you just fold like you know you're going to?'

We were in our cave at the back of one of the deep fissures that scored the embankments of the dump. An old piece of sacking was draped over the entrance as a curtain. Its loose russet weave filtered the light so that inside it was always dusk. The okes had been trading cards for hours and it was grating on me.

I already had the whole South African and British touring sides for the season, minus Hennie Muller, the Windhond, who couldn't be bought for any money and who, I had come to believe, existed only in myth. It'd almost driven me mad, cost me my whole pack, but I would not give those Kellogs bastards the satisfaction. Now I collected the badges you peeled off the inside of soda pop bottle tops. I had Mickey, Donald and Porky Pig, it was Goofy I was after now. Last week I scavenged around in the rec club garbage – dug out eight bottle tops; six Donalds and a Porky Pig. There's no bloody justice in this world.

Tommy blew Mitch a noisy kiss. That was when Mitch noticed his split lip. It was bruised and swollen too. Tommy glanced up and caught him staring. He looked away again. A tiny droplet of blood had oozed out of the slit and stood lividly against his white skin. He licked it away. I could taste the metal on my own tongue.

I was flipping through the *Johannesburg Crime Report*. Johnny bought it every week. It was crammed with pictures of all the murders they did in Jo'burg – women with their throats slashed, blood all over the rumpled sheets on the bed. The dog-eared rags were the only entertainment in the cave – well, except for what was buried in the secret chamber we dug beneath the floor: a pack of dirty cards. You know what I mean. Rod stole them off some Pole in the changehouse at the goofies one day. We took turns staking out the last cubicle in the boys' toilets at school, and charging the okes sixpence a look. There was always a queue wrapped right around the back of the shithouse.

Sometimes we made fires out of damp bits of kindling and tried to light stolen fags, jamming the butt between puckered lips and jutting our chins into the feeble flames. The worst was trying to light stompies: you practically singed your eyebrows off trying to spark up one of those bad boys.

'How many boxes of cereal did your mommy buy you to get that Jenkins anyway?' Tommy needled Mitch.

We were all a little edgy about the skid-kid race at four o'clock. Any given Sunday we'd race each other for the pot, never less than three bob. Davie Rabinowitz would untie his shirt from around his waist, spread it on the ground and we'd form a ring around it.

'Tickie?' Mitch would ask.

'Fork it over, sweet cheeks.' Davie'd wink.

Davie's grandfather came from Lithuania and their family still owned the Jew store on the mine. The shelves inside it were groaning with tin trunks, bits of mirror, Zam-Buk and whatnot for the black mine workers, but round the back there was an eating house where, my dad reckoned, Mr Rabinowitz bootlegged blue ruin, tanglefoot and hellfire water. Davie liked to brag about it, but his sister Cynthia said their father did no such thing, it was all lies and slander, and told Davie she was going to tell their ma.

We'd dig into our pockets and drop the coins onto the shirt. They'd gleam seductively before Davie knotted it and tied it up to the branch of a tree. Davie offered double or nothing on beating the seventeen-minute record, but only Tommy was heroic and dumb enough ever to take him up on it. We raced each other for money, sure, but team races, that was different. And today the race was against the gangers.

The gangers, or their fathers at any rate, were the day's-pay miners. Day's-pay didn't live on the mine for the most part, didn't qualify for housing, I suppose, which put the families even from R Row down – the engineering corps of boiler-makers, mechanics, fitters, and the underground shift bosses – above them.

They were immigrants, the gangers. There were Welshmen and Poles and Italians and God knew what else. Every time the Chamber of Mines went on one of its recruitment drives, a fresh boatload arrived from somewhere. Okay, so the artisans were immigrants too, but they had an apprenticeship so that was all right. And these days, there were droves of Afrikaners from the Platteland. Their hotel was the Transvaal Hotel and my ma said their wives had to collect their pay cheques or they'd drink them. Johnny reckoned he'd been in three fights at the Vaalies and he only went there twice. He never went to their other hotel in West Krugersdorp, the White Pick – although everyone called it the White Pig. They said curfew for blacks didn't start at nine o'clock in West Krugersdorp: it started at sundown.

Anyhow, gangers would never, ever get their mine-captain ticket, or at least that's what Mr Erasmus bored into us at school. It was inscribed in the Mines & Works Act, which was the law. If we ever hoped to join the mine as a learner official, then by God we had better get down on our two knees and pray we got that matric certificate.

They were called gangers on account of the gang of forty black miners who worked for them underground. I'd seen them in the old Lancaster East mine workers' cottages; they lolled around on the *stoep* in their vests and pants for the whole flippin' world to see. No wonder Rod's ma went berserk the day Mr Wazowski got caught in his vest with his braces dangling down his pants in the street one Saturday. Mrs Clack had spotted him when she was out patrolling with her dogs and reported him to Ginger Steward, the mine manager. Mr Wazowski got a fine for public indecency. After the last race against the gangers it was a bloodbath, if I'm being honest.

'I can't stand it any more,' Rod announced. 'I'm going to get in some practice laps.'

After he and Mitch had mooched off to the track deep in the plantation behind the dump, I stretched out beside Tommy on the mangy rug Mrs McAndrews had given us. I crossed my hands behind my head and stared up at the dome of the roof. Neither of us said anything for a while.

'It's Cece,' Tommy said at last. He gently pressed the pad of a finger to his lip. 'I got home too late,' he said, 'last night.'

My chest constricted.

'Ma,' he shook his head, 'she does nothing. Because he leaves her alone, mostly. I mean, she has to have receipts for all her groceries and that but ...

'You know, when I was a *laitie*, she'd come into my room afterwards and rock me to sleep. She'd whisper, "Don't cry, don't cry." But Cece she just leaves to wet the bed. She's always sick or scuttling off to the Mission for more praying. *Jisis*. Why can't she go to the Anglican church? Maybe it's the stone walls, it looks ancient – the place has dignity, man.'

Personally I thought Sunday worship in the drab little hall of the Krugersdorp Apostolic Faith Mission was a whole helluva lot better than the arse-numbing drone from the pulpit in the Anglican church. Down at the Mission, Pastor Mullins had to yell to be heard over all the hallelujahing and stomping and clapping. There was speaking in tongues and baptisms down by the Monument Dam and faith healings, when Pastor Mullins would lay hands upon the head of the cripple, who'd throw down his crutches and leap across the stage.

The Apostolic Faith Mission was supposed to be a nigger church, born of the slaves in America. Ma always said there was a whiff about the place, but I could see why the whites stole it.

'You still her special burden of prayer?'

'Yup.'

It grieved Pastor Mullins that such an angelic child had hardened his heart to the Lord. Mrs Michaels looked fraught when he said that, her lips drawn tight over her teeth.

'Chris?'

'*Ja*, Tommy?'

'I have this dream about her, about Cece ... the same dream, over and over. I've been having it since I was six years old. I dreamed it again last night.'

I stared at him, but Tommy just stared at the roof.

'In the dream, I'm somewhere underground, in the mine. I'm trying to climb down a shaft, but it's so narrow I can hardly get through it, and it's dark. The way ahead is blocked, the rock closing in on me, smothering me. I can't breathe. Then I push through into a cave, and I can stand again. I can see my hand groping along the rock walls that seem to ... to glisten. And I have this feeling, this powerful feeling, that Cece's in there, in the darkness.'

And for a moment he looked at me with naked eyes.

'No wonder I bloody spend all my time thinking up ways to kill him. Poison. Stabbing. Pathetic, really.'

'What about arson?' I said. 'We could cut the pipeline to the petrol tank in his car. There'd be like an explosion. He'd be blown to smithereens. No evidence.'

'*Ja!*' said Tommy. 'They'd find bits of him all over the veld. There'd be nothing to bury except pieces of gristle.'

'Maybe some teeth and a few shattered bones!' I added savagely.

Suddenly Tommy grabbed my wrist and twisted it so he could see my watch. 'Come on, you madman, move your arse,' he said, scrambling up. 'We're going to be late.'

But I knew Tommy's urgency was not for the race.

I'd lost us the last one against the gangers. On the final lap, with sweat from my stringy hair singeing my eyes and blood smeared over the 'WR Rockets' emblazoned across my vest, I was still in the lead, but as I skidded around the base of the last tree, its peeling bark a blur in the dappled light, I tripped on the pedals and the ganger took me. As we tore across the finish line, the plume of dust in my wake created enough room for doubt, though, that both linesmen stuck their fingers up in the air. The West Rand Rockets were leaping up and down and whooping, and the O'Flynn brothers were trying to hoist me onto their puny shoulders, staggering around, knees buckling, when we noticed the gangers doing the same. Things turned ugly after that.

'You bloody cheats, man!'

'*Ag, voetsek!* We creamed you okes!'

'Please, man. Get off his shoulders! You were bloody choking on Rocket dust!'

The okes were strutting around now, tuning the other okes and whatnot, when Tommy walked right to the front and just stood there staring until everyone'd gone quiet and was checking him. Errol Terblanche took a step forward and stood right behind Tommy's left shoulder.

Tommy narrowed his eyes and said, real slowly, 'Listen, Viljoen, you okes saw your arse and you know it. If you want to fight us for it, that's all right.'

I knew the truth, so did Tommy: it was I who had been staring at the ganger's peeling shoulder blades, at the vertebrae jutting out of the skin pulled taut over his spine as we crossed the finish line. But Tommy wanted the fight.

Viljoen told Tommy the West Rand *poephol*s could go piss on their rocket, and that was it. The last thing I remembered was lying under a tree, peering up at the flaking bark, thinking about how that same tree was going to end up in the pitch dark propping up one of the tunnels hundreds of feet below us, as blood dripped into my eye from a gash above the eyebrow. I still had the scab.

For a moment I stepped off the edge; in the clash of fear and lust that bred courage, in the stark infliction of pain, and even in the receiving of it, a deeper hurt was soothed. Like when he carved his initials into his arm with his army knife. As the tip of the blade pierced the delicate skin, a thin rivulet of dark blood welled out, and I saw that Tommy enjoyed it. He dug deeper. I looked down at the pale skin now as he twisted my wrist and I saw that the wounds were septic, livid around the ragged edges, and I saw he liked that too. I was afraid.

4

The Secret

Cece

I was baptised in the Church of Zion. At first I thought that
meant I'd be good all the time, but I was wrong. Sometimes
I was downright bad, even in Sunday school: I got to fiddling
with Lulu's hair and chewing my pigtails instead of thinking
about Jesus, and one time I was busted for singing, 'Yum,
yum, piggy's bum' in the yard.

Lulu was my favourite doll. I had to spend just about the
whole livelong day taking care of her and my other dolls and
all my creatures. These were my creatures so far: two tadpoles, almost frogs; one tortoise with a mangled hind leg
from Vilikazi and TJ. I used to have three tadpoles – Tommy
caught them for me in the Violet Dam, but one died. I found
him floating on his back in the jam-jar where he lived on the
kitchen window-sill. I scooped him out real quick so his
friends wouldn't have to look at him any longer.

It took me the longest time to tame the tortoise. Each day
he poked his head out a little more until he bit the chunk of

tomato right out of my hand. Eventually he let Tommy and Chris feed him too, but he liked me the best. Ma said she wasn't going to put up with that scaly reptile coming into the house any more, but once she'd taken to her room with her headache, he could've been dining off my plate for all she cared, so long as I didn't make a noise for pity's sake.

She always drew the curtains, but lying on her bed, her hip bones jutting out of her carefully smoothed skirt, she still shielded her eyes with the back of her hand, which clutched a small white hanky. Jeepers, I hated those things: horrible, scenty-breathy-smelling rags that Chris's ma was always licking and rubbing on my face.

My other dolls were Peggy, who was a peg doll, and Dot. Dot was a pom-pom with a sewn-on face. Lulu's face was made of porcelain: it could've shattered like glass in an instant, and so beautiful she just looked doomed for this world. I was awful careful with her, though, and hadn't ever dropped her. After Daddy ripped her arms off and threw them in the garbage, Tommy dug them out for me and sewed them back on, which is how come the stitching looked so bad, but I didn't mind.

After that I hid them all. Lulu's hiding-place was the old shed. Tommy let me use the McQueen – their car that was parked in there – for her cot. Chris told me that Lulu's nursery was a *stink gat*. 'The pong must make for sweet dreams,' he said.

I stuck my tongue out at him and he started laughing.

'*Ag*, don't worry, Cece. I only know what's under those planks over there because we had to use the thing at our house for so long. *Jisis*, going for a piss in the middle of the night in winter was bloody terrible.'

He pretended to be peeing knock-kneed.

When C Row got their modern conveniences, Paddy O'Flynn's dad honked his false teeth down the lavvy after a three-day bender. He lifted the manhole cover over the sewerage pipe and we all had to peer down it while he yanked on the chain back at the house.

I liked Chris. He was nice. Lots of times he'd let me ride on the handlebars of his bike. If I didn't already have a brother, I'd have liked him for one. The people I liked the best were: Tommy, Chris, Vilikazi and Chris's ma. Missus Jameson was her name. Vilikazi's skin was black, which meant he was from the Tribes of Ham. Here in Africa we got them. Pastor Mullins said they were living in darkness, but in actual fact they lived in the compound, which Ma said was a bit too close to Club Road for comfort.

The baddest thing I ever did was to Tommy. How I did it was like this: Mrs Clack spotted me worshipping at the Jerusalem Apostolic Church of Zion with Vilikazi. No one had ever noticed me tagging after Vilikazi before, nobody ever even noticed Vilikazi – well, unless he made a hash of something. People looked right through him, like he was a black ghost, but old Mrs Clack sure as hell noticed when I followed him to the Church of Zion.

Mrs Clack wore big floral smocks and smelt of germicide, and she had a beard budding on her chin. The old blabbermouth couldn't march her great wobbling behind over to our house fast enough to ask Daddy what in God's name was I doing leaping around in the veld with the Tribes of Ham. I said Tommy was supposed to be watching me, and he didn't, he just left, so it wasn't my fault. Then I got to feeling bad about that. I got a guts ache and sneaked into his room that

36

night and told him. Tommy started laughing and said he didn't hold it against me and to go back to sleep.

It was a lousy, yellow-bellied thing to do anyhow. After all Tommy's watching out for me. Now I worshipped at the Jerusalem Apostolic Church of Zion in secret. I had a lot of secrets as it was, some I kept because I swore a oath. One time I shimmied up the quince tree so I could spy on Chris in Lulu's outhouse. He was straddling the McQueen, holding its axle like a microphone, howling about hound dogs. Then he started doing revolting things with his bottom and I fell out of the quince tree and he made me cross my heart and hope to die if I ever told. I crossed my heart and spat.

The biggest secret I ever kept was TJ. It was Tommy and Chris who plucked him from the jaws of death in a sack full of his dead brothers and sisters. They found it in the papyrus that clogged the banks of the Violet Dam. Sometimes, just before I fell asleep, TJ curled into my belly, I'd think about those dead puppies, drowned like the sinners in the Bible. I thought maybe TJ was spared for a divine purpose. 'For there by the grace of God goes he,' I said.

Tommy snorted. 'What people mean when they say that, Cece, is there by the grace of God goes someone else.'

When Tommy pulled him out from under his shirt and put him all sodden and limp in the crook of my arms, I thought he could bid this cruel world goodbye. I hid him under my bed wrapped up in the winter blanket I snuck from the trunk. Slowly his fur dried out to a soft, pale yellow, like my hair, just as velvety as whipped cream. I loved to stroke him, his loose skin wrinkling into gentle folds over his rump.

Now, on top of all my other sins, there was the food I stole from the larder for TJ. I didn't count the bits I took from the chicken bucket. I ate bits out of the chicken bucket myself when I was desperate. Cheese rinds and crusts and things. They tasted jolly good.

Once Tommy gave TJ a dead rat, but TJ wouldn't eat that stinking thing. I didn't blame him, even though Tommy called him a ungrateful mutt. Tommy did a lot of stealing for that ungrateful mutt hisself. One time Mrs Clack nicked him stealing from the single men's quarters. He'd flung the sausage links through the mess hall window to Chris and me, then climbed out, just as Mrs Clack was walking past on the far side of the road. She stopped when she heard the thud. Chris took my hand. 'Just act normal,' he hissed. We started walking away, all harry casual. I kept putting one foot in front of the other, trying not to look over my shoulder, but it was like an itch. I had to scratch it, had to. I whipped my head around and saw her watching us with narrowed eyes. I turned back, but I couldn't do it. I let out a little shriek and we just broke for the rec club grounds, scared and laughing, her nasty little dogs yapping like mad.

We belted it all the way to Tommy's cave.

'We'd better lie low,' Chris said. He was willing to bet his arse that Mrs Clack had already snitched us out to the matron.

'It'll be her word against ours,' said Tommy. 'And you know damn well there's not a soul in this town who's going to believe us.

'Sickening,' he added.

'Why doesn't that old hag do everyone a favour and die?' asked Chris. He couldn't understand why she clung so grimly to life despite the sheer pointlessness of it all. He thought he could hear her runty little bloodhounds out combing the dump.

I wasn't scared of the hounds. I'd bet if a pack of rabid wolves was after us, Tommy'd just turn around and kill them one after another. Strangle them with his bare hands, or maybe stab them with his Swiss army knife. It had four blades and a corkscrew and a thing for taking stones out of a horse's hoof. He stole his milk money to buy it, and then he used it to carve rude pictures on the door of the boys' toilet at school.

We hid in the cave for ages, Tommy and Chris getting into stupid arguments.

'So who'd you reckon would win in a fight between Batman and Superman, hey?'

'*Ag*, don't be a *poephol*, man. Batman doesn't even have any real super powers.'

'Well, what if Batman shoved a rock of kryptonite up Superman's *poephol*?' Chris didn't see why Batman shouldn't win. He figured, if the worst came to the worst, he could mow Superman down with the Batmobile.

In the end Tommy said we had to turn ourselves in. My tummy did a flip-flop, but I knew Tommy'd do it. One day at school, after he'd mooned Mr Erasmus outside his window, and Mr Erasmus said not one kid was going home until he knew whose sorry white buttocks had been blocking his view, Tommy stuck his hand up in the air, even before Cynthia Rabinowitz could. Tommy always had a shrug lurking just under his shoulders, and he sure made me laugh. Once he made me laugh so hard milk squirted out of my nose. It was when he was doing the Bible reading and he said Noah's 'arse' instead of 'ark'. He didn't even wait to get slung out of assembly for that, just walked out the door – slouched is more like it.

Cynthia was the one who snitched on Tommy for arranging the clay-*lat* fights with the Afrikaans boys at Big Break.

Our school was dual medium. Dad said it had been since the Nats came to power and there was bugger-all the Chamber of Mines could do about it. But after the boys had eaten lunch together in the summerhouse, they split up for the fight at the bottom of the grounds. Me and some of the other Grade Two kids climbed out under our fence and sat in the shade of the trees to watch while we ate our sandwiches. I'd peel the thick slices of bread apart and peer inside. If you got anchovy paste there was no way in heck anybody would swap with you.

'Hey, Dirkie, want to hear a joke?' Tommy would start.

I didn't think Dirkie wanted to hear it.

'When the Queen visited South Africa, they took her to see Table Mountain, and as she reached the top, a whole orchestra played "God Save the Queen". Next thing, Verwoerd reckoned, *ja*, okay, he's also going to climb it, and as he reached the top, you know what they played for him?'

Dirkie narrowed his eyes, but he waited for it.

'"*Bobbejaan Klim die Berg*",' said Tommy. Chris would start singing, 'the baboon climbed the mountain', and laughing so much he could hardly strip the leaves off a swatch with his teeth and flick a lump of clay at Dirkie.

Now those fights take place down by the Violet Dam, at the edge of the blue-gum forest, far from the prying eyes of Cynthia Rabinowitz. I thought it was darn peculiar that Tommy seemed to like her so much, even if she did have a Teppaz portable gram.

40

After Tommy told Mrs Tarrantino that it was him who'd stolen the sausages, he said he'd had enough of this *kak* and told Ma. Just like that.

'Must you drink tea like that, Tommy?' she said at supper, and he said he didn't know there was another way to drink tea and that we had a dog, named TJ. He thought she ought to know.

It was one less secret for me to keep but, like I said, I had lots of them. Some I kept because I was afraid. I saw Ma stealing from Daddy's wallet once. She saw me and turned pink and went all breathy out like she does. She hissed in my ear-hole that if I ever told, then Tommy would get sick and die. So I can't.

I tried to tell Ma that I wasn't never going to tell Daddy what she did, and maybe she didn't trust me since it turned out I'd stab you in the back without flinching just to save my own skin, but I'll tell you what, she didn't say nothing one way or the other about taking that hex off Tommy. She just told me to hush in that high shrill voice and fluttered her hand near her mouth. I could see the little embroidered posy poking out of the crumpled hanky. So it was a jolly good thing I had got the power of the Holy Spirit, which is a damn sight more powerful than any curse you can name.

I didn't know what I'd do without Tommy. I tried hard to be good – no backchat or anything. Mostly I just kept quiet. I was good at keeping quiet. I'd got so good at it, I could be standing right next to you and you wouldn't even know I was there. Still, on Saturdays I was in the way, and one minute he was just as nice as you please and the next I was eating a bowl of raw liver. Some things was meaner than razor strops.

It was my fault. I'd pulled a yuk face when Ma unwrapped the package from the butcher's and Daddy saw and then I couldn't say sorry for stuttering, which made him angrier, and then my raggedy fingernails were scraping at that rash thing on my arm again and, oh, boy, that did it. Next thing I was blubbing and trying to spoon raw liver into my mouth. I sat there for hours. Ma left for Bible Study and there I was alone with him, watching me, slowly turning his hat in his hands, sweat that smelt like spoiled fruit popping across his brow.

The droplets glistened in the light, made fuzzy with moisture and moths, twirling and sizzling against the bowl that hung from the ceiling. Already a thick layer of dead ones coated the bottom. It looked like a dark smear from underneath. I knew how they would feel: brittle, crispy. Why did they give in to its deadly pull? My pigtails were spiralling in the mugginess.

I got a spoonful into my mouth, but I couldn't chew. Daddy told me to stop snivelling and swallow. I gagged and dropped the spoon. It clattered to the floor and there was Tommy, cupping his hands, too late. I honked it all up. Tommy stared down at that puddle of gummy liver on the floor by my feet and then he looked at Daddy. Just looked. I sucked in my breath and listened. Daddy snorted. 'Don't make me laugh,' he said. Then he backhanded Tommy across the mouth, told him to mop up that slop and left for the Union Club.

5

The Boxing Club

Chris

Tommy breathed deeply. The boxing ring basked in the glow cast by the heavy crystal chandelier suspended above it. Rigged up in the middle of the former grand ballroom, it was soaked with the sweet sweating smell of hope, and the sour smell of despair. Jock, who presided over it, said it was the smell of gods and demons, laced with the glorious past and its decay. It was the smell of a temple, a shrine, as intoxicating to Tommy as perfume or spices or incense.

Beyond the ropes, the dust-mote-flecked light was swallowed by the shadows billowing from the mangy curtains draped over the walls. Punch bags swung from hooks in the ceiling, like carcasses in an abattoir, their dim reflection strangely fractured in the jagged crack that ran the length of the stained mirror mounted behind the bar. Boxing gloves spilled from a crate onto the polished mahogany counter.

It was a ruin when they turned the old Millsite rec club

over to the boxers. The mine had been swallowed by West Rand Consolidated at the turn of the century; along with all the smaller outcrop mines on its fringe, Violet, Lancaster, Flora, and the rec club had long fallen into disuse. Now it was famous. When I asked Dad to sign the permission slip to join, he said that Millsite had produced some of the finest boxers on the Rand and who did I think I was kidding? He'd hesitate to back me in a bout with my four-year-old sister Maggie, for Chrissake. Ma said she'd have me know she was not setting foot in King Solomon's again if I turned out to be Jimmy Wilde reincarnate.

Again? King Solomon's was the most famous boxing arena on the Reef. Sometimes I got the feeling I didn't know my own mother. I mean, mostly she was just Ma, too busy wiping snotty noses and walloping backsides for either of us to see past that, but sometimes I'd catch that wistful expression on her face at the sink, and there was that time at the Robinson Lake picnic, when the women played touch rugby against the men. I'd never seen her dimply pink knees before. The women all cheated outrageously, stuffing the ball under their blouses and running out of bounds, and Ma pushed Dad into the lake. She was flushed and giggling, and for a moment I stopped jeering and cheering with the other kids on the sideline because it was like I'd glimpsed a stranger.

'You're late for *opfok*!' Doc barked.

I hadn't even seen him lurking on the far side of the ballroom. We hurried out to the quad, which was littered with scuffed wooden benches and a motley collection of dumbbells, and lined up with the other seventeen members of the junior squad, which included eight of us ungraded *laities*

44

between eleven and fifteen. Two years and not yet graded, but time was up. My breath grew shallower.

'His first fight is a rite of passage that no man ever forgets,' Jock had said.

I kept telling myself not to be such a pussy, not to listen to Jock's bullshit, but there was something so damn cold-blooded about it.

Bald except for a flaming moustache, the old-fashioned handlebar kind, Jock was short and stocky but sinewy as a strip of biltong, and gassy with hot air. The speech he made on our very first day should have given me a clue: 'Boxing, boys, is the closest to godliness you will ever come in your mostly wretched lives. It bestows all the virtues you will need in your quest for glory. It teaches humility, but not sub-mission – to get up when you are on your knees, when the pain has taken your breath, when you are blinded by your own blood, and your fear. And though the time will come when you cannot rise again, you will find that there is honour even in defeat.

'Boxing can heal the wounds of the heart, and from it comes the chivalry and pride that stop you hitting a man when he is down. It is the sport of brotherhood and solitude, love and madness, ugliness and beauty, strength and mercy. It will make you soar on the wings of angels and drag you to the gaping mouth of Hell. Oh, yes, boys, boxing will make you believe in God.

'Welcome, gentlemen, to the West Rand Consolidated Mines Boxing Club. You are privileged to number among its class of '58. My name is Hamish McGinty. I am a Celtic mongrel and your manager. You may call me Jock.'

It didn't sound like blasphemy when he said it, but the

funny thing was, one night when Pastor Mullins came calling with a satchel full of tracts, we discovered he was a heretic.

'What the hell is he doing here?' muttered Tommy, when he saw the pastor.

Jock strode forward and offered his hand. Pastor Mullins flashed one of his skittish smiles and took it. 'What may I do for you this evening, Pastor?' Jock greeted him.

'Ah, yes, well, it's not so much what you can do for me, Mr McGinty, it's what you can do for Christ,' he said, with a flourish. 'Especially in the position of . . . influence you find yourself over so many fertile young minds.'

'Look, Pastor, it's my job to teach these boys how to box, nothing more, nothing less.'

If he'd thought that would put an end to it, he'd underestimated Pastor Mullins.

'Would you have these young souls stray from the path of the Lord? Satan is casting temptation in their way. The road to Hell, Mr McGinty, is paved with the pleasures of the flesh. Would you have their very souls on your conscience?'

That did it.

'Look, Pastor,' Jock said, his voice rising, 'I am singularly uninterested in these boys' sins as, I suspect, is the Creator of the Universe. Why God would create the world, conceal all evidence of Himself from His creation, and then incarnate Himself as man in order to have Himself tortured and killed in atonement for our sins is indeed mystifying. If He wanted to forgive our sins, why not just forgive them? It amounts to executing an innocent to pay for the sins of the guilty. And since He didn't actually die, I personally feel a bit cheated, to say nothing of the injustice of being granted eternal life merely for believing in Him and His sin-wiping resurrection from death, particularly from the vantage of those who have been sinned against. Frankly, if one didn't know better, one would think that it was man, fearful of his death, who created Heaven along with its gatekeeper, God, in his own image.'

There was silence. Pastor Mullins's eyes were bulging. He grabbed his satchel, which had fallen to the ground, and fled. Jock sighed ruefully, 'I'm sorry about that, boys.'

'Jeepers, Jock, I'm not,' said Tommy, eyeing him with something close to reverence.

'Well, I regret it. That millions upon this earth are convinced they will survive their own death is their business entirely and it's not for me to tamper with your immortal souls.'

'So when you're dead, that's it, the end, worm fodder?' I said, aghast.

'Christopher, let's put it this way, when I look up above me, I see only sky.'

Tommy gave a low whistle.

'And, since I can't take it back, I'll say this too: there is poetry in this view of life, boys. The sky is not empty. It is infinite, crowded with stars, millions upon millions of them and their secrets, awaiting discovery. Is the splendour of the heavens really diminished by the absence of bugled angels?'

Jock came from a place called Ndola in the Copperbelt in the far northern reaches of Rhodesia, close to the Congo. There were great forests up there, he said, where the trees had names like Masasa. They grew so tall and so entangled in their upper reaches that they blotted out the sun. 'It's dark down below, boys, a never-ending twilight.' Those trees had stood since ancient times, their great serpentine roots strangling one another in the earth, their soggy, rutted trunks lush with primitive life: fungus, lichen, velvety mosses.

When he spoke of those trees, it was with longing in his voice. He'd gone to school in England where they taught dead languages, like Latin and Greek, and he'd graduated from the Royal School of Mines before he'd come here, but he said it was time for him to come out of the bowels of the earth and bask in the sunlight. Jock loved warriors and poetry.

Doc's blasts on the whistle conducted the drill, which ended in wind-sprints punctuated with enough sets of sit-ups and push-ups to make you vomit. Doc reckoned the gut muscles had to be as hard as a machine boy's. He had been a ganger in his past, and he swore that some of his machine boys could rest the hundred-and-thirty-pound jackhammer against their stomachs while they were drilling. 'You could bust your bloody knuckles on those muscles,' he said grimly.

Before the machines, drilling was done by hand. The boys would hammer in unison, Doc said, chanting. 'Their favourite was "*Isiburu Chigwani*" – "The White Man Is a Fool",' he told us, laughing, his face creasing around the waxy scar tissue over his brows.

Doc was pairing off sparring partners and I gloved up. *Jis*, I loved the feeling of my hands swaddled in those Invincibles. Jock made us wear ten-ouncers. 'I don't want any kid getting hurt in my gym, do you hear me?' he'd say.

I didn't think Doc would have such a problem with it. He was a good trainer, though, Doc.

'Rodney, come here, my boy, you're up with Christopher.'

'Rod, Mr Groenewald, it's Rod.'

'Doesn't no one ever call you Rodney?'

'No.'

'I knew a Rodney once. Rodney the Rotter, they called him. Grease monkey on the railways, or maybe he had his shunting ticket. Chased after girlies. Looked like bloody Paul Newman, I'm telling you. Came from a pig farm in Rustenberg. *Jisis*, there was broken hearts lying smashed on the tracks from here to Springs. One day, he just dropped dead. Syphilis, they said. Or was it gonorrhoea? Rodney the Rotter, till his *slang* rotted right off.

'Come on, Christopher, make him chase you, make him work for it,' he said, leaning on the ropes.

I was back-pedalling round the ring, weaving and ducking. From the first day he'd allowed us into the ring, Doc had concentrated on defence. 'If he can't hit you, you can't go down, got it?'

It was hardly what I'd bloody waited for for so long. Doc had punished us for months before we were allowed to climb through those ropes. Hell, I spent hours skipping and shadow boxing. I practised on the punch bag until I reckon I was running through the whole gamut of punches in my sleep: uppercut; right cross; straight left. I did it all just to get into that ring, but the speed ball I genuinely loved.

It was the hardest thing to crack. Like the jump rope, the speed ball was all about balance, switching your weight from one foot to the other quicker than you could blink. Jock showed us only once. 'Count with me, boys. One, two, three, four,' he said, clicking his fingers. 'Now, I drive my left fist straight through on the count of one, my weight on my right foot. Then I rock over to my left on two, and punch the bag with the butt of my left fist, like I'm sticking it with a knife.

Then I drive through with my right fist on three, my weight still on my left. Now I rock back over to my right foot and knife it with my right on four.'

He speeded up slightly and I could see how the bag moved in a figure of eight.

'Watch my hips swivel as I shift from foot to foot. *Gluteus maximus* is where the power comes from, understand?'

'You mean the arse?' Rod asked gleefully.

There was a snigger from the junior squad. Jock shifted into high gear, hitting the bag in a steady four count that had it smacking the platform in an unbroken rhythm, his waist twisting with every punch as he moved his feet in a half-circle beneath the platform and back again. The bag was a blur. When he stepped away, he was breathing easily.

I started on the ball screwed into the specially lowered platform, going haltingly through the motions, until the switch in balance became more fluid, and I was able to speed up. I can flurry it like a pro now. I stand there in front of it, the ball a blur in front of my gloves, lost in the lovely *tut*-tut-tut, *tut*-tut-tut, *tut*-tut-tut, *tut*-tut-tut of leather on leather.

Anyway, to make it into the ring only to get told I must pass the time bobbing in and out like a bloody blowfly seemed pathetic, but you had to trust Doc. He was once a prize fighter.

When he'd first come to Johannesburg – been driven, he said, by the English.

'In those days, there were grogshops on every corner, a whorehouse around the back and, man, the whole place was devoted to the vice of gambling. There was horse-racing, cock-fighting, cards and dice. Kruger always said the gold was a gift from Satan, and I tell you, it's a wonderful kind of city that men build once the Devil has truly taken a hold of them.'

He sighed. 'In 1914, I made three pounds ten shillings on my first fight. I was seventeen years old and I never looked back. Hell, after a few years, I had quite a name on the Reef. I knew it when the okes started throwing fights with me. One night, in a fixed fight with Freddie Battalino, *ou* Battalino lay down in the third round. *Sommer* stretched out right there on the floor of the ring. Ref says, "Get up!" Battalino told him to count.' Doc was laughing so hard, he nearly fell off the apron. 'The crowd were chanting, "Fix! Fix!" The din was terrible, man. I remember looking across Pat Flannigan's beer hall to this lamp Flannigan had hoisted onto the bar counter. The stem was a statue of a woman, classical, draped in a toga, bearing a torch aloft. Hell, she looked bizarre, all gilt and ebony reflected in the mirror behind the bar, illuminating the pack of men braying like rabid dogs. Battalino was persuaded at gunpoint to finish the ten rounds.'

So when Doc told me I had to play the Artful Dodger in the ring, I didn't argue. And I loved him for these stories, for making us members of the fancy. I begged for more. 'So what happened, Mr Groenewald?'

'His seconds watered him down with Castle Draft and he came out fighting dirty. Low blows and a foul mouth.' Doc puckered up. '"I kiss your mama,"' he said. 'He socked me in the balls and I sagged against the ropes, got burns where I slipped out of his reach. He thought I was still off balance and charged, but I was waiting for him.' He laughed throatily. 'I pivoted, then jammed my right hook straight into the bastard's sciatic nerve in his arse. He thought he was going to die.

'You never start this *kak*, but when a fighter steps outside of the Queensberry Rules, you do what you got to do to get respect. And the fight game, boys, is all about getting respect.'

Jock wouldn't even talk dirty. When we asked him to teach us a few tricks, he told us it weakened a boxer. 'No, boys, once a boxer becomes a street fighter, he gets sloppy, loses his speed. In the end, street fighting corrupts the soul of a boxer.'

But he wasn't the one who had to face Fats Vorster in the change-house at the goofies. He waited for you in there with his goons. They'd jump you, hold you down, pull your trunks off and yank your thingy. Sometimes they shoved your head down the bog too. The water gushed up your nose as they flushed.

Doc blew the whistle to end the sparring match. 'Nice work, boys, nice work. I reckon you might even be ready for your first real bout in the ring. It's a shame you've never seen a real fight in your life, though.'

'You ought to come down to the Luipaardsvlei garage some time,' Rod chirped.

'Oh, *ja*, sorry,' said Doc, pityingly. 'You don't need to bother to turn up at the rugby field on Saturday night, then.'

I looked up sharply. The jabber around the ring died.

He was leaning casually against the ropes, looking down at the squad who'd closed in around us. 'They call him a joke, man, but I reckon, *ja*, I reckon he might just have one last fight in him. If you want to find out why Hamish McGinty's ring name was Stout, then get your arses to the ring that will sprout in the middle of the rugby pitch between now and Saturday night after the fête. Make sure you stay under the stands. We're going to give those book-ies a proper snotty.'

6

The Mine

'I would not want to find myself with those toes dangling off my feet when your father gets home,' Ma remarked tartly to Mona.

Neither did I. I didn't want anything spoiling Friday night. The cold bath and the smoked snoek were bad enough. The bathwater, heated weakly by the geyser mounted over the cast-iron stove in the kitchen, turned cold after a few minutes anyway, and by the time I got to perforate the scum with my bottom and wallow miserably in its two inches for a few minutes, it was downright cold, and worse on Friday nights because of the hair-washing that went on.

Ma turned back to the stove and snatched up the curling tongs; mean-looking things, blackened from the fire. Her hands were gloved, but Mona's scalp was spared nothing. She screamed as the tongs grazed her skin again. Maggie was perched sulkily on Mona's lap. She had to sit in front of the stove waiting for her hair to dry. She started screaming too as Mona brushed it out, so that Ma could do it up in rags. Our kitchen was a hair torture chamber. Ma and Mrs O'Flynn from next door had spent all afternoon perming each other's.

'Ooh, Peggy, I love it!'

I wrinkled my nose. 'I'd think twice before dousing my head in that stuff. The smell alone could strip paint.'

'Perming lotion is the only thing that separates us from men and the animals,' Ma said. 'There is no such thing as natural beauty.'

'And we can't all waddle off to Bombshells every week, like some I know,' said Mrs O'Flynn, sourly.

She meant Mrs McAndrews. Mr O'Flynn was a mine captain, same as my old man, and apparently that meant perming your own hair.

'Well, I'm not sorry,' said Ma, 'looking at that frightful poodle do she's sporting. That's what she told me it's called, by the way – right before she told me how much it cost. And instead of telling her I was blooming relieved I couldn't afford it then, I just smiled at the sow before I could help myself.'

'That's because you were brought up right, Peggy. A Row doesn't equate to class. I've seen her at church without gloves, you know.'

'Well, it could've been worse,' said Ma. 'She could've left home without her girdle.'

And the two of them fell on the floor, laughing.

Mitch once admitted his ma took him to Bombshells for his crew cut. Rod had looked ill. Then he'd licked his lips. '*Bombshells?*' he'd said hoarsely. '*Bombshells?* What's the matter with you, man? I would never, but never, agree to have my hair cut if I knew my ma was taking me to bloody Bombshells. I'd sooner die than go to Bombshells. And if I *had*, I'd chop off my own balls before I admitted I'd been in there.'

Mitch had said there was nothing he could do: Mr Erasmus had sent a letter to parents banning duck-butts on account of the fact that they interfered with physical training and were attended by a lamentable disregard for attire, including shoes, and at times, a sullen look.

Rod told Mitch that he must never speak of it again. But on the day of Mrs McAndrews' next appointment, a surging crowd was pressed up against the Bombshells window. Anyone who'd ever known Mitch turned up – hell, okes who'd never met him turned up. Dirkie and his gang had sworn to be there. In the end, the glass of the shop front was so grimy from greasy fingers and thrusting tongues you could barely see inside where Mitch was almost crying for shame.

The smell of smoked snoek wafted round the kitchen, mingling with Ma's hair. It wouldn't move for days. It was all for the United Party fête tomorrow. Maggie's hair had to be in ringlets. The fête couldn't go fast enough as far as I was concerned. It was tomorrow night I was waiting for. My insides squirmed deliciously. After the long strips of torn bedsheets had been tied pitilessly to Maggie's head, she got a spoonful of cod-liver oil. Ma thought cod-liver oil cured anything. You got an extra dollop of it on Sunday night.

Squatting on the polished cement step outside the kitchen, I could see Tommy and Cece out in the back garden. Tommy was lying on his stomach, a stick in his mouth, TJ clamped to the other end, tugging with all his might. Cece was kneeling in the dirt a few paces away, tending the vegetable patch that Ma had given her beside

Maggie's. She took a dainty sip of her ginger beer. Beneath the sinewy string beans, I noticed a few wilting little petunias. TJ was straining on his haunches and growling through his clenched teeth.

I could see the tender welts across Tommy's thighs below his grey flannel shorts. He finally got bust renting out our deck of dirty cards. I'd also got jacked for writing with my left hand again. As soon as Mr Erasmus's back was turned, that pen snuck into my left, I smudged the ink and Mr Erasmus did not even want to hear my excuse. Writing was a helluva problem for me. I was better off in woodwork where we made lots of useless things – a letterbox, a door stopper once. The girls had to sew peg bags and bibs for babies.

The rest of the time we just chanted things over and over. Mr Erasmus said if we thought this was bad, then just wait until we saw the Act. They did not hand out captain's tickets to bounders who flew by the seat of their pants, that's for darn sure; they handed them out to those who knew protocol and followed it.

Tommy was a lot more cut up about our deck of dirty cards than his sore arse.

'What if your poor mother had happened upon this filth under your mattress?' Mr Erasmus said, as he flipped grimly through the deck, 'She'd weep no less if she'd beheld the obscene spectacle of her son violating himself.' When Mr Erasmus looked back down the long, dreary course of his career as a schoolmaster, he could not recall an abomination as foul as this.

'And you know what that dirty old bastard's doing with those cards right now,' Tommy muttered out the side of his mouth that was champing on the stick.

Frankly, I was relieved. Those shifts in the boys' toilets were bloody gruelling, man.

'I'd like to give her one, hey?'

'*Ja.*' I'd laugh nastily, even though I was never really sure what 'one' was.

I felt bad for Cece, though. Tommy had found her snivelling under the bougainvillaea on the playground. 'Tommy, my *broekies* are wet,' she'd whispered.

The toilet blocks at school had no roof, although the cubicles stank anyway, and the toilet paper was kept on the teacher's desk in the classroom. Izal Germicide. Coarse grey sheets that didn't soak up anything anyway. Girls had to announce whether they needed one leaf or two. Cece had waited until she was desperate, and then her teacher had said, 'No'.

'Hey, Tommy, maybe Mitch can charge the okes for a eyeful of Mrs Darlington when she's bathing?'

'*Uh-huh*, good idea – you can call your business Peeping Tommies.'

The voice floated down from somewhere above me. I glanced up and saw ten blood-red toes dangling down from the window-ledge.

'Just *kidding*,' I said.

'Sure,' Mona said, rolling her eyes. 'And I wouldn't dream of wearing nail polish to the dance after the fête tomorrow. Hey, Cece, do you want to know what *we* used to sing behind Miss Pempraise's back?

'"*Glory, glory hallelujah,*
Teacher hit me with a ruler,
So I hid behind the door with a loaded .44,
And she ain't my teacher no more."'

Me and Tommy joined in loudly on the 'ain't my teacher no more' bit. Cece's hands flew to her mouth and her eyes sparkled.

An African Monarch butterfly was flitting around Cece's flowerbed. It settled and, still gently fanning its orange wings, began to sup. If attacked, Jock said, it would fake its own death, then spray a poison drawn from the milkweed plant. He had a macabre fascination with the insects that plagued us around here.

The front door slammed and I twisted around to see Dad disappear into the lounge at the far end of the long passage. I glanced at Ma, who was paralysed in the act of twisting a lock of hair around the tongs. Something was wrong. Our house at the end of C Row was one of the oldest on the mine, and beneath where the pitch of the green tin roof tilted there was a deep wrap-around veranda, which had been partially walled off for a lounge. We called it the museum. My dad's heavy tread was suddenly muffled as he reached the horrid floral swirls of the Persian rug.

Tommy hopped over the hedge, and I passed Cece and TJ over to him before I ran back inside and down the passage. Dad was sitting on the couch. He'd removed his Bogart hat and was running his hand through his hair. I noticed for the first time that it was thinning and more silvery than blond. He lifted his pale blue eyes to Ma. 'Three fatalities,' he said softly. 'Two timbermen and their boy. They were working in the East Shaft when part of the wall collapsed on top of them. We tried to get down there, but they're buried under God knows how many tons of rock. Christ,' he said, looking haggard. 'Three weeks before it's sealed for ever and it claims another three lives.'

'Oh, Patrick.' Ma sounded stricken. 'Have they told the men's families?'

Dad nodded. 'They're not going to make an official announcement until the day after tomorrow – trying to quash a Chamber post-mortem since the shaft's going to be closed anyway – but Ginger's gone to tell the wives himself.'

Ma made a strangled noise at the back of her throat.

'Dad, do you think they're buried on top of the cage victims?'

We were all crowded just inside the doorway, even Mona. Dad frowned at me, but I couldn't help it. There were always deaths on the mine: ground falls, rock bursts, mud rushes, underground fires and flooding. One night in 1924, thirty black mineworkers and one white had climbed into the cage at the East Shaft head to descend to the twenty-fourth level. They were about halfway down when the winding rope snapped. They say they heard the crack in the queues at the shaft head. There must be skeletons down there by now, the mutilated bodies of the new victims mingling with the bones.

'For God's sake, Christopher, have some respect, man.'

I shifted uncomfortably, trying to avoid his faded blue eyes, so like my own. Dad did not like those stories, no sirree. He liked to talk about the Millionaire Shield, awarded for a million fatality-free shifts by the Chamber of Mines, which was better than God, really.

'First mine on the whole Reef to get it, from bloody Randfontein to Springs,' he'd boast.

Only Tommy and I liked to pick over the gruesome details, lovingly fingering each one, polishing them up if they were a little dull. But Dad would talk about other good stuff if you could get him in the mood.

He loved the mine. He liked to boast that West Rand Cons began mining exactly one year after gold was discovered on the Reef. Cecil Rhodes was one of its founders, he'd have us know. You'd think he owned it, the way he bragged about it.

The best times were after he'd been to the club. He'd come weaving slightly on his bicycle down C Row, his sleeves rolled up, sit out on the veranda and ply us with stories. Ma said Maggie was not to listen to Dad's wild nonsense, but she snuck around the back and crouched under the low veranda wall, trampling Ma's bulbs again.

'Have I ever told you about the vanished murderer?' he'd ask. And he'd tell us again about the mineworker who'd stabbed his white boss and fled into the mine. The last word the dying man uttered was his murderer's name. The mine police staked out the shaft head to catch the killer when he came up from below, but he never did. The police and hundreds of volunteers launched a manhunt in the labyrinthine workings, but he had yet to be found.

I loved those times with Dad, the night sky hanging sullenly over the two of us as we sat side by side on the top step, my freckly forearm brushing his, waiting for the first spines of lightning to bring sweet relief. For a while, it didn't feel like he was out of reach.

Once, Dad came back from his shift flushed and grinning, a little sheepishly. He unwrapped a cloth on the kitchen table to reveal a lump of rock laced with gold. The ore on the Reef is called low grade – you have to mill about five tons of rock to produce one ounce of gold – but sometimes a geological freak concentrates the gold particles into paper-thin sheets sandwiched between the conglomerate and the barren rock beneath. I touched it reverently. Ma ordered him to surrender it immediately. Dad folded the cloth back up.

'I prefer to think of it as a sample,' he said, winking at me.

That night he grew strange: pensive, but feverish at the same time. 'Christopher, my boy, there is something profoundly unnatural about tunnelling miles below the earth in search of a metal that does naught but glitter, and in a lifetime spent on such a quest, I've touched the stuff only a handful of times. And yet, when I have, I too am touched by a kind of madness.'

A lot of the miners sold their 'samples' to dealers in Krugersdorp, but Dad kept his hidden in that sackcloth in an old boot in his wardrobe.

'Breaks your heart, man,' he punctured the silence in our stiff lounge. 'Oldest shaft on the mine, nearly three million ounces of gold out of it, and we'll end up having the funerals the day before it's closed for ever.'

Ma untied her apron and sat down beside him.

'And now it's all changing. We're bloody mining uranium for the Yanks to make atomic bombs, for Christ's sake.'

7

The Corpse

It slapped me in the face as we punched through the swing doors. Hell. Grinding out of the jukebox, the music had a ... a *dirty* sound to it. Men heaved and sweated grotesquely in its flickering light. Millsite was something else when the pros were training.

'What are you *laities* doing here?' Doc asked, without glancing up from his swabs and jars of Vaseline petroleum jelly that he was laying out with military precision on the gleaming mahogany bar counter.

'Couldn't stay away.' Tommy shrugged.

Doc held up a vial of clear liquid to the light.

'Adrenaline chloride solution,' he said. 'Holy water. Sometimes you can't stop the bleeding – the cut's too deep or too wide, the boy's heart is pumping too hard. Sometimes,' he winked slyly, 'it takes another shot from the opponent right in the cut itself to drive the constrictor into the blood.'

'*Jisis*,' said Tommy.

'Blood running into a boy's eye can stop a fight real quick, so if I stop the blood, I save the fight, and that boy loves me more than his ma. I'm worth every penny of my cut of the purse. 'Bout two per cent,' he added, 'especially if the boy's a bleeder, like your *boet* over there.'

He nodded towards Johnny, who was in the ring, working the mitts with Jock. Jock was swaying like a cobra in front of him.

'That's why Sweet Johnny's a good draw,' said Doc. 'Because he's tough and because he's pretty and also because of the blood.'

I woke up this mornin', Lucille was not in sight
I asked my friends about her, but all their lips were tight

I could hear the sax grooving over a heavy backbeat, and now the oke was actually moaning. I'd never heard anything so raunchy, man – it was outrageous. It was like I'd been struck by lightning. Johnny turned and looked down at me from the ring: he had a wolfish grin on his face. Rivulets of sweat streaked down his torso.

'I thought we'd never hear that sweet tickie-swallower sing again!' said Tommy.

Our efforts to crank it up with crudely cut tin tickies had been a total flop.

'Only reason I train the juniors,' Doc said drily.

He hated the jukebox, ever since he'd watched such a contraption suck the marrow out of a bushveld dance. 'It was always Oom Sarel's fingers that breathed life into the dances. When they swept over his concertina in the *vastrap*, you couldn't keep your feet still, man. There was still dancing in the *voorhuis*, peach brandy in the kitchen, but when Jan Cruywagen ripped off the green curtain he'd draped over that gramophone, Oom Sarel said, in that case, he'd never again play at a dance. It wasn't easy for me to think about the bushveld dances of the future after that.

'*Ou* Cruywagen was getting altogether too many ideas about himself, turning up wearing a collar he'd ordered from the Indian store. I wasn't jealous, you understand, I was only annoyed that a person such as Jan Cruywagen was making a fool of himself by wearing a ridiculous thing like a collar.

'I pointed out to him that the gramophone did not play "Sarie Marais", and nor did it play "Vat Jou Goed en Trek, Ferreira". Then I asked him if it wasn't very strangulating sitting there like that with a noose around his neck, and if he knew the reason why his peach brandy tasted like piss next to the *mampoer* I distilled from the maroelas.'

He was chuckling.

'Jan Cruywagen said I was a Philistine. His language was hotter than anything I had ever heard – except once, and that was when Stoffel van der Merwe said what he thought of Cronje's surrender to the English at Paardeberg. I'm only glad Oom Sarel never lived to hear the likes of this.'

'Head first, Johnny!' Jock shouted.

'If you want to hit your opponent in the body, go to the head first, that's to get him to lift his hands, see?' Doc explained. 'If you want to go to the head, hurt the body to get the hands down. Trick him. The fight game is like poker. You have to know how to lie.'

'When are you going to teach us how to fight like that, Mr Groenewald? To attack.'

Doc looked at Tommy. 'Glove up.'

He was waiting for us in the ring when we got back. Jock was on the apron.

'Okay, Chris, you're up first.'

As I swung under the ropes, Doc retreated to a corner and crouched down.

'Okay, Chris, let's see what you can do.'

Me and Johnny looked at him in disbelief.

'*Ag*, I didn't tell *you* to hit *him*, did I? Just hit him, Chris, now!'

Johnny shrugged at me. There was a snolly dangling from his left nostril. I hit him with my straight right. He didn't even flinch. The snolly quivered a little, but that was it. He smirked. I felt like I was down behind the Luipaardsvlei garage.

I started throwing frenzied punches. I was grunting and sweating, my carefully sculpted *kuif* plastered damply to my forehead, but my blows just glanced off Johnny's gloves.

'Slow down, Chris,' Doc urged. 'Get your balance first and the speed will come.'

'With balance comes leverage, with leverage comes speed, with speed comes power.' Jock's voice resonated around the ring. 'It's balance behind power, Christopher, not muscle. Get your stance right, stay on the balls of your feet, slow down, let *him* tell you when to punch him. You'll find your reach.'

It had a way of penetrating, Jock's voice. It could drop to a whisper and you could still hear it. Man, you could hear it when he wasn't even there.

I closed my eyes, slowed down. The music throbbed in my veins, and I began to move rhythmically, springing off the balls of my feet, shifting my weight smoothly. Then I rocked forwards to generate momentum off my big toe, throwing the full weight of my body behind the punch. The jab caught Johnny right in the middle of the solar plexus and I could feel my glove sinking into the relaxed muscles, winding him with a *lekker* 'whoosh' sound. Tommy whooped.

'You got it, kid! Now move – you've got to keep moving to throw your opponent off balance and without thump in his punches.'

Jock always said a boxer must be schooled in the theory of the sweet science. 'Tough ain't enough,' he said. 'You've got to learn to think in the ring. And breathe, always breathe.'

We loved him, tried to live up to him, but at the same time, well . . . if he wasn't telling you about all the wondrous things he'd done, he was busy telling you about all the wondrous things he was going to do. He'd almost struck it rich loads of times, and he was about to again. All he had to do was find that volcanic intrusion crusted with gold, and he was on the verge of that.

'It was years ago, we were rustling out of the East Shaft – though I shall deny it under oath. I was blessed, or cursed, depending on your viewpoint, to have been born in a place that breeds rogues and rebels and general moral laxity.'

He liked that bit of seasoning. Rod and Mitch rolled their eyes at each other. You had to cringe for a oke who actually told you he was a rebel.

'Anyhow, we were using the old disused incline shaft that opens out further down the ridge. I had a handpicked gang of *ntshontsha*s smuggling iron pipes up to the outcrop workings. Hell, the biggest danger came from the bragging.

66

'One night I was down in one of the drives off the main shaft when I saw the gleam of visible gold next to a running dike. As soon as I had purloined the explosives, we blasted, opened up the stope, and when we returned, true as God, we found Fairyland – the whole footwall was covered with gold, very fine it was, very beautiful. Doc prostrated himself right there on the gold filigree floor and kissed it.'

He squeezed his eyes shut, shook his head.

'We were rich, until the Good Lord decided to set us on the path to righteousness. We'd carved out too much of the column that had been left to hold up the roof. Two nights later there was a heavy rockfall and Aladdin's cave was buried. I believe it must still be there.'

He'd forget he'd told us some story, and he'd tell it again, except some of the details would change. One time he'd announce that boxing was the greatest of all sports, greater even than rugby, and that until we'd learned to defend ourselves with nothing but our bare hands, he'd thank us not to contradict the one-time holder of the Northern Transvaal welterweight title. The next he'd tell us he almost made it to the nationals in '32, but was beaten on points in the Northern Transvaal championships. Bloke from Witbank Colleries – 'Bastard,' he spat.

If you ever called him on stuff, he'd look wounded and ask, 'Have I ever lied to you?' It was the same with the promises he made – except if you counted the empty ones.

'Okay, Chris, that's enough,' Doc shouted.

The music was pumping louder and I looked across to where Rod and Mitch were jiving in front of the jukebox, twisting and grinding across the sprung floor of the forsaken grand ballroom of the Millsite rec club.

'*Jisis*, it's a pity you okes can't dance, though, hey?' Doc said, grimacing. 'You *laities* can bugger off now. We've got a fight in six hours!'

Trudging back along the ridge, I couldn't pull my eyes away from the East Shaft headgear that hulked like some great mechanical insect poised to suck the blood out of the earth.

'Come on, Mitch, we've got no bread, china. The bookies don't take IOUs.'

'Hey, you okes want to know a secret?' The words just fell out of my mouth.

'*Ag*, come off it, Tommy, you honestly think you can hustle the okes for a gawp at Mrs Darlington's bottom?'

'The profits on bare flesh are endless, you poor schmuck, and that it's never occurred to you to exploit that bathroom window next door fills me with a mixture of pity and disgust. You're going to wind up just another grunt, stuck down that hole in the ground. Please, let me teach you how to put two and two together to make, I don' know, about a million bucks – we'll go into partnership. We'll need someone to do the dog work and someone to handle the money.'

Mitch shook his head in disbelief. 'Do you think the okes have forgotten how you gypped them at the ladies' change-house? Two and six it cost me, "no wanking", you said. *Jisis*, I've been trying to forget what I saw in there ever since, but at night, when I close my eyes ...' he shuddered '... Mrs Clack's blubbering arse is burned onto my eyeballs. The lesson I learned on top of that ladder is that some people won't think twice about blinding you for life if there's a quick buck in it for them.' He drove his fist into his palm for emphasis.

'Will you lot cut the gas?' I said. 'Do you want to know about a *bona fide* hush-up or not?'

'You're full of shit, Chris.'

'*Ja*, you like to lick shit, and there's three dead bodies in the East Shaft and nobody knows about it. How's that for shit?'

I felt a little queasy now that I'd blurted it out. I started garbling on about the accident to quell it. When I'd finished, Tommy walked off.

'*Ag*, come on,' he said scathingly, over his shoulder. 'You *know* we're going to go and look.'

We followed Tommy into a clump of blue gums a short distance from where the loco tracks ran out of the mine's throat. I scanned the terrain ahead: it was deserted. The area around the shaft head was cordoned off and I could see men milling around by the change-house, but it was quiet further along the ridge.

'Odd man out?' Rod asked.

We flicked our bottle tops into the air. They spun upwards, glinting in the sun, then fell to the ground with a soft clink. Three heads and a tail. It was Mitch. He didn't say a word. He turned and looked through the trees at the tunnel opening into the ridge of rock. Our eyes followed. An empty cocopan was stranded in the mouth, arrested on its way out of the shadows at the brink of light when they'd shut down the works.

Last year on my birthday, Dad took me down the mine for the first time. I hoped he couldn't tell from my face how my gut somersaulted as the cage plunged downwards. I'd eyed the great iron wheel in the wind-house as we filed past the queues up to the cage. *Jis*, I hadn't known men could make things so big.

The old *oom* hoist driver caught my eye from his booth, just as the great winch was grinding into life, winding the thick coils of rope up from the deep, feeding them over the wheel at the top of the towering headgear and down onto the grooves of the greased reel in the wind-house.

On its descent to level thirty-three, the cage rattled past thirty-two other gaping holes left by those who had gone before us – the old, abandoned tunnels propped up by beams, stretching eerily away into the darkness.

When gold was first discovered on the Witwatersrand, fortune-hunters descended in droves. Many came from the diamond fields of the Cape. Ruined down the Great Hole of Kimberly, they scraped together the stage-coach fare and headed for the Transvaal. But they were destined for more heartbreak: the gold was secreted in hard pyritic ore, and could not be freed with the rudiments of a sluice box and a prospecting pan. Once a man had hacked out the rock with a pick and shovel, he still had to crush it and mix the powder with water to form slurry, then apply a delicate process of chemical alchemy, using mercury and, later, cyanide to recover the gold. So although they lined up when the public diggings were proclaimed, each clutching four pegs, and ran at the shot of a gun to stake a claim, all they could do was strip off the topsoil to expose their shelf of the Reef and wait for one of the big speculators, who had already mopped up the *mynpacht* to the farms along the ridge, to buy them off.

Harvesting the gold on the Witwatersrand proved so formidable that no small mines survived either. The outcrops that jutted along the ridge of the great saucer-shaped Witwatersrand basin turned out to crest a series of parallel reefs that plunged southwards at an angle to great depths.

Extracting the gold seam, which ran like a layer of icing through the earth, necessitated sinking deep shafts, blasting with dynamite to free the rock and hoisting it to the surface. Huge stamp batteries were needed to crush it, and even the big mining consortia spent that first year waiting for them to arrive by ox-wagon from the railheads. Within six years of the discovery, no more than eight conglomerate mining houses controlled all the gold mining on the Witwatersrand gold fields. West Rand Cons was more than three thousand feet deep now.

It was warm as I stepped out onto the main drive, the air dank, musty. A huge safety poster nailed to the hanging wall by the cage showed a small black child reaching up to a man's hand, an acacia-shaded *kraal* in the background: 'Their future is in your hands!' it read. I touched the jagged rock that shone beneath it; it was wet.

Tunnels branched off in either direction from the main staging area by the shaft. We turned right and pushed through the huge sprung doors that swung slowly back on their hinges behind us.

'It's to keep the draught flowing downwards,' Dad said. 'If they don't block off the drives, the fresh oxygen is sucked down the tunnels higher up the shaft and the lower ones get starved.'

As I tramped down the tunnel behind Dad, it was the noise that shocked me. The terrible symphony of the pumps that droned day and night to staunch the endlessly rising water, the whining blades of the huge ventilation fans, the growling locomotives that drove the chains of cocopans, was all but drowned by the horror of the jackhammers. I looked up into the stopes – the narrow crevice, just wider than a yard, cored into the rock at about shoulder height – that stretched steeply up into the darkness. Inside each cell, separated by a column of rock, crawled the two-man jackhammer teams. Jammed up against the rock face, the machine boys gripped the handles of their convulsing drills, sweat sluicing their dust-caked chests. And everywhere, water seeped, trickling down the sabre-toothed courses of the stopes, leaching out of the hanging walls, gushing in streams under the raised cocopan tracks that ran up the old incline shafts still used to haul men and machinery.

Seeing it all changed how I saw my dad. Brave. That was the word that popped into my head, like a bubble oozing up through the slimes dump soup.

'Hey, Jameson, this your new *pikinin*?'

'My *laitie*, Christopher, and you better watch out. He's going to be your boss one day – underground manager, hey?'

And the men laughed. Even though it was eternally night down there, it was like standing in a patch of sun.

Dad told me to wait back at the cage for him. 'Sit here, boy. Don't move, don't touch anything, don't bother the men.'

I sat there not moving, not touching anything, not bothering the men.

Boy, I did not want to crawl on my knees down into that hole to see a corpse. I wasn't even sure I wanted to see a corpse – I couldn't stomach roadkill, for God's sake, jammy bullfrogs and stuff – but at the same time, you know, I had to. Mitch's eyes swivelled back to us. Desperate.

'It's best not to think about it,' Rod advised.

Mitch nodded fiercely and ran.

I watched as he sprinted, stooping, towards the cocopan.

He reached it, looked back once in our direction, and vanished into the darkness.

'Poor bastard. My balls are shrivelled so tight I think they're going to get sucked back inside my body,' Rod said, squeezing his knees together.

There was silence for a moment. Suddenly Mitch popped up on the other side of the cocopan and jack-rabbited it back over to us. He hunkered over when he reached us, his hands splayed across his knees, blowing. Shame radiated off his body in waves.

'It's number two hundred and two,' he gasped.

We stared at him blankly.

'The cocopan, man,' he said, flinging his arm back in its direction.

'What the fuck are you talking about? Get your arse back over to number two hundred and two, then,' Rod barked at him.

'What time did you say the cave-in happened, Chris?' Mitch asked intently.

'Two minutes past two,' I said baldly. 'That's what my dad said.'

'What time is it now?' Rod asked, looking curiously from Mitch to me.

I was the only one who wore a watch, a cheap piece of junk I'd got from the Jew store. 'Two minutes past two,' I said, although I knew it lost time.

'That's spooky, man,' said Rod, holding his hands up.

'No way am I going in there again, okes,' said Mitch. 'It's an omen.'

'Balls,' said Tommy, clucking his tongue. 'That doesn't mean anything.'

'No, man,' said Rod, worriedly. 'I'm telling you, you go down there now and it's like giving God the finger. Maybe we shouldn't be going looking for dead bodies, hey, okes? I mean, sometimes, at night, I get to picturing those bodies down there in the sump, coiled up in the rope. And then I can't sleep, you know ...'

Ja, I knew. Sometimes the gelatinous eye of a corpse staring through the murky water crept into my dreams.

'And what if we find these bodies and they're grim? I know I'll wake up in the night and it'll be them miners under my bed, all mangled and gory, but moving somehow, dragging themselves on their stumps. If I hang my arm down—'

'Shut up, Rod.'

Rod shut up. He looked relieved.

'Tommy, man,' I said, swallowing, 'let's just split. You know this is dumb anyway. There's a fight tonight and we're playing kiddies' games.'

'*Ag*, all right.' He shrugged. 'I've got to get home anyway.'

We shoved off.

'Hey, Rod? You know you're too old to be wetting the bed?'

'Fuck your hand, man.'

'I don't need to – I've got your mother.'

'*Wooooh!*'

Do your balls hang low? Do they waddle to and fro?
Do you tie them in a knot? Do you tie them in a bow?
Do you throw them over your shoulder like a continental
    soldier?
Do your balls hang low?

As we ambled across the veld, shirts tied around our waists, the sun bronzing our bare shoulders, throwing a *lekker* baritone on the last note, my mind kept straying back to that last birthday down the mine. My future was a hazy smudge on the horizon, but the thing my old man had said, about me being underground manager, it'd stuck in my throat. That night, I told him that when I grew up I was going to be a speedway racer. I don't know why I said it. He told me good luck, it was nice to see I appreciated my good fortune and the terrible sacrifices he'd made and to go to bed. I said, 'You can't tell me to go to bed. I'm twelve years old.'

He scraped the chair back from the table, stuck his finger between my eyes. 'I'm warning you, shut your gob and go to bed, little boy.' My eyes were smarting.

8

The Fight

Skulking outside Tommy's gate, I was listening to the strains of the gumboot dancers in the darkness. I hadn't yet heard the curfew sirens wailing across from the mine and the town hall, yet a deep, tribal sound was pulsating from behind the high compound walls: the thump of gum-clad feet in the dirt, the pounding of the drums.

Jisis, it gave me the *grils*, but at the same time it got me right in the guts, like rock 'n' roll. There was something about it that was raw, thrusting. I didn't know how they could keep going through the night: the shift started at bloody four in the morning.

You'd see them queuing at the shaft heads in their thousands, stamping and blowing on their fingers in winter. The white miners took their time over a cup of tea in the shaft change-house. When the black mineworkers trudged back late in the afternoon, they were naked from the waist up save for a hard hat. Mitch's uncle was the compound manager. Sometimes he let us go with him to watch the films they showed in the compound.

Mitch sat up on a stool by the projector with Mr McAndrews, all gangly-legged and grinning, but we had to squat on the ground with the rest. I especially liked the mine safety ones about the *mampara* who buggered everything up. Last year Mr McAndrews got this troupe called Lo Six to come up from the East Rand, and we got to watch them sing 'Tikoloshe'. Hell, it was *lekker*.

Sometimes we went down to the zoo at the entrance to the compound. The blacks would sit and watch those bloody monkeys for hours. We'd hunker down next to them and throw things at the cage.

Mr McAndrews reckoned you had to keep the Zulus separate from the Shangaans, who had to be kept separate from the Ndebele, who had to be kept separate from the Tonga, and so forth – especially after Wenela started recruiting Tropicals from Northern Rhodesia and Nyasaland. He said that when they first arrived here in the thirties, loads of them had filed their teeth to a sharp point. Even back in the twenties, fighting had broken out in the compounds one Christmas between Pondo and Sotho and continued underground for days. Hundreds were wounded, some were killed. But usually they all worked together underground: machine boys who had to climb into the steep, narrow stopes to do the drilling; pipe boys who laid the pipelines that wound through the tunnels behind the miners like iron serpents; winch drivers; loco drivers and the lashers, the poor bastards at the bottom of the stoping gang who did the shovelling. Vilikazi had a winch ticket. He'd started out as a miner's *pikinin*, getting his lunch ready in his box and whatnot, and look at him now.

Only the white miner could handle the explosives, though. Blasting was not a Native Occupation. Well, except for the *tshisa* boy, of course. At the end of a shift, the *tshisa* boy helped the miner charge the blasting holes with explosives, then had to light the fuses with his *tshisa stik*. Fuses had to be lit one by one in a set order and started only when the *tshisa* boy got the signal from his neighbour: '*Tshisa lo hol!*'

Then he ran.

Even though my old man was plain disgusted by it, not all the tales we liked to chew over were about blood and gore. Some were about heroes. One time two white miners tried to save the *tshisa* boy when a charge went off prematurely. He was blown into the ore-pass, and even though seventy other charges were burning, they climbed in after him to save him. He was already dead when they found him.

I was getting twitchy now. I'd told Tommy I wouldn't knock, that I'd wait for him outside at seven o'clock. I was here on time, which was a bloody miracle considering all hell had broken loose at my house, what with Johnny going out looking like a ducktail, and Dad threatening to *klap* him even if he was seventeen, and Mona bawling because Dad wouldn't let her go to the social at the Catholic church on account of the Lebs and the Porras and other poor whites, and the babies bawling too, and now I'd been waiting for at least ten minutes and there was no sign of Tommy. There had to be trouble brewing in there. It was the most important night of Tommy's life so far and he was late.

Eventually I couldn't stand it any more. I lifted the latch and inched open the gate. The hinge whined, and I ducked inside. I crept across the lawn, past the ember eyes in the windows, and round the back of the house, darting under the quince tree to the open door of the kitchen. I peered inside and spotted Tommy's back framed in the doorway to the passage. He stood rigid.

'Psst!'

His head jerked round and he saw me beckoning to him from the back door, but he merely frowned and shook his head, almost imperceptibly. We both jolted at the sound of glass shattering.

'Christ, Cecelia! Christ almighty!'

Mr Michaels's voice was coming from the front room. I could hear the clench of his jaw, the fury in the guttural roll on the *r* in 'Christ'. Tiny shards of glass glinted viciously in the soft amber glow spilling from the doorway.

'Sorry! I'm s-s-sorry, Daddy!'

I could see her in the passage now. She was on her hands and knees, she seemed to be trying to pick up the pieces. Neither Tommy nor I moved. Then Mr Michaels's silhouette appeared in the pool of light and I shrank back against the wall outside the door. I squeezed my eyes shut, and when I opened them, Tommy was pressed against the wall beside me.

I heard a low, grizzly noise coming from inside. Then a shriek. Jesus.

'Get off of it! Get off of that dog, Cecelia!' Mr Michaels roared. 'I'm going to teach the *brak* a lesson.'

There was a dull thud as something slammed against brick and then Mr Michaels's heavy tread as he advanced towards us. I crouched down by the outside drain. My nostrils flared in the putrid air seeping out from under the algae-slicked grid.

'D-d-don't hurt him, Daddy. Please, Daddy, don't hurt him.'

They must have been just inside the doorway. I could hear her gulping air, swallowing her sobs.

'Don't worry, D-d-dad, I'll get rid of him for you.'

She was trying to sound soothing, but the slight stutter betrayed her. I looked at Tommy. Why didn't he help her? Why didn't I? He cringed against the wall.

There was silence for a moment and I became aware that I was wringing the skin on my left wrist. Then Mr Michaels grunted and TJ was flung out the back door. He sailed through the air in the moonlight, impossibly high, before he thumped to the ground and lay still. Tommy slumped, his face blank.

Mr Michaels's footsteps retreated down the passage and the front door slammed.

I realised I'd been holding my breath and I gasped as Cece rushed out to TJ. Tommy followed her. 'Come on, Chris. What the hell are you doing just standing there?'

I shoved off against the wall with an effort and the three of us knelt around TJ's broken form. His eyes were closed and he wasn't moving, but as Cece tenderly laid a hand on his flank, he whimpered softly.

'He's alive.' Tommy exhaled.

After a while, though, as TJ regained consciousness, it became obvious that he couldn't move. He lay utterly still, not even trying to drag himself towards Cece as she coaxed him, and he made no noise at all. Only his eyes looked searchingly from her to us.

'Tommy?' she said urgently. 'We have to help him.' Her breath was coming in quick, ragged pants, but no tears.

I cupped TJ's muzzle gently, his whiskers felt prickly in my palm. 'Let's take him to Doc,' I said in a flash. 'He can fix anything – he's a cuts man!'

'Chris, you genius!' said Tommy. 'But we'll need a stretcher. Let's use the McQueen carriage.'

When I spied it just inside the doorway of the outhouse, God forgive me, I felt a surge of savage reluctance to sacrifice it. The tomato box was attached to four big wheels and an axle, with a rope for steering. The car's construction had taken me ages, and such was its strength and grace that we'd won every race we'd ever been in, Tommy hurtling down the *kaalgat* slide in the dump like Speedy Gonzales. Besides, we could detach the wheels and had a nice sideline in axle rental. I had a stack of IOUs for two and six under my mattress. Then my churlishness passed and, without a pang, I grasped the crate to rip it from the undercarriage. The truth was we were getting too old for the damn thing.

I ran back outside and placed it on the ground beside TJ. It was lined with a sheet Cece must have nicked from the ironing-board, and we gently lifted TJ and laid him on the faded cabbage-rose print. Then Tommy and I each slid a hand through the top slat on either side and limped down the road lugging it between us, splinters digging into my palm. We were trying not to jolt TJ too much, and ended up doing a sort of quick shuffle. Luckily, we didn't have far to go to the rec club. Cece jogged along behind us.

Tommy was swearing under his breath: 'Shit, man, shit! Sorry, hey, Chris. I couldn't leave. Cece won't leave TJ, and you know Dad goes for him now because she loves him. She's getting clumsier around him too, makes it worse. Christ, she's brave, though. Sometimes I make myself sick,' he spat.

When we staggered into the rec club foyer, it was deserted, but when we burst through the doors to the locker rooms, Doc was still there, thank God, with Mr Clack, a dark-suited stranger, and Jock.

He was sitting on one of the benches as Doc knelt in front of him, wrapping his hands. He was wearing his fighting togs, silky red shorts, and was naked from the waist up. Doc looked around as we entered.

'Mr Groenewald! Please, Mr Groenewald?'

He and Jock got up and walked towards us. Jock looked lean and tapered, but his shoulders hulked over a stomach like plaited rope. Me and Tommy lifted the tomato crate for them to see TJ curled up at the bottom. Doc looked at us questioningly.

Cece from behind the crate said, 'Daddy ... My dad ...'

'He fell, Mr Groenewald,' I lied, 'but it was from real high.'

'Jesus, man, what the hell's this?' said the suit. 'Who are these *laities*? Get them out of here.'

'I'm sorry, Mr Groenewald, but he can't move, he seems to be ... paralysed.' I swallowed as I said the word.

'You shouldn't be laying this *kak* on Mr Groenewald now.' Mr Clack clicked his tongue at us. 'We're late.'

'*Ja*, but this dog is still a pup, if he's fractured a growth plate ...' said Doc.

Jock, who hadn't said a word until now, spoke directly to Doc: 'Look, it's all right. Stay. If you don't make it in time, Johnny can second for me.'

Doc shook his head for a split second, then nodded. 'All right, let me finish wrapping you first.'

He took the box of TJ and placed it on the folding

82

massage table, then followed Jock back to the bench. On the slats beside Jock there was a roll of gauze and two of tape. The half-inch was for use between the fingers, to tape down the layers of gauze protecting the knuckles. I could tell that Doc had set them out from the way they were lined up like surgical instruments.

Doc knelt down again and carefully tore off six strips of half-inch tape, each about nine inches long, sticking one end of each strip to the edge of the bench. Jock extended his hands, and Tommy and I crowded in behind Cece, who was leaning curiously over Doc's shoulder as he began to wrap them. I marvelled at how soft those hands were from being steamed over and over again in gauze and leather and sweat.

'Always be careful to protect the eight bones in the wrist, the fragile bones across the back of the hand, the thumbs and the knuckles,' he instructed. 'The wraps must be tight, but not so tight as to cut off circulation. I've seen blue hands before, seen fighters miss because they couldn't feel their hands.'

Then he gloved Jock's hands and taped his laces at the wrists, wrapping the tape towards the thumb to compact the stuffing in the gloves. The suit, who had observed the whole process in silence, nodded curtly and stamped the taping over the laces. It was to certify that there'd been no skulduggery and that only eighteen feet of wrapping and eleven feet of zinc oxide sticky tape had been used. Suddenly I felt guilty for intruding on this sacred ritual.

'Vaseline,' said Doc.

He unscrewed a jar, daubed some of the jelly on Jock's forehead and smeared it across his face and arms.

'Okay, go,' he said, rising and grasping Jock by the shoulder. 'I'll be there as soon as I can. You probably won't even need me – nine losses on points.'

Jock shrugged into a beautiful shiny blue gown, 'Stout McGinty' stitched on the back, and pulled a towel around his neck.

'Good luck, Jock,' I said. My voice sounded thick.

'Won't need it.' Jock grinned. 'You heard the man – thirteen fights, nine losses on points.'

'What's that mean?' piped Cece.

'It means our opponent is a pug, a one-punch Johnny, a slugger,' said Doc.

'It means he's no boxer,' said Jock, winking at her, as he and Mr Clack and the suit pushed through the door.

Doc turned back to us. 'Come on.'

He moved back to the massage table, gently lifted TJ out of the crate and examined him, lifting his eyelids with his thumb and peering into his eyes, splaying the paw on his hind leg. After a minute Cece, who'd followed him and was flitting anxiously behind him, blurted out, 'Please, Mr Groenewald, is he all right?'

Doc said nothing and continued examining TJ, carefully running his fingers along his spine. There was silence in the room. Then he turned and lifted Cece up onto the massage table beside TJ. '*Meisietjie*,' he said, in his thick, guttural accent, 'I don't know without an X-ray, but if the growth plate on one of the vertebrae is fractured, it will protrude right into the spinal cord – even if it isn't severed, the compression alone will cause permanent paralysis – in which case the best thing for the animal is to put it out of its misery.'

Cece's face grew taut, but she nodded. I glanced at TJ.

He was lying there docile as a lamb, one eyebrow cocked, as though he was listening.

'But in this dog's case, I think, there is hope. I was feeling along his spine for the tell-tale crepitus – scratching – and all I found was a lump. I think it might just be haemorrhaging producing a spinal concussion. And look here,' he lifted the forequarter of TJ's hind leg and pinched the paw. TJ's leg jerked.

'See? That response tells us that even though he's paralysed now, there is sensation – the message is still getting through to the brain.'

'He's going to get better?' Cece almost whispered.

'I don't like to make promises, but let's put a compress on that swelling to stop the bleeding and encourage tissue shrinkage, and I reckon he may be on his feet again within a day.'

'Thank you, Mr Groenewald, sir,' said Tommy.

'That's Doc to you little buggers,' he said, grinning.

I wondered whether his patience on a night like this had anything to do with the leopard that haunted his dreams. He'd told us about it once, a long time ago, and sometimes she haunted me too.

He was spending the night under the stars, just off the Government Road to Naboomspruit – he'd decided to do it on a whim after he'd spotted the government tax collector coming over the *bult*. Doc said he didn't know about stars in other parts of the world, but one thing he could tell you about stars in South Africa was that the best way to look at them was lying under a Withaak tree, one end of a fallen branch that the white ants had been eating for the last seventeen years lying in the fire's embers, which you'd nudge with your toe, every once in a while, just so. After looking at the stars that way for a time, he'd rested his eyes.

He woke some time in the night to the unspeakable howling and cackling of the hyenas, and it was coming from somewhere very close by. The fire had gone out and he got up to wake the *kaffer*. 'Mules are very sensitive creatures,' he said, 'and you know how they get when they hear those ghoulish noises.' He thought it would be better if the fire was stoked up. It was taking quite a while to wake his *kaffer*, though, because the *velskoene* he was wearing were the wrong kind and had soft toes. Eventually he rolled his blanket over and found that the *donder* had run off. And that's a *kaffer* for you.

'*Kaffer*s?' he said. '*Ja*, I know them. And they are all the same.'

The Hottentot would also have run off, mind you, but he wouldn't have stolen the biltong as well. That was where the *kaffer* was different.

By now the noise in the bush was so loud and so close that Doc thought he'd try and see where they were: it was better than sitting and waiting for them to come and tear his face off at any rate. He crawled on his belly through the drift towards the noise until he came upon a pack of hyena circling a tree; some were trying to claw up its trunk. Poised in the branches above was a leopard, a small animal hanging limply from its mouth. The hyenas were so excited that not one even noticed Doc.

He fired his Mauser into the air and the thieves fled, but not the leopard. He thought this was strange, but didn't know what to do now. He was only a few yards from the tree and the leopard was staring at him, its eyes glinting in the darkness, and he knew he could not turn his back. Then the leopard climbed slowly down the tree and began to walk towards him. Doc did not run, he said, only because he could not move at all.

As the creature drew near, the moonlight was bright enough for him to see the whiskers on its muzzle. And then he understood. The leopard's paw was broken. It limped towards him, its right front paw twisted back to front, dragging in the dust. When it reached Doc, it dropped the bundle in its mouth and he saw that it was not its prey after all, but a squirming little cub.

The leopard flopped down in the dirt and crossed its hind legs. It rested its chin on its left front paw, the way a dog sometimes does. The cub was gambolling in the dirt, clambering over its mother, chewing her ears. The leopard looked straight into Doc's eyes, and blinked slowly. Doc stood for a long time before that leopard and her cub, and then he walked away. He never saw her again, although a few days later he saw the *aasvoëls* circling up there above the drift.

He was rummaging now in his cold box. He retrieved a compress and bound it to TJ's back, wrapping the tape around his middle, while TJ gnawed at Cece's fingers.

'If we *bopa* him up, it will also keep him nice and *styf*, see?'

He finished with a strip of Elastoplast to hold the bandages firmly in place. 'That's it,' he said at last. 'Take him home and give him some water and rest. He must not jump up on anything, okay?'

Doc was moving swiftly as he gave instructions. He lifted TJ back into the tomato box, hoisted his bag over his shoulder and was heading out the door as he said, 'Anyway, his back will be a bit *eina* for a few days.'

'Thank you! Thank you, sir, Doc,' Cece called after him. She was beaming at him for all she was worth.

'See you *laities* under the stands,' he said, over his shoulder.

'Tommy, TJ can't go home now,' I said urgently, as the door swung shut. 'We're late, man. Just tell Cece to wait here till after.'

'I can't,' Tommy groaned. 'If my ma gets back from prayer circle and Cece's not there, she'll raise hell.'

'Ah, for crying out loud.' I grabbed the box. 'You piggyback Cece, then. Goose it!'

'Don't be *dof*, man. We can't jar his back like that.'

So we crawled back down the road past the rugby field, which had been lit up specially to taunt us with everything we were missing. The men from the workshops had constructed a boxing ring in the middle of the field. The electricians had rigged four huge lights on wire strung from four poles set into the ground some ten feet from each corner of the ring. Clouds of moths whirled madly beneath their tin shades. The stands had been arranged in a huge oval around the ring. Every oke had a ringside seat and there looked to be about a thousand men packed onto those groaning benches. As we passed, a thunderous roar went up from the crowd, followed by a collective moan.

I was so desperate to get there now, I was panicky, tears stinging my eyes. After we'd finally dropped Cece and TJ off and got bawled out by Tommy's ma, we flew back to the ground.

The din from three hundred yards back was unholy, man,

88

but it was all over by the time we got there. Our only shot at watching a real fight before our own and we'd blown it. The crowd had gone *tekere*. Fighting had broken out at the base of the ring, okes were clobbering each other; a knot of them overturned the judges' table. We could see the slugger from Randfontein, limping to his corner. He hulked over his seconds, who were serving as crutches under his armpits. The ref stood completely still in the middle of the ring, and as Tommy and me stood on the outside, watching, it seemed to be sobering up the crowd. At last the noise died down, and some okes weighed in to pull the brawlers off one another. Then, when there was total silence, the ref beckoned to Jock, who was squatting on his stool with his back to us.

As he rose, I realised it was not Jock.

He stepped forward and the ref grabbed his hand and raised it high in the air.

'The winner by a knockout in the seventh round, Whitney van der Linde!'

With a clear view now across to the far corner, I watched in disbelief as Jock got up. He bowed blindly to the Randfontein slugger in the centre of the ring, his eyes swollen slits, and the crowd went wild again.

'He lost,' said Tommy, with an ache in his voice.

We tried to get to the ring, but as the boxers left, Buster Burnstein clambered through the ropes for the payout and the mob set upon him. I was trying to shove my way out when I bumped right into Mrs Tarrantino, the moustachioed matron in charge of the single men's quarters, and the only woman at the match.

'Mrs T, sorry, man. Hey, Mrs T, what happened out there?'

Mrs Tarrantino smiled beatifically at us. 'It was ... *magnifico*.' She sighed. 'It is Italy, Christoforo, who boasts the world's great lovers, the fighters, the dreamers, who have suckled from the bosom of *la bella vita*.' She clenched her fist. 'His name may be McGinty, but I *know* it is Latin blood that pumps in those veins.'

Then she turned and bellowed up at Buster, 'You bloody *skelm*!'

'Did you lose money on him, then, Mrs T?' Tommy asked sympathetically.

She snorted. 'You must be joking? Buster had him at four to one. Not even those odds could tempt me. He was always going to be crucified.'

'Woah! Look at Sugar Ray Jameson, the kid's a bull terrier!'

I was in the ring, fighting a phantom Rocky Marciano, except it was deserted ringside but for Tommy, commentating from the stands, his hands cupped over his mouth for volume.

'He's spotted an opening, fired one of the best left hooks I've ever seen. It's landed smack on Rocky's jaw and he's sagging against the ropes. The kid's storming after him, clubbing blows to the head and, yes, oh, yes, it's the champion who's slumped to the floor. He's struggling to get up ... He's on his knees, but the ref's completed the count. And it's Sugar Ray Jameson who takes the world heavyweight title with thirteen seconds left in the fight. *Waaaaah*.'

I leaped around the ring, punching my fist in the air. Then I flopped down onto the canvas and Tommy climbed through the ropes and lay beside me. We stared up at the night sky: sultry, briny with stars. Sweat slicked the back of my knees, and I didn't care any more that we'd missed the fight.

'Funny,' I said warily, 'I never knew until tonight whether Jock believed his own bullshit. And now, it makes me see … Christ, he's making a fool of himself.'

I was breaking an inviolable law.

'There's a difference between what you wish was true, and what is,' I said defensively, but Tommy didn't even flare.

'*Ja*,' he agreed. 'But the thing is, I still *want* to believe him – that the world is better than it is … that *I* am.' There was something flat in his voice. 'You're going to bale out of that jive contest, aren't you?'

I stared at him, dumbstruck.

'I saw your name, it was on the list posted up on the bulletin board outside the town hall.'

Sodding bastard organising committee. I squirmed.

'I don't blame you.' He looked at me thoughtfully, and I could tell he was trying to make up his mind whether to say something or not.

'It's the same as our first fight. I thought, you know, it'd be my one chance. The rest of the time,' he shrugged, '*ag*, you know how it is, you're just a kid, no clout, trying to do things to prove you're brave, but really they're just dumb, and when it counts, you're gutless. But in the ring, you have to stand up, eyeball to eyeball, you can't run and, one way or the other, you're going to find out what's under your skin.'

My senses grew sharper. I could see every pock on the canvas floor.

'But that's just bullshit,' he said, his voice hardening. 'Like you say, wishes and fairytales.'

I thought about Tommy cringing with me outside the

back door and I wanted to tell him what I knew was under his skin. I wanted to drive back the shadows that were slowly shrouding him, but I couldn't get the words out. Some things were too hard to say. They came from somewhere inside you that you'd long ago smothered, and if you tried to say them, you felt hot tears behind your eyes and you had to choke them back down.

'Tommy,' I said, with sudden ferocity, 'I am dancing in the Krugersdorp Junior Jive Contest. If I come stone last, I will still have got up on that stage. I don't care if they laugh at me, if they lob rotten tomatoes at me. Great steaming pats of cow dung won't keep me from that stage.'

'*Jisis*, Chris, and you call me crazy,' he said, but his eyes shone.

'And don't bloody blab it all over town, okay?'

Still I said nothing of the wings that only I could see, and the night drifted sluggishly along, close and sticky and buzzing with crickets.

9

The Church of Zion

Cece

The women's ululating thrummed with the dust as the men's boots pounded into the ground and, man, oh, man, I could feel the power of Umoya.

Standing before us Ntate Ezekiel called out, 'Peace in the church!'

It was the greeting, and I lifted my hands and shouted, 'Amen!' My voice was lost in the mighty chorus. I am of the ama-Ziyoni, the Church of Zion.

Kneeling on the ground, grit digging into my flesh, I was the only girl on the men's side. We were a raggedy congregation of miners, women from Madubulaville and me, all facing the bare dirt stage that was ringed by the *mokhukhu*, who had fallen silent as the preaching began. Many preachers and people would be called upon to testify between the choir singing in fine harmony, and I don't mind confessing that I didn't understand a word of what they were saying, but it didn't matter, because I was waiting for one of the prophets to call me.

The prophets were the ones carrying staffs. They roamed up and down the aisles beckoning to people to follow them into the special pen. When the Holy Spirit took a hold of them, some of them staggered backwards, some even fell, and then they started trembling from head to toe and blowing and panting like a dog. One old man stooped and wrung his hands behind his back. I even saw a prophet slithering like a snake and hissing. Their staffs were powerful channels, and so were their holy whips, which they carried at night to defend against *tsotsi*s or the *tokoloshe*.

I'd been praying with all my might for one of the prophets to call me. I even said no thanks to Tommy to go with him to his cave this afternoon. He looked at me strange and wanted to know what the hell'd got into me, but I'd already made Vilikazi promise to take me, even though he muttered and shook his head and carried on grumbling all the way down the railway tracks to where the church was. If you were going to split hairs, there wasn't really a church: we just knelt down and worshipped straight under God's washed-out blue sky. TJ looked like he was going to hang hisself. He tried to scramble out of the gate behind me, and when I slammed it on him, he slunk down to the furthest corner of the fence with his tail drooping behind him. Every time I looked over my shoulder the whole way down Club Road, there he was, lying with his middle all bandaged up and his nose mashed against the chicken wire.

I thought I would fail the gate test. My heart was thudding as I walked under the arch and got sprinkled with holy water – doused, more like. I bowed my head as the prophet dipped his hand into the tin and flicked the water over me. He did such a good job of it that water was running down the back of my neck. I kept expecting him to grab me by the shoulder and pull me away, but nothing happened.

Holy water is mighty powerful. In the Bible, it says the Spirit of God is hovering over the waters, and after Ntate Ezekiel blessed it, the Holy Spirit was present *in* the water. You could drink it as a healing potion or wash with it, and sprinkling holy water was a sacrament. Sometimes you had to mix it with ash or salt or Sunlight soap, so as to make you honk to flush out the evil. Even when someone died, you sprinkled holy water in the grave, lest the dead one had been bewitched. Then his vestments and his badge – a silver star on a green flash – and his membership ticket were laid on top of his body. That way he could prove that his tithes was fully paid up when he got to the gates of Heaven.

I was beginning to fear that it was because I was not baptised, not properly anyway. You had to get dunked three times by the prophet in living water, which means running water, a river, which you called Jordan no matter which river it was. That was the way you received the Holy Spirit.

Pastor Mullins would've told you the same thing, except he cared mainly that your sins had been washed away and that you had been saved from eternal damnation in Hell. Nobody around here seemed too bothered with salvation of their soul. Far as I could tell, most of the people were a darn sight more worried about things here on earth, and the main point of getting baptised was to get a hold of the power of the Holy Spirit. I was just hoping like hell that the prophets' power would still work A-okay for the unbaptised believers.

The prophets had been given the gifts of the spirit. Pastor Mullins said that the *charismata* were the proof that the gospel was true. Whenever He gave the gift of tongues at the Mission, I'd climb up on my chair to get a good look at the ones blathering and writhing around on the floor, but no one ever understood a word they said and, frankly, you had to wonder if the Holy Ghost knew what He was doing. One way or the other, He didn't waste time speaking in tongues in the Church of Zion.

He was pointing at me. That old one, all hunched over. I was nudging Vilikazi and staring at his crooked finger and my tummy was slick with oil. Vilikazi got to his feet and I clung to his hand as we followed the prophet into the place where they whispered the secrets they had been told. I felt eyes on us as we passed into the ring of sticks. Vilikazi knelt down and tugged on my hand.

'Ntate,' he said, and I bowed down low as I could, my nose practically scraping the dirt.

The prophet squatted in front of us and did some grunting. Then he turned to Vilikazi and began speaking in a low voice. Vilikazi said, 'Hmm, hmm.' After the prophet had finished speaking, he looked deep into my eyes and I saw that his were yellow and feverish.

'The prophet,' Vilikazi said gravely, 'he says he knows from where your suffering comes. He is the seer.'

The Church of Zion preached that evil came from Satan, the dark side of God. Suffering was God's punishment for disobeying Him, or the ancestors, just as God punished the

Israelites. But mostly evil came from the wickedness in human hearts. Someone who had not forgiven you could go to the *molôi* for *muti* and get you. Evil could even come from God if someone prayed against you and God answered their prayer. Because God loved some people and hated others, according to the Bible.

'There is one who has hatred in his heart. He is behind your pain.'

Well, I knew who that was. Most of the time people did not know why they were sick or had lost their job or had their passbook stolen or were barren, although they might have a pretty good hunch, but it was only through the revelations of the prophets that you could know who it was you had angered and needed to make peace with – the ancestors whose spirit was bound to yours, or someone on this earth. I didn't need that part. What I was here for was ... *deliverance*.

'Hold out your hands,' Vilikazi ordered.

I stretched them out, and the prophet took them in his old gnarly ones. They felt cool and dry. He turned my palms upwards. They were scored with sweat and dirt. Then from a little pouch tied around his waist he retrieved a large darning needle.

Oh, boy, why me? Other people were cured with holy water or smoke or ropes that had been prayed over. You could get protection from lightning or magic by pinning a strip of blue cloth to your clothes or from stringing copper wire across your gate. A droplet of dark blood welled up on each palm as the prophet pierced it with the needle.

'The poison must be bled from your body,' he said to me in English.

I sighed as it dripped onto the ground between us, mingling with the dirt. This was why I had come.

Ntate Ezekiel said the spirit came from God. The spirit, Umoya, is that which gave us life, and what bound us to Him, and to all life. It was power. To live is to have power; to sicken or die is to lose it. *Amandla* was the word. I rolled it over on my tongue.

And I saw in Tommy a weakening. I saw him hiding against the back wall and I was afraid. The fear was the poison in our blood, slowly spreading through our bodies. Tommy was losing his spirit.

And so I had come here. Ntate Ezekiel wielded more power than any *sangoma*, even those possessed by ancestor spirits found at the bottom of riverbeds, he said. The Holy Spirit sure stuck it to them.

A long time ago, when Ezekiel was only a boy, there was a terrible drought in the land. One day, the Spirit caused him to prophesy during worship that before the sun rose there would be an abundance of rain. He continued in prayer all through the night and was only aroused by the rain falling upon his back. Hundreds were saved that day.

With my own eyes I had seen him cast out demons from a woman possessed. She was kneeling quietly with the other women, but she had an unwashed look about her. As soon as prayer was offered, she began laughing uncontrollably, tearing at her clothes. It took ten men to subdue her. They tied her down with ropes and forced her to drink holy water. Ntate Ezekiel prayed over her for three days and she was released from bondage.

I knew I could trust the Umoya to drive out the evil. The old prophet groped around his robes and pulled out a bag of tea leaves, which he laid on my palms. The crescents of his nails were huge and very white. Sweat stung my impure blood. Pleasurably.

'You must drink it every morning before you go to school,' he instructed. 'It is the tea *ya bophelo* – the tea of life.'

The noise from the pounding of the drums and the *mokhukhu* had grown louder. It was time to go back. We stepped out into the clap of sunlight, and I felt new inside. The men were leaping in the air, 'Lifted on the wings of faith,' the old prophet whispered hoarsely in my ear. His breath was sour. They slammed down into the ground, stamping out evil under their great boots.

'They hunger for Moya,' he said, 'dancing and dancing until they are filled with its power.'

Vilikazi marched straight down the aisle and out of the makeshift entrance, and I was forced to follow behind him, burning with shame. We squatted under a gnarled old Karee tree and Vilikazi mopped his brow.

'Did you get what you came for, *bazalwane*?' he said, screwing up one side of his scowling old face.

'Oh, yes, Vilikazi,' I said, licking my salty wounds.

Vilikazi hawked. His spit frothed there on the ground in disgust. I frowned at him. 'Well, I don't think the Lord will like that.'

When Vilikazi first came to Johannesburg he'd had a dream in which his grandfather had come to him and told him to find this place. He obeyed, and Ntate Ezekiel saw him and said, 'I know you.' He prayed for Vilikazi, and the sleeplessness that he'd suffered since he'd left his home troubled him no more. That was years ago, but Vilikazi'd better reckon on never sleeping again, after how he'd paid them back.

The people had begun streaming out of the church, veering past us like we were lepers. One of them clicked her tongue at us. Vilikazi was definitely the leper, but I had to sit next to him. He'd left the Church of Zion since it forbade doing political things. The great Lekganyane, who was the leader of all the multitudes of Zion, taught that to seek worldly power was a sin. Christians should pray and abstain from politics. That was why members of the Church had respect. You could ask anyone around here: the whites would look to employ Zionists because they were humble, they did not steal, they were not members of trade unions and they obeyed the government. They could be trusted.

I was not so sure about Vilikazi. When he went to the fights in Jo'burg he went to meetings too – and I didn't think they were about boxing. He'd be deader than a dead dog in the street if he ever got busted. Vilikazi said the black man's Church was a prison. He said it served the high priests of Apartheid. He didn't know why they'd even bothered to split from the Apostolic Faith Mission. Well, I can tell you: it'd be a cold day in Hell before Pastor Mullins ever let a black come strutting into his church for Sunday worship, so maybe that's how come. Vilikazi reckoned the prophets were worse than the herd-boy miners, saving their wages for *lobola*, running back to the Bantustans when their *tikits* expired on the twenty-ninth day of the twelfth month of every year, propping up the *kraal* and the past that was gone for ever. He said it took doing that for about twenty-nine years to work it out.

'*Eish!*' He gestured angrily at the river of Zionists flowing past him. Then he took my face in his huge black hands. 'It is fear that brings you here, *bazalwane*. It is fear that makes

100

Africa fertile soil for the evangelists, but hear this,' he said, lowering his head so his face was only an inch from mine. 'In the slumyards of Jo'burg, the Black Spots, when they cry "*Amandla*!" the people answer, "*Awethu*! Ours!"

'*Awethu*!' he shouted to the faithful, but they were deaf to him.

'It means,' he said quietly, '"power to the people". It is inside of *you*.'

10

The Republic

Chris

I was aiming at her heart, just below the beacon that was her red eye, but as I rolled down onto the ball of my foot, something startled her, and through my sights I watched her lift into the air on wings like dappled sunlight. I fired, too late, and the shot ricocheted through the forest as the dove flapped gracelessly out of range.

'Bugger it!'

'Should call you bloody Big Foot,' tuned Tommy.

'Ah, shuddup.' I kicked at the mulch underfoot, but it struck me as odd. It was always strangely quiet in those woods that mottled the slopes of Noordheuwel to the north of town, just the sighing of the boughs in the wind, nothing else, and I knew the mulch had muffled my footfall. We ambled on for a while, saying nothing. Tommy was cradling his BB gun like it was a baby.

'Hey, Tommy, remember when Rod got his BB number one?'

'*Ja*,' he said. 'He brought it to the Scout Hall on his sixth birthday.'

Jisis, we'd buzzed around him like flies all afternoon. Rod had the power to choose who could touch the air gun and who could not.

'By the time it got to the bloody *Dib Dib Dib*, I was crazed with lust. You know, I can honestly say that is the only thing I remember from our five years in Cubs and Scouts.'

'*Ag*, come off it – you don't remember how to tie a knot? Build a lean-to if you're lost in the woods?'

'Nope. Only thing I remember are those bloody campfire songs. You want to know the words to "Davy Crockett"? I'm your man. And tossing the whole can of kerosene on the fire – that was a *lag*.'

You got badges when you passed the tests, paddled a canoe or whatever. If you got them all, they gave you a merit certificate that said members of the order may use the letters SAS after their names. I don't know who they thought they were fooling.

'Hey, if you're such a Boy Scout why don't you invite Cynthia to hang out in your lean-to, maybe cook a toad in the hole?'

I stroked the muzzle of my No. 3.

'Wonder what sort of guns they'll have in the future?' Tommy mused. 'Like in the year 2000. Ray guns? For blasting those little green okes.'

'*Ag*, please, I haven't got time for this sort of crap any more,' I said, with as much scorn as I could. 'We'll be long dead by then anyway.'

'Uh-uh,' Tommy said, frowning. 'Well, not unless you're planning on croaking before your fifty-fifth birthday.'

'*Jisis.*' We'd be alive in the year 2000.

'It's like you just bought me a ticket for Sputnik. Those Russians probably have ray guns already, man. They're probably sting-raying the crap out of the Martians right now.'

'Jeepers, but we'll be old toppies, though, hey?' I added, a bit appalled. I'd never thought about being old before, older than my old man.

'Hey, check that,' said Tommy. I followed the aim of his gun to see the huge Victorian house looming through the trees.

'Spackman House Boys Correctional,' I said, awed.

'*Jisis*, man, why'd they make it look so creepy?'

Ma would love it. She pined for all things English, even though she'd never set foot in England. Dad loved to tell us how her father, who'd been grubbing around in the tin mines of Cornwall, was so gullible that when the train stopped at Krugersdorp and the runners from the mine – who were paid a bonus of a pound for each new recruit they signed on – called out, 'Johannesburg!' he got off. It was no coincidence, he'd say, that that was the year they opened the jail. Ma'd roll her eyes. Spackman House, with its shingled turrets and Gothic arches and eerily stained glass window-panes, was straight out of her most sordid fantasy. There seemed to be no sign of life about the place. No plaintive cries from the boys getting reformed at the end of a stiff cane, no lights from its ghostly windows, and darkness was falling.

'Let's get out of here,' said Tommy. 'Race you!'

And we were both flying through the woods, pitching down the steep slope towards Monument Dam, high on our unstoppability.

Even though we took the shortcut behind the old dump,

it was late as we wandered down the main drag, past the mine offices towards the workshops. The gardens outside the mine manager's office were immaculate. I was just past them, tiptoeing along on the loco tracks where they crossed the road, arms outstretched for balance. I had to make it to the sheds without toppling. I could almost smell the blood-metal tang of the machines in there, standing in mind-numbing row upon row, staring at me in ominous silence, until their gears meshed with a snarl.

Tommy was slashing at the hydrangeas with the barrel of his gun. *Jisis*, Slimy Roth, the gardener, would do his nut if he checked him. One time Tommy walked on the grass outside the reduction plant and got summoned to Ginger Steward's office for a bollocking, and now here he was lacerating old Ginger's bloody hydrangeas with his BB No. 3.

Tommy reckoned there was a charcoal sketch mounted on the wall behind Ginger's desk of the two wandering prospectors, both named George, who had discovered gold on the Reef. The story went that when one of them stumbled over a rocky outcrop on the Widow Oosthuizen's farm, Langlaagte, they noticed something odd about the crumbly sediment: it was peppered with pebbles, and looked like a kind of confectionery the Boers called *banket*. They panned it and found a rich tail of gold. Tommy said the sketch was of them kneeling in the dirt and crushing the *banket* in a mortar with a pestle. We had to take his word for it – none of us had ever seen the inside of old Ginger's office.

'Come on!' Tommy goaded, over his shoulder, while still thrashing the hydrangeas. 'You're going to make a total *poephol* of yourself, man.'

'Thanks a lot.'

'All I'm saying is, how do you think you're going to crack a rock 'n' roll dance competition if you're too chicken to go to a real dance?'

I had to agree. So far we'd only ever been to the end-of-term social at school. All the girls lined up on one side of the room and all the boys on the other, and we'd do the waltz and the foxtrot and all that malarkey. There were two jive numbers, right at the end. But the sessions at the town hall, that was where it was really happening. Rock 'n' roll all night. With the Lebs from the Catholic Social and the gangs from Roodepoort fighting the ducktails on the steps. Only one waltz, the very last dance. They'd never let the likes of us in, though.

'Tsk, tsk, tsk.'

It came out of the darkness, quietly, almost a whisper. My heart stopped in my ribcage. There was the sound of a match scratching. My fingertips tingled and I peered through the gloom to the far side of the road. I could make out the silhouette of the Cape Dutch gable soaring above the wrap-around veranda of the building opposite, 'Engineering Dept. 1938' moulded onto its façade, but it was difficult to see anything beneath it. As my eyes probed the darkness, I could just make out the form of a man leaning against one of the pillars stationed along its length.

'Tommy!' I hissed.

He stopped slashing and looked over.

'You *laities* are dicing with death,' said the disembodied voice, followed by a grating laugh.

'Dad?' said Tommy, sounding fearful.

A small orb glowed in answer, followed by the acrid smell of tobacco.

106

'Come over here, boys.'

I waited for Tommy to cross in front of me before I followed warily. As we reached the red-polished cement of the veranda, Mr Michaels laughed again. 'Ah, out hunting, then, boys? No trophies? *Ag*, shame, not even a pigeon for the pot, or a small rodent for the taxidermist?'

His laugh ended abruptly in a gargled cough. When the spasm passed he swigged from a brown-paper bag.

'Sit down, man, pull up a chair.'

It felt surreal sitting there beside Mr Michaels on the smooth, cold floor of the Engineering Department veranda, and none of us said anything at all.

'Dad,' said Tommy, breaking the spell, 'aren't you supposed to be at the Union Club?'

Instead of *klapp*ing him, Mr Michaels just waved his brown-paper bag dismissively. '*Ag*, I couldn't take it any more,' he said. 'I had to get out of there. It's pathetic, bunch a pompous old farts spilling their whisky and spouting *kak*. It's over man, over. Any *poephol* can see the Union is dead.'

This was news to me, but I wasn't about to try Mr Michaels's strange mood by arguing.

'Yup, while Smuts was strutting around Churchill's war cabinet, the Nats stole the election, and now it's just a matter of time. The Brits still can't quite get behind the Apartheid slogan – we English don't like that sort of thing, boys, we find it all rather crass. We were quite happy to go along with the Native Land Act and suchlike, but all this ranting about *bloedvermenging* is quite distasteful, and now we've got Verwoerd, and Treason Trials and Triomf.'

Triomf was what they built on top of the rubble of Sophiatown. Sophiatown was a slum close to downtown

Johannesburg, heaving with violators of the Immorality Act and other felonious types, so last year they razed it. Then they fumigated it and built Triomf on top. Only Afrikaners live in its neat rows of drab little houses.

'And how long do you think those Broederbonders are going to put up with saluting the Union Jack and singing "God Save the Queen", hey? So we can sip gin at the Union Club and dance the foxtrot at United Party fundraisers, but, frankly, we're a joke.'

Tommy sucked his teeth. He was trying to sound helluva fed up with the state of affairs. I was feeling pretty chuffed myself. Mr Michaels was talking to us like grown men. I supposed it was because we weren't a bunch of pompous old farts spilling whisky and talking *kak* – we were dumb mutes.

'And who are we anyway? "English-speaking South Africans" – we don't even have a proper name. We're just a feeble little knot of orphans hovering on the fringes of the great clash of nationalisms unfolding in this land.' He burped, and swigged from his whisky, then offered the bottle to Tommy and me.

I took it from Tommy in disbelief and nipped from its neck. It blistered down my gullet and tears stung my eyes. I wanted to gasp, I was trying so hard not to, but in the end I couldn't stop it. I clawed at my throat and panted next to Tommy, who was smirking at me as he handed the bag back to his dad. But his eyes had a dazed look, as if his dad sitting around in the pitch dark talking to him like a man was as good as slugging half a jack of whisky.

'Jesus, we orchestrated the whole damn thing. With the Martini-Henry in one hand and the Bible in the other, we smiled politely while we ground up the black tribes and the lost white one too, and then discovered the source of Mammon – the gold. It's true, though, what the Afrikaners call us: *soutpiel* – salty dick – because we have one foot in Africa and one in England. It erodes our loyalty to South Africa, even as it broadens our horizons. We're a bunch of lukewarm patriots, and that's what crippled us. Gold is not a bond that binds. We never trekked, we never fomented a new tongue, we were never defeated in war, we never had to pick ourselves up out of the dust. We do not burn with a sense of grievance or mission.'

That was what Doc had. 'The land was scorched,' he'd tell us, bitterly. When his pa came home from the war, he'd found the cattle dead from the *rinderpest*, and his wife and youngest child mouldering in graves at the pleasure of his lordship Kitchener. '*Ja*, you *Engels*,' he said knowingly. 'When was the last time you set foot in the old Burger's Hoop graveyard? *Hey?*' He shook his head disgustedly. '*Ja*, I know, bloody never. You make sure you take a big detour past it.'

'*Ag*, come on, Doc, it's bloody spooky.'

We all nodded, although only Tommy could get away with saying stuff like that.

I sometimes traced the words engraved on the face of the obelisk erected outside it: 'In honour of the mothers and children who died in the Krugersdorp Concentration Camp 1899–1902, *vir vryheid en vaderland* – for freedom and fatherland.'

Without livestock, the plough and the blimmin' packets of seeds sent from Holland didn't make for a promising start, but Doc reckoned his old man had had guts. Hell, he'd ridden with General de la Rey's commando, he was a Boer, he said, rolling his *r*s with gusto. 'So we pitched the tent below a ridge, and me and my pa, we tried to make out.' He lapsed into silence. 'But, *jisis*, then came the drought. The land grew as bitter as us living on it. One day, my pa strode out onto the *stoep* of the little raw brick house we'd built, and stared grimly at the horizon. He wiped the sweat from his brow with his sleeve but said nothing. I stood beside him and watched as a dark cloud spread slowly across the sky. In the end, it blotted out the sun. The locusts descended in their own darkness and took possession of everything. Every blade of grass, every leaf quivered with them. And that high-pitched *chirruping*! It was unholy, man. Filled your whole head. Sometimes I wake up in the night screaming – I can still hear them in my dreams.

'After that, my pa squatted on his haunches, scratched some figures in the dust, and then him and his eldest brother, who had the best piece of land, had a long talk out on the *stoep*, full of sighs while they tapped their pipes out on their *velskoene*.

'In exchange for a wagon and a span of oxen, my uncle took me and my pa's land, and Pa went out on the road, hauling fresh produce from the farms to the great sprawling mining camp that had sprung up to the east of Langlaagte. But then they built the railways, and Pa couldn't pay for the fodder. So he fetched me from his brother's and headed for Johannesburg.

'Hell,' he said, with a shudder, 'I can still see him now, shuffling along door to door in his baggy khaki pants, begging. Each day he went out at dawn to join the queues at the mine gates, and dreamed at night of the land. He hated the city – he was afraid of it, to tell the truth. It was the citadel of Anglo-Saxon power and Jewish blood money, where he was looked down on, where he was scorned. The language was English and he was a foreigner. He hunched over the newspaper sniggering at Hoggenheimer, but he had to wait until the blacks went on strike in 1907 before he could get in as scab labour. Still,' he winced, 'to be stood over by a taskmaster with a stopwatch, to be checked on each time you went for a piss or stopped for a smoke.'

'Bunch of boneheads,' I said disgustedly. That was what my old man reckoned Paardekraal was for – a shrine for them to nurse their grievances. 'There's nothing like nationalism nicely curried with a bitter dose of self-pity,' he said.

We'd passed it as we'd hurtled past Monument Dam. The monument was built on top of a pile of stones that had something to do with the revolt against the British, so the Boers could get back to scratching in the dirt. Whenever they got the chance, the Afrikaners loved to dress up in clothes from the olden days, the women in long dresses with little bonnets on their heads, and trek off to Paardekraal, where they rigged up an ox-wagon – and made speeches and whatnot.

The big one was in '38, when they'd staged a re-enactment of the Great Trek and the Covenant with God, to mark the centenary of that sacred saga. They built nine ox-wagons and named them for the heroes of the story: Piet Retief, the martyr, Andries Pretorius, the victor of the battle of Blood River, Dirkie Uys, a boy of fourteen, who had died beside his wounded father rather than flee from the Zulus, Johanna van der Merwe, who had survived the massacre when her mother hid her under her own body, and so on. They set forth from the Cape, symbolically fleeing the yoke of the

111

British Empire and their *kafferboetie* ways once more. They rumbled slowly across the hinterland passing through little *dorps* and the whole thing dragged on for months.

As the wagons groaned northwards towards Krugersdorp, Dad reckoned the Dutchmen had gone into a frenzy. The *dominee* from the NG Kerk strutted around appointing committees and whatnot, men grew beards, and when the column rolled into town, they staged a big laager at Paardekraal where babies were baptised and the *dominee* fell off his horse as he rode in to deliver his sermon. The pilgrimage culminated in a mighty rally on a hill outside Pretoria, where the great Voortrekker Hoogte monument was erected. There was a torch marathon, symbolising freedom and white civilisation.

'Three thousand crazed torch-bearers from the Voortrekkers cadet movement wound their way up the hill. From a distance it looked like a river of fire,' Dad said grimly.

As they reached the summit, each torch was hurled into the flames of a huge bonfire, until the chain of light was consumed in a great conflagration. Then there were calls for the creed of *Blut* and *Boden* – blood and soil.

'Christ almighty! We should have known what was coming.'

Now they clogged the ranks of the civil service, the railways, the mines. Whenever Dad came back from the post office or the railway station he'd be ranting about sheltered employment for dim-witted in-breds. 'I have the violent urge to run out and slash the freeloading bureaucrats' tyres while they're slumped over their desks waiting for five o'clock to roll around.'

You could feel the resentment, from both sides, seething just under the skin. Dad said they were choking the life out of this place.

'*Ag*,' Mr Michaels said stoically. 'We English might have had our balls chopped off, but we console ourselves that politics is a dirty game, particularly in a situation that demands the constant suppression of a swelling black population – best left to people who have fewer qualms about doing what has to be done.'

And I felt as if a shadow had fallen across the land. So much hatred had bled into the soil, I could feel it roiling beneath my feet with anger . . . or was it sorrow?

'Come on, boys, help me get home before I bloody drown in my self-pity.'

11

The Dance

'*Jisis*, okes,' Rod said, rubbing his hands together gleefully. 'This is the big time!'

'Keep it together, Wazowski. You got to keep it together, my china.'

'*Jissee*, those chicks are with it, hey?' said Mitch, flicking his wrist as a bunch of girls in their forty-five-yard skirts flounced up the steps of the banqueting hall.

We were approaching the town hall from the western side of Commissioner Street. Tommy didn't want to overtake his old man on the way to the Union Club. We were almost opposite the hall outside the magistrates' court. Mitch leaned against one of the old horse posts and kicked up his heels one by one to check his ankles.

'Hey, okes, you reckon my stovvies are orright, hey?'

'What you worried about, man? Your ma did it for you. Check mine. It's a total bloody *gemors*!'

All the rest of us had stitched the hems of our own pants together and it looked like it. Plus we were going to have to unpick them on Sunday night. School rule: nothing under sixteen inches. I'd done my best with half a bloody tub of Brylcreem too, but when I checked my *kuif* out in the bathroom mirror, all I could see was this *krul* that kept springing out of place. *Jisis*, this being cool was tougher than it looked. We were loitering now. Just killing time. At this rate, we weren't actually going to make our début social at the town hall.

It looked even grander at night, with its white façade all lit up from below. It was an old colonial building, arches galore, and a huge portcullis jutting out below the spire of the clock tower. Princesses Elizabeth and Margaret had stood and waved from the balcony above it in '47. I didn't really remember it, but Johnny and Mona were in the parade waving their Union Jacks. It was right before the Afrikaners gained power, but the bloody hairybacks stayed home on that day, I can tell you. Next thing I spotted Johnny and the greasers loping up the steps, Texans dangling from their lips.

'Come on, you bunch a sissies,' Tommy prodded.

'Look, Tommy, I've been thinking ...'

'You do that with your left hand or your right?'

'I just thought you should know that I'm not going to let you bully me any more.'

'Of course you are.'

Actually, I was dying to go, mostly on account of Pastor Mullins. Last Saturday night of the month he marched down Commissioner armed with a satchel full of tracts with headings like *Sinner Saved from Hellfire*, past the Majestic and the Victoria, dodging the fights going on all the way down to the town hall.

Pastor Mullins's sermons on the Sunday after always came from the Old Testament. They were a whole lot grittier than the pathetic stories about the meek and whatnot you got in Sunday school up at the Anglican church. And Pastor Mullins got helluva worked up about them too: little flecks of spittle flew from his mouth and you didn't want to be sitting in the front row, that was for sure.

In the Old Testament, God would smite the sinners left and right. If he didn't smite them personally, he got the children of Israel to stone them. Pastor Mullins's favourite Old Testament story was the destruction of Sodom and Gomorrah. And the main point was that, frankly, Sodom was a joke next to Krugersdorp, these days, what with all the boozing and fornicating going on.

Occasionally Pastor Mullins brought a well-known boozer trembling to his knees before the Lord. Jeepers, when the singing and hallelujahing, and praising the Lord, really got going, some of those repentant sinners began crying and confessing their sins and the whole congregation fell quiet as they lapped up every last salacious drop. I reckoned plenty of them wouldn't have minded committing some of the fleshly sins, but they could forget about their mansion up in Heaven if they did. And Heaven was a damn sight better than the crackle of hellfire and the dreadful wailing of the everlastingly condemned. Afterwards, we sang 'Take Me To the River' loudly.

But it wasn't every week that he got one – you knew when you saw the special pew where they lined them up standing empty. On those weeks, we heard about the fallen instead.

'Oh, yes, my brothers and sisters,' Pastor Mullins would

say, in a quivering voice. 'The Devil was hard at work in Krugersdorp last night.'

Kneeling on the steps of the banqueting hall, Satan's filthy music pulsating in his ears, he'd looked down upon the wretched face of the poor sinner fallen from the grace of Our Lord, Jesus Christ, a great burden of sorrow weighing upon his heart.

I knew we were supposed to be thinking, Boy, I'm glad I'm not that oke, lolling around drunk on the steps of the Devil's main lair, I wouldn't want to be him, man, but actually, I was thinking I'd like to check out the Devil's main lair.

And that jive contest was starting to bite. It was Dad who did it. Tommy'd kept his mouth shut, like he promised, but when Johnny – is there no mercy in this God-forsaken world? – checked my name on that list outside the town hall, he came home and announced it to the whole family. He was laughing so hard, I swear he wet himself. I stared blandly at him, pulled every rude sign I knew under my chin, while he howled and slapped his thigh, but actually, I sort of wanted to see their reaction.

Ma stared at me dumbstruck, but Dad ... he was actually angry.

'You telling me you're going to get up on stage – in front of actual people – and jiggle your arse like a jungle bunny?'

He looked at me with something like disgust and I had the urge to pull the finger at him.

'Okay, girls, let me demonstrate what it'll be like for you when you grow some balls!' Tommy taunted. Then he legged it across the road and vaulted over the chain-link above the low stone wall onto the strictly forbidden mani-cured lawns below.

'Okay, okes, me too. I'm going in!' Rod announced, and we all followed, but down the path to the banqueting hall. I mean, why chance it before you'd even got in?

The foyer, when we got inside, was foaming with petticoats, which was just as well, considering it was best not to be checked by Mrs van der Watt, who was seated behind a desk at the door selling tickets. It wasn't the two-and-six that was the problem, it was the fact that we were under-age – and how the hell had Tommy snuck in already?

'They say she's got X-ray vision, man.'

We were at the back of the throng, our arses pressed against the wall by the lavvy. I glanced inside the girls' one – there were hordes of them in front of the mirrors, smearing on lipstick, backcombing their hair, spraying it with that stinking lacquer, spitting on mascara. I shuddered. Mitch leaned forward to check Mrs van der Watt again.

'*Ag*, bulldust, man. Mrs van der Watt is a joke. Watch this.' Rod hunkered over, darted through the crowd and past a flurry of girls at the door, without Mrs van der Watt even glancing up.

I couldn't take it any more. I had to get in there. My heart was bloody hammering in my bony chest, but I gulped some air and ran for it. I slunk past the X-ray eyes and straight into the hall.

Hell's teeth, man. Great balls of fire were bouncing off the bloody rafters and the floor was jumping. Pastor Mullins would have had a *poep*. There must've been hundreds of couples jiving out there. It was dimly lit and I just saw tulle and bobby socks flying through the air. I spotted Tommy against the wall, with Rod and Davie Rabinowitz sitting next him, like some sort of Brylcreemed imp. How the hell did he get in, man?

'Where's Mitch?' Rod shouted, as I joined them.

'Didn't make it.' I shrugged.

'They don't grow them so daring in A Row,' said Tommy.

Look, his old man was an underground manager. After a while, though, I had to face the fact that we were just sitting there like bloody wallflowers, man, and I couldn't see what was going to change that. Not even Tommy had the balls to ask a chick to dance.

'How the hell are you going to get up on stage if you're too *skaam* to set foot on the dance floor?' he yelled in my ear.

I shrugged glumly.

Pastor Mullins had told us that Jerry Lee Lewis was possessed. He was born a poor boy, though his ma and pa mortgaged their farm to buy him a piano so he could nurture his God-given gift for music. Yet he forsook Elmo and Mamie and the Lord when he was expelled from the Assemblies of God University in Texas for playing the Devil's music. 'Great balls of fire' comes straight from the Book of Acts. It was the seminal moment in the Pentecost – the descent of the Holy Spirit upon the followers of Jesus Christ – when the Holy Spirit manifested as cloven tongues of fire and the Apostles spoke in languages they had never known. When Pastor Mullins heard the blasphemous strains of 'Great Balls Of Fire' as he ministered to the fallen on the steps of the banqueting hall, he was as sure as he was of the Lord God Almighty that Jerry Lee Lewis *knew* he was playing for the Devil.

119

I spotted Johnny with a pretty blonde girl. She was wearing an Alice band and he was sweeping the floor with her. I was clicking my fingers along to Chuck Berry carrying on about rock 'n' roll music when he swung past and shouted, 'Hey, Chris, you cats are really jiving, man!'

I knew Tommy was feeling like a bit of a chop too because he started looking for trouble. He nudged me and nodded towards the entrance. A few okes were shoving their way through the throng, and I could hear some kind of commotion over the tub-thumping: shouting, a girl's high-pitched scream.

'Come on,' shouted Tommy, getting up and sidling along the row of chairs that lined the wall. I was right on his heels when Johnny grabbed my upper arm and pulled me towards him.

'Hey! Stay out of it, Chris, do you hear me?' he said urgently, into my ear. He looked at me hard while Chuck swore he'd only dance to rock 'n' roll, and then he was gone again. I hesitated for a minute, and then I ducked after Tommy as he slipped through the door.

Out in the car lot on the western side of the town hall, by the market square, there was a flippin' fleet of rag-top Thunderbirds and Zephyrs and big, jacked-up Chevys, all chrome and fins, not a damn Wolseley or Oldsmobile, with its boot stuck out as far as its engine, in sight. Man, I hated those Sunday-afternoon drives: sitting in the back seat bored brain-dead, I'd wind up telling Maggie that hers was in fact the worst seat in the car, so then we'd have to take turns wedged in the middle, elbows chicken-winged on Ma and Dad's backrests. From our vantage at the top of the steps, I could see okes lounging against the fenders and smoking. I gave a low whistle. 'Check those sweet chariots, man, I could weep.'

But Tommy couldn't take in the hot rods because his eyes were drawn to the pavement in front of the car lot. He bounded down the steps and out of the portcullis into the huddle at the bottom. Behind me, Johnny Otis had a cat named Willie doing his Hand Jive.

'Who is it?' a man shouted up at me, as he hurried across the lawn dogged by a couple of old chuggers from the Majestic. I shrugged back at them. The hand jive kept bawling out of the hall.

When I turned around, Tommy had vanished. I followed him down, and jostled my way through the crowd until I got to the edge of a clearing. It was rimmed with ducktails, greased to within an inch of their lives. There were about twelve of them, maybe thirteen, circling like vultures around the two who were propping some oke up under the armpits for a third to batter in the face.

It was Fats Vorster's brother, Boet. Christ. Now I knew what Fats was destined for: when he was done with the change-house, he was headed straight for the steps of the banqueting hall.

Boet was getting clobbered. He sagged between them, slavering, his eyes dull, as the greaser smashed his face. Some of the vultures had knuckle-dusters on. I felt ill. Next thing the mob surged and I lost my footing. I stumbled against the wall, frantic to get up before I was trampled. There was a bellow and four or five huge beasts crashed through the ring towards Boet. The one in the lead yanked the greaser behind his shoulder, half spun him into his fist, and his nose exploded. He staggered backwards, clutching his face, moaning. The two greasers who had been restraining Boet released their grip. Boet roared and charged into the ranks of vultures. All hell broke loose after that. The crowd that had closed in scattered. I was scrambling backwards, trying to reach the steps. As I finally felt my heel against the bottom one, someone grasped my shoulder. I looked up to see Tommy just above me.

'Come on!' he yelled, pulling me up to him. I turned back to see the fight. It was wild. There were okes on the ground and others standing over them, kicking and kicking with thick-soled boots. Suddenly, at the edge of the fight, I saw Boet moving in on a greaser he'd cornered just below us against the steps. The greaser was lank. His once-coiffed hair fell limply across his face and, looking down at him, I realised he was hardly older than we were. Boet pulled his shoulder back and hit him with a straight right below the heart. The kid went down without protest and I heard a sickening thud as his head hit the concrete. Boet was kicking him in the head over and over, but the greaser didn't even squirm.

'Hey, Boet, better get off him,' one of his goons shouted, pulling his arm. Boet turned, wiping his mouth on the back of his hand, his chest heaving. Then, as his mate let go of his sleeve, he turned back and savagely kicked the kid again. I didn't know how much more I could take.

That was when Tommy moved. He leaped on Boet, almost trampling on the kid lying prone on the step below us.

'*Tommy!*'

I felt like someone was pushing a thumb into my

122

windpipe. I had to get him out of there. Two greasers moved in on Boet with Tommy hanging onto his back, one of them punching him in the short rib. Tommy slid off and I jumped over the kid and reached out to get a hold of Tommy, but my hand just swiped the back his shirt.

Strong fingers gripped me under my armpits. 'Get the fuck out of here!'

It was Johnny. He lifted me into the air, turning me sideways, and dragged me back up onto the steps. I was struggling in his grasp, trying not to lose sight of Tommy over my shoulder.

'Let go of me, man, Johnny!'

He stood on the step above me, one hand still on my shoulder, looking keenly at me. 'Chris! Stay away from this shit, man! Don't you get it? There's no way back.'

'I can't, Johnny. I've got to help Tommy. I can't leave him out there.'

His eyes, intensely blue, searched my face. He shook his head. 'No, Chris, you got to let him go.'

I pulled away, turned back to the fight, my eyes raking for Tommy. I spotted him standing a little way behind the two greasers who were punching one of Boet's goons on the ground. His arms hung limply by his side. 'Tommy!' I screamed hoarsely.

He turned towards my voice, saw me standing on the steps with Johnny, then stared down at the crumpled body of the kid below me. I was staring down at the kid too now, at the blood pooling under his head, and more than anything else in the world, I just wanted to get away from there. I wrenched free of Johnny, jumped over the greaser and landed right in front of Tommy.

'Tommy, come back with me, man.'

His eyes stared vacantly past me at the kid lying at the bottom of the steps.

'It's not like he was lost, Tommy,' I shouted. 'He came looking for the fight.' I was searching his face, trying to get him to see me. 'He's not Cece.'

Tommy was looking at me now, frowning, struggling to hear my words, and then Johnny was hauling me back up the steps, and I let him. Tommy's bewildered eyes caught mine one last time before he turned back and lashed out with his right foot, kicking the goon, again and again.

That was when I heard it, that song. It was flooding out of the dance hall, and it was like it was calling me back. Johnny was pulling me through the foyer, but it was the song I was following. When we got to the doors, we could *sommer* just walk in, Mrs van der Watt'd given up long ago.

The kids inside were going crazy.

'Oh Lucille, please come back
Where you belong
I've been good to you baby,
Please don't leave me alone.'

I stood on the edge, bovine, as long minutes passed, and next thing, it was Tommy yanking me out onto the dance floor, and me and him were jiving like it was going out of style, man. Blood was splattered down his shirt, but he wasn't bleeding.

'Lucille, baby, satisfy my heart'

Tommy was throwing back his head and laughing, and I was laughing so hard I got a guts ache and I never felt so alive, man. The knowledge that I'd deserted Tommy filled my lungs. A shadow had fallen across the light inside me and I kept dancing wildly, laughing and laughing, surrendering to the darkness.

12

The Museum

They're black. *Jisis*. I had a hot copy of *Stage & Cinema* that I'd smuggled out of the girls' room, right from under Mona's coir mattress where it lay nestled on the sagging springs, and now I wasn't even sorry that I couldn't get my thieving mitts on Johnny's *Johannesburg Crime Report*.

He'd eyed me over the top of his Mickey Spillane when he saw me casually leaning against his window-sill – did I think he didn't know what a dirty little rotter like me was planning? I liked to go through his stuff when he wasn't there, see if I could find anything.

'Hey, listen to this,' he said, his eyes returning to the last page. '"How c-could you?" she gasped.'

Johnny put on a falsetto as he quoted from *I, the Jury*, which he'd only read about a thousand times. He recited Mike Hammer's line without having to glance at the page: 'I only had a moment before talking to a corpse, but I got it in. "It was easy," I said.'

He was snorting with laughter as he snapped the book

closed and whacked my fingers with it as they stole towards the discarded *Crime Report* on the sill over his shoulder. Johnny'd always loved his pulp detective novels. When I was a kid, he used to make up his own versions for me. Jack the Ripper bedtime stories. Man, they were brilliant: lying in the dark, Johnny's voice breathing life into a dwarf, a widow, and someone called the Fat Man, who'd turn out to be ghoulishly thin and wear a gold ring engraved with his initials. There were people who went missing, until Johnny followed the trail to a dingy hotel room, 'just big enough for a bed, a chest of drawers and a corpse'. Johnny would be found holding a smoking gun. The smell of perfume or Turkish cigarettes was always significant, and the dwarf's dying words about a falcon would turn out to be the *nom de plume* of a master criminal who'd eventually have Johnny in his clutches, look at him with deadly eyes, and know he was lying.

Funny, the other person who always loved those stories was Mona. She'd steal into our room and curl up at the bottom of my bed to listen, then silently slip out at the end. Mona was born a twin, but her brother died at birth. I'd never asked her how she felt about that – must've been kind of weird. She'd have made a good character in one of Johnny's stories with a ghost like that in her past, but Johnny didn't tell those stories any more.

After he'd tried to break my fingers with the spine of *I, the Jury*, I gave up on the *Crime Report*, crept into the girls' room and whipped *Stage & Cinema* as a booby prize. And now here I was, sprawled on the floor of the gymnasium next to Tommy, staring at page twenty-seven, flabbergasted.

'Hell's teeth! Did you know they were black?'

'Who's black?' asked Doc, pummelling the speedball.

'Little Richard, man. Check here,' I said, stabbing a finger at the picture of a sweating, screaming black man with his eyes squeezed shut, head thrown back, mouth agape.

'Richard? How's the oke black with a name like Dick? Dirty Dick, as it turns out.' He was cackling as he pummelled. 'So now you listening to *hout* music? First that bloody pervert, Elvis, singing about hound dogs and God knows what else, and now a bunch a bloody *hout kops*.' Doc had to stop pummelling, he was laughing so hard. 'Jesus, what's next?'

Tommy came over to check it out. 'They're not like our blacks, see?' said Tommy. 'Look they're American blacks. That's different.'

'Black is black, *ou* pal,' said Doc, darkly. 'Where do you think they came from?' He went back to pummelling.

This was a bloody revelation. I started thumbing through the pages, taking a lot more of an interest all of a sudden. Up until now I'd just checked the cover. When it was Elvis or James Dean, I rolled it up and stuffed it down my shirt front and snuck into the bathroom, where I propped it up on the basin and practised my sneer in the mirror. Marlon Brando's was also good. You had to look *lekker* pissed off. I reckon that's why my old man and the other farts hated him so much, Elvis. It was just rude, man. That and his Pelvis. When I tried it out, though, I just ended up looking like a dog before a fight: lip curled, ferrety teeth bared, nothing cool about it, man.

And now it turned out rock 'n' roll wasn't just rude and the Devil's music, but it was cranked out by black okes too. Next thing Tommy'd spotted another one: Fats Domino.

Johnny smacked through the swing doors.

'Well, ain't that a shame,' he said, as he made his way over to us.

'You *piepie jollers* want to hear Beethoven roll over? Chuck Berry too.'

'Chuck is black?'

'Black as the night, went to jail for hijacking too,' he added. 'Half those jive cats are black – taking back their music, which was stolen and tamed for whites. "Whitebreading", they called it.'

First their church and now their music. Funny how it kept coming back to Africa. I was pretty sure the old *vrots* on the Morality and Decency Committee at the town council were not aware of this fact either or they'd slap a ban on Chuck's shiny black arse so fast his head would spin. I suspected that David Davies on LM Radio knew, but he was safely out of reach of the long arm of Piet Meyer and the Censorship Board, barricaded in Radio Palace in Mozambique scoffing prawns.

David Davies loved to tune old Piet Meyer: 'This one's for you, Piet. How *you* doin'?'

It was whispered that Piet Meyer was high up in the Broederbond too, but there was bugger-all the old git could do about the airwaves.

Doc reckoned it was a good thing we couldn't dance, now that it turned out it was *hout* music we were listening to.

'You're wrong, Doc. These kids do know how to dance already. They just don't know they do.'

It was Jock.

'Get in the ring, Tommy. Christopher, you too.'

'Trust me, Jock, they can't dance. You shoulda checked

these débutantes at the banqueting hall on Saturday night. It was bloody embarrassing, man,' said Johnny, helpfully.

'It's true, Jock, we made a arse out of ourselves.'

'Look, I don't care about your performance at the vaunted socials down at the Krugersdorp town hall, dazzling though I'm sure those occasions must be. I care about your performance in the ring. You still think boxing's about punching? You think it's in the shoulder, the fist? That it's not. A great boxer is a dancer. A great boxer is pretty to watch, even if you only watch his feet. It's all in the footwork, boys. Hey, Johnny, let's have that tune again by this Richard fellow.'

Johnny shambled over to the jukebox, and next minute 'Lucille' was blaring all over the gym again.

'You hear it?' said Jock, cocking his head.

'*Duh-da-duh-da, duh-da-duh-da . . .*'

He was clicking his fingers to the slower back beat.

'It's a metronome so loud anyone can dance to it. Now get up, Twinkle Toes – let's see you move.'

Soon he had me and Tommy weaving around the ring to the rhythmic drumbeat under the driving piano.

'Brilliant, boys, this is better than the speedball!'

'*Ag*, congratulations,' said Doc. 'So now you got a pair a bloody ballerinas. Look at them. Two little queers dancing to *hout* music on a souped-up gramophone.' And he was guffawing again.

'Can't call yourself a man until you've tried it,' said Tommy, as he jived past the ropes Doc was leaning on.

Johnny reckoned he still wasn't going to ask us to dance next week at the session.

'It's all in the foundations, Johnny, and these boys have rhythm in their big toes.'

I hadn't thought about that night. I tried not to. Tommy and I dodged it – it simply did not happen. But it swelled in the gulf between us. He'd tried once that Sunday morning afterwards. 'How cool were we on that dance floor, hey?'

'So cool you shit ice-bricks, man.'

'Although maybe I should've taken my shirt off before, you know … Orright, maybe I just should've made like Buddha and stayed out of it.'

He faked a laugh, raked his fingers through his hair, looked at me in a way that gave me such a tight pain in my heart I didn't know what to say. So I said, 'Forget it, man, you were just cruisin' for a bruisin',' like it meant nothing, and he said, 'Hey, what's a little blood on your threads?' like it meant nothing.

But it did. In a 'Hand Jive' heartbeat he had made a choice, and so had I. And, with the brutal clarity of hindsight, I looked with longing upon the freedom we squandered. Right up until the instant I turned my back on him, I was still free to choose, just as he was in that moment before his father turned into the dark corridor and saw him.

It doesn't seem like much, when what you do won't make one bit of difference, but when it's all you've got, possessing the freedom to choose is a kind of power. Once the choice is made, possibility dies; what you will do has become what you have done – and, sometimes, who you have become.

We had a choice – that's the point, you always do – between courage and cowardice, between loyalty and betrayal. You don't save yourself by hiding behind a wall; somehow, with the smell of the drain curling in your nostrils, you're still a victim of what you feared. That much I knew was true.

131

Jiving around the ring to jukebox rock 'n' roll seemed so far away from secret guilt and shame, it was like it didn't happen, like everything was still the way it was, or the way it was supposed to be anyway. I was caught by my sudden need to turn away so the whole of the West Rand Cons Boxing Club didn't see the hot tears of an almost-thirteen-year-old cry-baby.

After Little Richard's last scream faded away, Jock took a long look at us, and then told us to get in the back of his pick-up truck, which was parked outside. 'There's something I want you two to see.'

I was stuffing my rolled-up copy of *Stage & Cinema* down the waistband of my pants when Tommy asked if he could borrow it.

'*Ja*, but you'd better give it back before Mona finds it missing. You know I'm prime bloody suspect if she does,' I said, as we pushed through the swing doors.

Hanging onto the back of the Morris Minor branded 'West Rand Cons', howling into the wind, we roared out onto the Main Reef Road. We were headed east towards Johannesburg, past Luipaardsvlei, and were somewhere between Durban Deep and Rand Leases when Jock pulled into the car park in front of an old hotel in a crunch of gravel.

It was Willie Smith's. Everyone knew it: Willie was a legend on the Reef. My old man came drinking here. I'd never been inside, though. I crunched after Jock to the entrance of the hotel, feeling mighty impressed.

I squinted up at its ivy-festooned façade. Beneath the red roof, it clambered hungrily over the mock-Tudor beams inlaid in the whitewash. It was so densely matted it was like a living, breathing wall of vines draped over the arched windows, which struggled for light. Willie was one of the Empire boxers, from the glory years, spoken of in hushed tones around Millsite. He had made it all the way to the Paris Olympics in '24 where he'd won gold in a pair of Everlasts sent specially from Solly Goldstein's gym in Johannesburg. Above the ebony door set to the side of the main entrance 'The Willie Smith Bar' was stencilled in ornate lettering.

Before we entered, Jock said, 'When I was a kid, I queued for four hours with my father to watch one of the greatest fights I've ever seen. It took place at the Royal Albert Hall on the sixth of October 1927. Willie was the underdog. Few men thought he had any hope of defeating Teddy Baldock, but the champion fell for one of the cleverest double bluffs ever pulled off in the ring. Willie was declared bantamweight champion of the world. The press hailed him as one of the greatest natural boxers since Jimmy Wilde.'

Jock paused and shook his head. 'Willie was so light on his feet, in the film, it looked as if he was floating.' Then he pushed the door open and we followed him inside. As we entered the bar, a dark, curly-haired man standing behind the heavily wrought brass cash register glanced up. His eyes crinkled at the edges when he grinned. 'Hey, Willie, you old has-been,' Jock greeted him.

'Hamish. What's an old mongrel like you doing drinking with a pair of whippersnappers?'

Jock laughed. 'Just wanted to give them a quick history tour.'

'You two in the squad?' Willie asked.

I stared at him with a mouth full of teeth.

'*Ja*, Mr Willie, sir,' Tommy squeaked.

'Take your time,' he said.

My eyes roamed the bar in the dim light seeping through the spokes of the wagon-wheel windows. Barrel chairs clustered around tables occupied the centre of the room, which was flanked with maroon velvet booths. A large fireplace dominated the opposite wall, two moth-eaten buffalo heads jutting from the chimney. A half-naked strong man heaved a barrel of Lion beer in a picture by the door: 'For strength and health,' it said. A thermometer was nailed to the wall beneath it. Stale smoke and beer fermented in the bottle-green paisley swirls of the carpet.

Jock headed towards the first recess and we traipsed after him, but it was only when he stopped just short of it, without sitting down, that I finally saw why we were there. Mounted on the walnut partitions separating the booths was a whole gallery of framed photographs. 'The legends of the ring, boys. Go ahead, soak up the reflected glory.'

Kneeling on the velvet, peering closely at a frame, I made out a blurry boxer posing with his fists raised, one eyebrow cocked. 'Jack Dempsey' was etched onto a copper plate below it.

Tommy was kneeling beside me, 'Jimmy Wilde,' he whispered. I stared at the faint picture; Jimmy's ghostly eyes stared back. Tommy moved off, but I couldn't pull my eyes away.

'Hey, Chris, come here,' Tommy called. 'You've got to see this.'

I joined him in the next gallery. He was stabbing a finger at Rocky Marciano in a clinch with another boxer. Marciano, the puncher with bottomless guts, was the world heavyweight title-holder who'd shocked the boxing fraternity by announcing his retirement. I whistled appreciatively. Willie Smith's bar was the greatest museum on earth.

'Ah, this is what I wanted to show you.' Jock's voice floated over from the far side of the room. 'Henry Armstrong.'

Between 1937 and 1940, 'Hurricane Hank' won world titles at featherweight, lightweight and welterweight, and he fought a draw for the middleweight title. For four glorious months in 1938 he'd held his titles simultaneously. His record had never been matched. Tommy and I made our way over to the mantelpiece above the grate and stared into the grimacing face of a black man, his left eye swollen shut, sweat glistening on his brow. I recoiled in shock.

'In the same year that Armstrong held his four titles, Joe Louis held the heavyweight title.'

He tapped another picture and I saw a black man behind the glass wearing a deadpan expression.

'When the young champion beat Max Schmeling in a hundred and twenty-four seconds to avenge his solitary defeat at the hands of the German, the Nazis ordered the broadcast to be cut off when the Aryan's cries of pain were drowning the commentator.'

'Well, I'll be buggered,' said Tommy, standing beside me.

'Sugar Ray ...' said Jock, scanning the walls. 'Sugar, you black beauty, where are you?'

Sugar Ray Robinson was the greatest middleweight in history, and very possibly the greatest welterweight as well. Finally Jock found a picture of a black Sugar Ray captured in mid-air on his jump rope. He hovered slack-jawed a few feet above the ground.

'They say the crazy bastard drives a pink Cadillac, has his

own personal shoe shiner. He lost it a bit when Jimmy Doyle never regained consciousness after he'd knocked him out in the eighth round in Cleveland in 1947. Sugar dreamed the precise circumstances of Doyle's death the night before the fight and was only persuaded to go through with it by Doyle's own priest.'

A siren sounded in the distance.

'The point,' he said, sobering up, 'is that greatness is not always found where you expect it. Get your arses back in the pick-up. Willie's customers will be rolling in now the shift is over.

'Cheers, Willie,' he called to Willie, who had disappeared into the back somewhere.

Tommy and I shared the cab with Jock on the way back to West Rand Cons. We were both quiet. In just over a week, the Southern Transvaal Junior Championship would bind us for ever to this fraternity. By strange coincidence it was on the same night as the Krugersdorp Junior Jive Contest. Oh, well, screw it, I still couldn't dance, even if I had found rhythm.

'Hey, Jock,' said Tommy, 'how come Willie Smith came back? I mean, if I ever made it to the Royal Albert Hall you wouldn't see my backside again in Nowheresville.'

'He made it all the way to Madison Square Garden,' said Jock, 'but that was where he made his mistake. Sold his soul to the Devil, I'm afraid.'

'I thought you didn't believe in all that hogwash, Jock?'

'I mean the Mob, Chris. The underworld has always flirted with the fight game. In Willie's day, the Mob virtually ran big-time boxing in America. Contracts were still haggled over in sweaty change-rooms, and a length of lead pipe got you further in negotiations than is proper. There were plenty of fights that looked suspicious. There was no way to prove it, though – only two people need ever know about it: the fixer and the diver.

'Anyway, Willie signed a five-year contract that bound him to the Mob. There was no way out. Any boxer who tried to leave his manager got blackballed by the Guild and would never fight again. Willie once told me that after he signed he was taken to a bar in 57th Street where his new manager showed him an album of Polaroids. The man didn't say a word, just sat there with a cigar poking out the side of his mouth, flipping mechanically through them one by one. The light was dim, but Willie could see they were stiffs. His manager told him they were renegades and to take a good long look. He had one fight in the US, which he lost, and then left the country.'

'Hell.'

The ring had always had a seedy sort of glamour about it.

13

The Prayer

Cece

I was the keeper of secrets. I was telling you that before. Now I had a new one: Vilikazi had to spend the night in the bushes in the cemetery. Man, if it'd been me, I'd've taken my chances with the police, rather than them ghosts.

Nestled in their graves, they waited. Sly, patient, hungry, their eyelids fluttered as the witching hour drew nigh. Slowly they unfurled, sifted through the earth and the probing roots of the trees, and drifted across the graveyard like mist. They were unutterably lonely. If you looked into their eyes, which were broken fragments of the earth's soul, you saw how you were going to die. Once I woke in the night and felt something moving furtively in the dark bedroom. My fingertips tingled and I saw my breath was cloudy. I asked Vilikazi if he felt the deadly chill as they passed. He said he didn't have nothing to fear from ancestors. Well, let's see, shall we? And that's what you got for sneaking around after curfew anyway.

He was in Madubulaville, at his old Makhulu's *shebeen* drinking *gwebu*. Vilikazi said only the sweet froth could soothe his throat after his shift yesterday. That stuff was disgusting, man.

'*Maningi tshik!*' Vilikazi's lip curled. 'That's what he says to me, the *mpasopi*. "*Mpasopi*" – *eish!*' He clicked his tongue. 'Fanakalo! When you come to the GMTS, they teach you the word for "miner" is "*baas*". I don't trust a language where the only word for government official is *mlungu ka lo guvment.*'

Dubula meant 'bang' in Fanakalo, like when the dynamite went off, but Vilikazi said in Zulu it meant 'to shoot' – although he reckoned it was some poor baboon who got shot for living under the stage of the town hall. Dippy name for a place, if you ask me, and it suited it.

When Vilikazi took me there once, after he'd stopped going to the Jerusalem Apostolic Church of Zion, my eyes nearly fell out of my head when a donkey cart came trundling down the main road with a piper and a honky-tonk piano-playing loony on its back. There was music blaring from gramophones inside every ramshackle house on the street and a dog that looked fit to have rabies was howling at a moon that wasn't there. The noise got so bad I thought everyone had gone raving mad. Vilikazi said a touch of madness was no bad thing.

I sat outside Makhulu's *shebeen* watching the other kids playing in the street until it was dusk. I wished I could play with them. They were fighting in the fading light when Vilikazi emerged, their faces gone blank with it.

Anyhow, I promised Vilikazi I wouldn't tell a soul how come he was so late for work. I was lolling drowsily in the gnarled old roots of the quince tree, tenderly ministering to my clutch of secrets. Plump quinces had fallen and ruptured all around me; ants and gauzy clouds of *miggies* gorged on the oozing flesh, and the sticky sweet perfume coated the back of my throat. TJ was snapping at the *miggies*, champing and shuddering. Man, that dog was driving me nuts. Vilikazi was on his knees a short way from me. 'Vilikazi?'

'What you want?'

'Why can't you walk the streets at night?'

'*Eish!*'

The sun was too bright today, he said, to speak of evil. I narrowed my eyes. Actually, if I'd had to choose, I didn't know if the graveyard was worse than sleeping in our house. The fear, as far as I could tell, had seeped into its walls, like damp, before I was born, if it wasn't always there. Maybe it was in the ground.

Around noon Tommy and Chris came for me. I felt bad just leaving Vilikazi, his hands in the soil, but I had to get out of there. I think Vilikazi knew why.

'Come on, TJ!' I yelled, from my perch on Chris's handlebars.

TJ dashed behind the wheels, all paws and flapping ears, grinning insanely, his tongue flapping out the side of his mouth. I don't think he even remembered the time he couldn't walk. I was trying to forget about it too. Since Tommy had peeled off his bandages, it was getting easier.

When we got to Chris's house on C Row, teenagers were sprawled all over the veranda – there were always loads of kids at Chris's house – Johnny's transistor radio was booming, and Chris and Tommy looked at each other like they'd just found a last gobstopper at the bottom of the bag. They glued their rumps to the steps of the veranda, even though Johnny told them to get lost. I liked Johnny. He was the one who taught me ghost lore, but only when it was just me and Maggie, and we were sworn to secrecy. He called us the pip-squeaks.

I headed straight round the back to the kitchen. I could see Missus Jameson through the window. She was laughing at something, her face lit as the fine lines around her eyes and mouth deepened. I stood shyly in the open door.

'Hello, little sunshine,' she said, when she saw me.

TJ barged past, pranced up on his hind legs when he reached her and started frantically paddling her with his paws.

'Get down, TJ! Cecelia, take your savage little brute outside this minute.'

I dragged TJ out by the scruff of his neck. He wasn't going to go willingly, that's for darn sure. He stuck his bottom down and dug in his paws, and I had to drag him across the floor with a look of doom on his face.

Missus Jameson gave me a big bowl of peas to shell and I sat cross-legged on the scrubbed table, shelling and popping peas into my mouth and listening to the lovely sound of one of the twins banging on a row of pots with a big wooden spoon, and the tinselly music coming from Missus Jameson's radio and her laugh – there was nothing dainty or prim or modest about it, it just burbled right out of her.

She wasn't always like this, happy, and I don't mean when she was cross. I knew she was still happy underneath all the hollering. I mean, I'd seen the shadows in her. Sometimes I'd find her at the window, and there was a stillness about her. Once, when it was strangely quiet in the house, she came out into the garden where I was watering my veggie patch and knelt down beside me.

'I like your flowers, Cece, a touch of whimsy in the midst of all these strapping string beans.'

'Thank you,' I said. Then I asked her why she was sometimes so sad.

She looked startled, but then she sighed and said, 'Do you want to know a secret?'

I didn't answer.

'I have six children. Strong, beautiful, their lives, with all their miracles and sorrows, ahead of them, and do you know, the one I think of most often is the one I lost?'

Mona's twin.

'She was only one when he died, Mona, but she remembered him for so long after he was gone, it was almost impossible. She wouldn't say anything for the longest time, but then we'd be at the market or somewhere, when she was two or even three, and suddenly she'd grip my hand and point to the crowd. "Mommy!" she'd say. "There's Patty, Mommy! Hurry!"

'I would always look – I don't know why, I couldn't help myself. And there was always a resemblance, sometimes just a whisper, a mop of golden curls, but unmistakable nonetheless.'

I listened. I wondered if that was why she told me. I was good at listening. Like I said, sometimes I think people almost forgot that I was there.

She sighed, a warm, damp sigh. I wanted to call her 'Mama', and sometimes I did, quietly, under my breath.

'Cecelia, you're gobbling more peas than you actually put in the bowl!' she chided.

I winked, my cheeks bulging. She waggled her wooden spoon at me and said it was going to be me who found my sorry behind out in the veggie patch picking more peas. And I could wipe that grin off my chops too. 'Love Letters In The Sand' was warbling out of the radio and she was swaying to the music and singing along in her lilting voice. Tommy hated Pat Boone – he and Chris called him soppy and said rude things about him being queer, but I just loved him to bits. As the sax started blowing, she swooped across the kitchen floor and scooped me up, and then we were spinning and spinning, and I hung my head upside down and I felt dizzy and swirly and the baby was squealing with laughter.

After she plopped me back on the table, I felt myself droop. Might as well face it, I'd been busting a gut praying, and you only had to look at the cold hard facts to know that God was punishing me. I'd begged and begged Him to let me and Tommy come and live here. I'd given Him the address and told Him I'd leave it in His mighty hands to fix it, but He was deaf where my prayers were concerned.

And why? I'll tell you why. Because of that unrepentant hellcat.

I had just about had it with Tommy and I told him straight. It was after he bunked church – again. Just got up and swaggered on out. I told him his slamming the door in Jesus's face was why we were still living at No. 113 Club Road.

'Ag, jisis, Cece, not you too, man. Don't let them brainwash you with that hooey.'

I told him they have an especially hot place in Hell for the likes of him and just wait until he felt the flames licking at his feet: that'd teach him a lesson. 'That's what Satan will

143

say, when he spots you being carried in on the shoulders of his foul minions. "Hello, Tommy, welcome to Hell. Guess you're feeling pretty stupid right about now."'

But inside I just wanted to cry and for Tommy and me to come and live here, and I had this scared feeling that Tommy really was falling, faster and faster. Something had changed in him. It was after that dance him and Chris snuck out to, and he came home with blood on his shirt. I saw him scrubbing at it in the basin with a bar of Sunlight soap, but the blood wouldn't come out, and I saw his face and I felt cold inside. I knew that he'd gone through some kind of door, and there was no way back. It wasn't like that all the time, mostly he seemed okay, but still I felt it lurking underneath, like a dark current.

14

The Compound

Chris

'You're late.' Jock was curt.

He'd said we could come along to the compound on Saturday afternoon – we surely needed all the extra training we could get. It was one week until our match.

'Why you wasting your time with the blacks anyway?' Mitch had griped.

'I'm not wasting my time,' Jock said brusquely. 'Show some respect, boy.'

'Respect?' said Mitch, sounding flabbergasted. 'Well, the Transvaal Amateur Boxing Organisation sure as hell isn't ever going to let them box, man.'

'The Transvaal Amateur Boxing Organisation isn't the only forum to box,' Jock replied. 'Just get to the compound gates on Saturday at three o'clock sharp.'

Jock's squad, when we arrived, was assembled in the middle of the quad, the men standing stiffly in rows, naked from the waist up. We fell in at the rear. Some of the men turned at the disturbance. I recognised most of them from the hours we'd hung out in the compound. That I hadn't known they were boxers until now made me feel strangely exposed, like we belonged to some secret brotherhood and I hadn't been careful enough. I spotted Vilikazi rummaging in the tackle and grinned. He winked.

The drill nearly killed us. Jock barked and we ran until I could see the men's slick torsos glistening through the mirage formed by the sun glinting off the roof into my stinging eyes. The men were singing throughout: a deep, booming hymn. It went on and on, the air searing my lungs, the sun bleaching the blue from the endless sky. It wound up with a twelve-minute routine in which we had to jump on and off a two-and-a-half-foot-high block.

'That's it, men, good work.'

The military rigour dissolved. I flopped down onto the bald dirt floor of the quad. Rod and Mitch buckled down beside me. Only Tommy still stood, doubled over, panting. The men were mocking us – Vilikazi blatantly guffawed, a sleek young man, who looked about Johnny's age, was jiggling his cupped hands under his nipples and catcalling about *amabele*. Tommy started laughing, but he still didn't have any air in his lungs and he keeled over, laughing and wheezing. I stared up at a vulture spiralling lazily on the hot thermals far above me, but eventually the thirst drove me over on my hands and knees to the jostle of men around the tap. The iron was corroded and slimy, but I gulped *manzi* until my guts cramped, then let the shockingly cold water run down my chin and neck, sluicing the sweat off my skin.

After Jock paired sparring partners, we sprawled out in the shade of the low, squat whitewashed building, beside the men perched on upturned crates and blackened tins playing dice around a crumpled board. Most of them were older, more grizzled. I didn't study their game, though: I was staring at the boxers. They were beautiful to watch.

I'd never seen anything like it before – their movements were fluid. The pairs practically glided around one another. My muscles were stiffening, but I couldn't move, couldn't tear my eyes from them. Light, powerful, perfectly balanced, their feet and fists in synch, they had grace.

There was a makeshift ring in the centre of the quad, just a roped-off square of floorboard, slightly sprung off a frame of planks, but there was a stool and a spit bucket placed in opposite corners. Jock was in the centre, strapping on the punch mitts.

'*Buya lapa*,' he called to a young boxer outside the ropes, slapping the mitts together.

Dlamini was his name. He began working the mitts, grunting as he threw punches in short combinations, his face a scowl of concentration.

'That's it! Put your left fist into that jab! Snap it,' Jock pressed, as he shuffled backwards.

We knew Dlamini from the Go-away bird he kept in his cell. He had raised it from a chick, but no cage held it captive. It was free to fly away whenever it wished, but it never did. It was perched on the gutter running along the roof of the compound building, tilting its crested grey head curiously. By now Dlamini was in the last of the usual four three-minute rounds on the punch mitts, which left my arms hanging dead from my shoulders.

We were sitting in the area set aside for floor work, and Mitch eventually hauled himself up and started skipping.

The sparring and the steady *whap-whap-whap* of the rope as it smacked the floor and harsh *kwa-waay, kwa-waay* of the Go-away-bird were just starting to make me drowsy when they cranked up the *gumba-gumba*.

Hell.

The music coming from the record-player was something else, man. I'd heard the jazzy sound of the Southern Rhodesia Cold Storage Commission's *tsaba-tsaba* band piping out of the radio hook-up in the compound before, but this was different. It sounded bluesy, I could hear the sax, but it had roots going down deep into African soil. It had that *lekker 'a wimoweh, a wimoweh'* beat, and a woman's rich, melodic voice was soaring over a deep, gravelly man's. I couldn't understand the words, but Tommy started seesawing on his buttocks and clicking his fingers in time to it.

'What is that, man?'

Some of the boxers weren't so much boxing any more as doing a sort of sashay in time to the music. A few other men had emerged from the doorway, outside which the *gumba-gumba* was standing on a chair. They were dressed like gangsters, white fedoras with black hatbands pulled low over their eyes, collars unbuttoned, cigarettes dangling from their lips. I was impressed, man. And their shoes, *jisis*, they were smart. They were jiving like I'd never seen jiving before either.

'*Kwela!*' one of the gamblers behind me shouted to Tommy. 'It's *kwela-kwela*.'

He was one of the old lags, painfully thin, his ribcage protruding grotesquely from his craggy skin. He always wore the same pair of ragged pants; the flap of a ripped pocket hung down, exposing an obscene buttock. I didn't know what his job was down the mine, but in the compound he was a bit of a *skollie* – the oke who could get it for you: tobacco, *skokiaan*, *dagga*, women even, they said. There was one on every compound on this reef, Vilikazi reckoned.

'*Kwela-kwela*,' said Tommy, limbering his tongue up. 'Orright, then,' he shouted, jumping up. 'Watch me *kwela-kwela*!'

And Tommy started jiving right there in the middle of the West Rand Consolidated Mine's native compound. It was irresistible, and before I even had time to think about it, I was up jiving next to him and the men were clapping and whistling and Vilikazi shouted, 'You better *passop*, Tommy, you'll be *in* the *kwela-kwela* with us next time.'

I could hear a pennywhistle now, piping out the melody.

'Hey?'

'The *kwela-kwela*, it's also the word for the police van. When they pull up at the *shebeen*, where you've been drinking *skokiaan* and dancing *pata-pata*, that's what they shout, the police: "*Kwela! Kwela!* Climb in! Climb in!"' and he roared with laughter.

'Come, like this.'

Vilikazi was heavy, and an old *madala* too, but, man, he could move. He was dancing alongside us now and I was trying to follow the way he was sort of rolling his shoulders and his hips. I'd just about got it when he *gooi*ed in this complicated footwork routine.

'Ah, Jeez, man!' I said, and he started laughing.

I dropped down onto an old tin to watch. Jock strolled over – he'd given up on the boxing – and kicked me off my stool. 'So, Christopher, what do you make of my other West Rand Cons boxing squad?'

149

I was sitting on the ground, knees bent, leaning back on my elbows. I gave a low whistle and slowly shook my head in answer.

'*Ja*, I know,' he said, grinning. 'And Wenela lured half of these boys straight out of the Bantustans only a year ago, maybe two.'

'Hey, Jock, you ever seen them when they first get off the train at Jo'burg Central? *Jisis*, they're *kak*ing themselves!'

I clenched my buttocks to make the point. You'd see them on the platform down by third class, cringing together with heavy tin trunks on their heads and fear in their eyes. Property of the GMTS – that's Government Mining Training School in official mumble, God Made Them Slaves to everyone else.

Jock nodded slowly. 'The distance from *kraal* to compound, Christopher, can't be measured in miles …' He trailed off, waving at the doorways yawning in the whitewash around us.

Although it was dark, I could see inside the barracks on the far side of the quad to the rows of concrete bunks stacked like slabs in a mortuary. The men had hung their meagre possessions on hooks nailed into the walls; a charred coal stove squatted in the centre of the room. Jock followed my gaze.

'But my point,' Jock resumed, 'is that my herd boys are quite something to be reckoned with. Would you not agree, Chris?'

'*Ja*, but where do they box, Jock? I mean, where do they get a proper fight?'

'Ah, Chris, there's a whole circuit in the slumyards. Migrants aren't the only type of black in this city. There's

150

another breed altogether – second and third generation city-born proles, who have slithered out of the state's grip. The rutted streets of the slumyards are teeming with *shebeen* queens, *tsotsi*s, the prophets of Zion, pennywhistlers who walk the streets playing requests for a tickie per seventy-eight.'

My eyes swivelled to the Chicago-styled gangsters jiving in the corner.

'*Tsotsi* promoters own the fight game in the slumyards. And in the gymnasiums of Jo'burg, well … Apartheid crumbles in the face of greed.'

'So can you teach me some *tsotsitaal*, then, Jock? Do you know any good swear words?'

'Alas, most of the choicer words refer to *dagga*-smoking and prison.'

'Oh. And what do you mean? About Apartheid crumbling?

He gave me a wry look. 'Apartheid, Christopher, is really about controlling the gates to the city. It is about keeping the *bantu*s out … Don't you know?' He cocked his head. 'The city is where a good native gets spoiled. It is from the indolent native in the city that the undesirable classes spring – the slumlords, the bootleggers, the prostitutes, the agitators. Much better they go back to the old way of life – nice, simple, tribal natives, living in the past.

'Apartheid promises to keep migrant labour corralled in the compound, five hundred yards of nice, bare, windblown veld between the Location and the town it serves, and to drive the rest back to the dusty little patches of leached Bantustan soil.

'But it can never satisfy the mines' insatiable hunger for men – Apartheid is strangling their supply of cheap labour.

Verwoerd says that when it comes down to it, we must choose to be poor and white – but the Rand Lords aren't willing to pay for a racist Utopia, and you can't switch off industrialisation, so Wenela keeps luring the herd boys to *eGoli* with a glitter in her eye. And so they come, pouring into the city, a strange, violent, dangerous place, where the dice are loaded, where you come knowingly to be sweated like a beast of burden.'

I sat there staring at the forest of legs twisting in the dust before me. Vilikazi squatted down right in front of me. 'The Basotho,' he mouthed. 'They say when you come to Johannesburg you enter the land of the cannibals. And at night, in the *shebeens*, *tsotsi* promoters haggle with white managers for their boys to slug it out for a share of the purse, while the *shebeen* queens sway to the *kwela-kwela* and keep pouring the beer.'

Then he was up again, thrusting his hips, his hands behind the wheel of an imaginary car. 'Come, Chris, try again.' He reached a hand out to me and winked at Jock. I took it and let him pull me up. Jock heaved himself up off the can and went to start packing up the gloves. The shadow from the compound block was stretched halfway across the ring by now.

'Chris?'

I spun around and spied Cece hesitating at the entrance to the compound. She hurried over to me and beamed when she saw Vilikazi.

'What are you doing here, Cece?' I said, scowling at her.

'Sorry, Chris, I know you're boxing, but Tommy told me I had to bring you Mona's *Stage & Cinema*. He said Mona's got pointy fingernails and I'd better hurry.'

'What did you want with *Stage & Cinema*?'

'Nothing,' she said. 'Tommy forgot it in your cave and he told me to go and get it for him and bring it here to you.'

'Good God,' said Jock, who'd made his way over to where Cece was gawping beside me.

He looked over to the far corner of the compound where Tommy had made his way over to the *tsotsi*s. Of course. He hadn't even noticed Cece's arrival.

'Tommy! Get here right now,' Jock bellowed.

'I know how to boogie-woogie,' said Cece, shyly, looking up at Vilikazi.

'Well, go, then, young lady,' said Jock. 'Let's see.'

Cece started wiggling her bottom impudently and Vilikazi convulsed. Tommy was squinting over his shoulder. He took in his sister, legs bowed like a chicken, her bum stuck out behind her, and sauntered across to us. 'Hello, Cece,' he said. 'Did you get it?'

Cece hiked up her skirt and, from the pocket sewn onto the gusset of those great bloomers of hers, pulled out a slightly more tattered copy of *Stage & Cinema* than the one I'd lent Tommy. She passed it to Tommy for inspection before he handed it to me. 'Thanks, Cece,' he said.

'*Ja*, thanks, hey,' I added.

'Thomas, am I to understand that you emotionally blackmailed your sister, clearly a kindergartener, into venturing alone into the canyons of the dump to retrieve a purloined copy of this magazine?' Jock said, gesturing at it in my hand.

'Oh, I wasn't alone,' said Cece, glancing anxiously from Jock to Tommy. 'I had TJ with me. And Lulu,' she added, lifting her arm for us to see Lulu dangling raggedly from her grubby hand.

'And where is TJ now, may I ask?' said Jock, addressing Cece.

'Oh. I tied him up outside to the bars of the monkeys' cage. They didn't seem very happy about it, actually.'

'Nevertheless, it's dangerous and you could have got lost for ever.'

'I wasn't lost,' she said pluckily. 'We were only late because we went also to Aladdin's cave, in the East Shaft.' Her green eyes widened slightly.

'Well, she's here now, so no harm done, hey?' Tommy interjected quickly.

Jock rolled his eyes. 'Another unwitting victim of exploitation.'

Tommy must've figured the dump would be safer than home, but I didn't say so.

'Come, young Cecelia, let us attend to your companion, TJ. You boys finish packing up those gloves and get them back to Millsite.'

Cece grinned impishly at me, her jade eyes slitted, but before she could follow Jock, Tommy seized her wrist and muttered, 'What are you talking about, Cece? What cave in the East Shaft? I told you to go straight to our cave in the dump, not to go wandering anywhere else. And the East Shaft's sealed off.'

'Well, it's open for us,' said Cece, stoutly. 'It's a secret and I'm not telling you – it's *our* cave, mine and TJ's and Lulu's.'

Then she turned on her heel and trotted off after Jock. Tommy looked at me, perplexed.

'Should you wish,' Jock called back to us, as she reached the gate, 'you may accompany us tonight.'

'Sure. Where're you going?' shouted Tommy.

'The slum of dreams.' He laughed as he turned away.

I could just see TJ outside the gate, tormenting the monkeys. They were enraged, shrieking and pelting him with debris from their cage floor. TJ had his muzzle pressed right up against the cage, his chest low to the ground, his haunches stuck jauntily in the air, yipping like a lunatic. Every now and then, he pranced back to chase his tail madly round in a circle before throwing himself again at the cage. The ragged piece of string trailed in the dust.

I started to climb into the ring to collect the gloves when Vilikazi stepped closer to me and said, '*Eh*, Chris, wait – it's not *Zonk!* magazine, but if you give me that *Stage & Cinema*, I'll teach you how to dance to *kwela*. What do you say?'

I hesitated for about half a second and decided: what the hell? If I could crack this, man, I'd be back in the game. The jive contest nagged at me. I wasn't sleeping at night. When the moon in my window-pane started sinking towards the horizon, I'd climb out of bed and sit on the steps of the veranda. I'd listen to the guttural chorus of the bullfrogs and torment myself about it. In my mind, see, it'd grown into a big, fat middle finger to my old man and all those Elvis-baiting *vrots* who thought you had to think like them. I wanted it bad, but I couldn't pull it off. It'd been eating me alive. I mean, I knew I had rhythm – I'd known it ever since that day at Millsite – but I still didn't know what to do with it. Until now. If Vilikazi could teach me how to put it into moves, I'd wipe the floor with those cats at the town hall next week. Mona had already been screaming for days about her stolen bloody magazine, and even though she suspected me, like I kept pointing out to her, she hadn't got any proof.

155

'*Ja*, okay, you got a deal,' I said.

'Nothing for *mahala*, hey?' he said, chuckling, as he helped himself to Mona's copy of *Stage & Cinema*.

'*Lekker*,' said Tommy, rubbing his hands and heading off towards the *tsotsis*.

'Look, man,' said Mitch, uncomfortably, 'I don't know. I've got to get home like yesterday. My ma, you know . . .'

'Then bugger off,' said Rod, amiably. 'Actually, I'll come with you. I don't know about all this jiving stuff, man.'

Vilikazi and I turned back to our dance steps as the *gumba-gumba* needle scratched over the vinyl once more.

'You like this,' he said. 'Afterwards I show you *pata-pata*.' He did a sort of shimmy with a rakish grin on his face.

It was Sophiatown music, he said, but not jazz from the salons – Aunt Babe's, the 39 Steps, the House on Telegraph Hill, no. This wasn't Black Velvet. It came from the back-yard *shebeens* and the all-night dance parties. The street urchins, nursed on *marabi* music, snatched the pennywhistle away from the MacGregor *stokvel* mamas' funeral parades, and they *gooi*ed in a bit of tea-box bass and now you had Dorothy Masuka singing '*Hamba Nontsokolo*' and 'Dr Malan'. Well, they'd banned it, but you could still hear it on the streets, on the trains, even in the jails and deep below the belly of the earth. '*Indoda Yempandla*' and '*Azikwelwa*', when those kids wouldn't get on the bus in Alexandra. And you could hear the strains of *tsaba-tsaba* and taste the *skokiaan* in the music and you got the *pata-pata* dance. It was jive danc-ing all right, but a dirty kind. *Kwela*, said Vilikazi, was pure Jo'burg.

Tommy's *tsotsis* were leaving and he came back to the boxing ring where Vilikazi and me were jiving. One of them waved back at him as they swaggered out of the gate. I asked Vilikazi if they were going off to do crimes, muggings and things. He started laughing and said they were going to the jive-dancing competition at the Bantu Men's Social Centre in Munsieville, the Location outside Krugersdorp. They mostly danced to *kwela*, but they liked rock 'n' roll too. He said the competition was brutal there. The basement ones in the slumyards were worse – they had to search the midnight streets for a stranger willing to serve as judge or there was fighting afterwards.

I kept on jiving with Vilikazi and tonight I was destined for the slums.

15

The Slumyard

The heat was fierce, and the noise. It started with the stamping of feet, hundreds of them grinding into the dirt in the gathering rhythm of a dance. Now the drums were pounding and the crowd surged forward towards the ring, bearing another wave of heat that slammed into my back.

'*Jisis*,' Tommy hissed at me, a sheen of pure ecstasy on his face. 'But I'm only *kak*ing myself now, hey?'

He was crouching below our corner beside me. The black boxer above us whacked Johnny with a solid one-two, one-two combination to the face, the second left-right even harder than the first. Johnny spewed gob across the ring.

'*Eish!*'

It was Vilikazi, wincing. The crowd roared its approval. His was the only black face not awash with savage delight. A deep gash had opened above Johnny's left eye. The ref called time to look at the cut.

'*O, God!* Here we go,' said Doc.

He didn't stop the fight, though, and soon blood had filled

Johnny's eye and was coursing down his cheek, mingling with the sweat.

The bell went and Doc vaulted into the ring with his stool. While he was squirting adrenalin into the cut, Jock watered Johnny down. He pulled out his mouthpiece and rinsed it in the water bucket before slipping it back into his mouth, murmuring closely to him the whole time.

'We got lucky there, Johnny – you were punching blindly at the end. Now Doc's magic's only going to last so long with a cut like that – we'll have to get you stitched up after- wards – and that promoter's looking to get a win for his boy.'

I looked across at the stage rigged up outside the *shebeen*. A few of the *tsotsis* were clustered around the microphone at the front to get a better view. They were Harlem Brothers. The one with a gut like Fats Domino's had his arm around a woman in a green satin dress. She shimmered like an angel above the ragged crowd. He was the promoter, the one who'd done the talking when we arrived. His thick, jewel- encrusted fingers curled around her cinched waist, hugging her tightly. She didn't look too pleased.

Her name was Dolly, that was what Vilikazi said, and she belonged to the Harlem Brothers. She and the Jive Maniacs always performed here at the Ritz Palais de Danse and it would've been a brave band that ever tried to play in their stead. It sure didn't look much like the Ritz when we walked through it to get to the boxing arena out back: a few rickety tables and chairs standing on a dirt floor only partly covered by a worn floral carpet, a shabby couch and a cheap pedal organ in the corner. The walls were plastered with old newspapers and copies of *Drum* magazine. Tommy and me huddled against it and studied the covers while Jock haggled with old Fat Gut. Somehow, even with his bald head and pale skin in that sea of black satin, he looked like he belonged.

'Reef girls forced into love,' read one headline, above a photograph of a black girl posing on top of a mine dump in a bathing suit. I nudged Tommy to check it out. Below it was another: 'Togoland riots – the truth'.

The joint was heaving – big, black mamas sashaying between packed tables creaking under empty bottles and enamel plates of congealing stew – and it reeked, man. I was relieved to escape outside into the relatively cool night air where they were setting up the makeshift boxing arena in the backyard, but the din and the stink had dogged us.

'Better knock him out in a hurry, because that ref will stop the fight the minute he figures his boy's ahead on points. You got it?' Jock said urgently.

'Got it, boss.'

Johnny was standing up at the ten-second warning and waiting for the bell.

'That's my boy,' said Doc, grinning. My stomach lurched as he skipped back out into the ring for the fifth round. The young black boxer's trainer planted a kiss on his forehead before he left the ring. Bra Theo, they called him, but he was also known as the Black Panther.

'Hey, *marashea*!' one of the onlookers taunted Vilikazi – it was a corruption of MaRussia, the migrants' gang, Sothos.

Vilikazi turned, and the man gestured crudely at him. Vilikazi cursed him with dashing style.

Johnny unloaded a nine-punch combination that had the crowd screaming. It almost dropped his opponent, who collapsed against the ropes, his legs spread wide. He looked like a lost child. But then, from his low squat, he charged straight into Johnny, his left fist jamming up under Johnny's chin and Johnny fell back.

'Sweet Jesus!' moaned Jock. 'That's why I love them.'

He glanced down at me and Tommy crouching by the canvas. His eyes were wet. 'I've seen tough fighters,' he said, looking back at the ring, 'ones who'll take shots to land shots, I've seen pretty ones, who're quick and slick and don't like getting hit, but you have to come to the Black Spots for the whole sweet deal. I love their heart, their discipline. I love that they're not afraid to love their dream. When they fight, they put it all on the line.'

Next thing Johnny'd knocked the African down with a left uppercut off the jab, followed by a straight right-hand.

'Like a flippin' fairytale!' Doc yelled excitedly.

The timekeeper and the ref were stretching the count, but they could've counted to sixty for all the difference it would've made. Johnny was back in his corner, Doc removing his gloves and cutting off the wraps, Jock wiping him down, when the straining zoot suit on the stage gave the thumbs-up and the ref finally called it.

'Better get out of here quick,' shouted Doc, gesturing to the mob. 'Backed their boy with money they earned with their own hands.'

He hustled Johnny back through the *shebeen* as Jock disappeared with Fat Gut, and then I heard the sax and the trombone, and Dolly's luscious voice was drenching the crowd. Under her spell, it seemed to swell and then, man, it started swaying to the music. The boxing ring capsized and the crowd pitched across it. Soon couples started to curdle from the mass. I could feel the vibrations through my feet,

161

coursing right through my body, and I wanted to join them. The lyrics of Dolly's song were full of soft explosive Xhosa clicks, as her honeyed, subtly piquant voice, like cinnamon, soared and fell to a raw groan with the cello. I was itching to get out there and join the pairs of dancers who were touching each other in tempo, skimming each other's bodies with their hands in a way that could only be sinful.

The saxophonist was going gaga. He was gyrating right next to Dolly, leaning backwards, his legs splayed apart, knees bent, the mouth of his sax thrust right under the mike. His eyes were bulging as he blew beside the shimmering Dolly. People were dancing with ever more abandon, flinging their arms into the air, swept up in his wheeling notes, and now I was dancing too, my body moving rhythmically without trying, pulling me into the beating heart of the throng. I felt drunk with the raw thirst for life here, the way the African soil thirsted for rain. I closed my eyes. I didn't know how long it had been; time seemed to have slowed. My shirt clung to my skin in the wet heat.

Then Doc was gripping my arm and propelling me across the floor of the collapsed boxing ring towards the door. He steered me through the fetid *shebeen* and out into the alleyway past the rag-top Chevy parked in front of the Ritz Palais de Danse and into the back of the waiting pick-up truck.

Trundling through the rutted streets on the way back, I slumped down low against the sides. On the way in I'd been straining to get a good look at Madubulaville, at the sprawl of rusted corrugated iron and flapping sackcloth that choked the backyards of the derelict buildings lining the street.

The place was swarming with Chinamen, Indian women

with intricately hennaed faces, scores of scabby children splashing in the rivers of sewage that flowed through shallow ditches, playing soccer with a soda-pop bottle beneath washing that fluttered gaudily from lines strung across the alleys. Barbers shaving clients on upturned Joko Tea boxes and women sieving *utshwala* over petrol drums straightened as we passed. A *sangoma* plying fortunes and cures, her hair matted with red clay, a snuff box stuck in her earlobe, watched warily as Jock wove past the potholes.

I was dizzy from the carnival of robes and chiffon saris that wound around the lavish piles of garbage and meat and spoiling fruit that lined the street. Bloated rats gorged upon gently putrefying delicacies. In the setting sun, sallowed by a thousand fires, the cathedral on the hill looked down with clemency upon the wretched.

Although I couldn't see the alley-riven huddle of shanties behind the stained façades of the buildings any more, I could just make out the stumbling forms of the drunks, eerily lit by the glowing coals in the braziers and the fitful gleam of candles. Beneath the muddy lanes there was a subterranean cellar of fermenting beer, sunk to foil the beer-raids. The stench from the open gutters wafted into the back of the truck.

'Hey, it's still better than in the Location,' Vilikazi remarked.

'Huh?' said Tommy.

'You see the *kwela-kwela*?'

Tommy shook his head. 'Nuh-uh.'

'That's why it's better than the Location.'

Vilikazi reckoned the police roamed the streets of Munsieville like dogs, and if you didn't have the right stamp

163

in your passbook it was *Kwela! Kwela!* for you. In Munsieville your pass was worth more than gold. Without it, you couldn't get in, couldn't move freely, couldn't even get out – well, unless you climbed through the tear in the fence up by the railway tracks. And not having your pass wasn't the only reason to *kwela* either. You could find yourself in the back of the van for owning a knob-kerrie, for sitting on the wrong bench outside the Court of Native Affairs, for trespass, nuisance, impertinence, or for possessing stolen property.

One time, Vilikazi went to stay with his cousin in Munsieville for a funeral, although the landlady made him pay rent because he was a Sotho and had the look of the *amalaita*. There was a raid: three o'clock in the morning, flashlights through the window and hammering on the door. He was dragged out into the street and kicked in the groin because he was a *skelm*, wasn't he?, and some crook stole his winch ticket and he spent the night on the cold, hard floor of the police cells.

It was a hell of a funeral, though: the *stokvel* women dressed in uniforms of tartan kilts and white gloves paraded through the streets playing the drums, *isigingci*, milk-tin rattles and five-shilling pennywhistles, accompanied by the voices of the *manyano* choir. The mourners followed, not marching in step, but dancing wildly, and the prophet Isaiah from the Zionist Church of the Nazarites preached about the immoral women of the slumyards.

Driving westwards on the deserted Main Reef Road from Johannesburg, I stared out at the sinister shadow of the abandoned headgear rising up over the East Shaft. It was late by the time we'd dropped Johnny with Doc at the mine hospital and Vilikazi back at the compound. My forehead was pressed up against the glass of the cab and I was staring vacantly out of the window as Jock tooled along the quiet streets towards Tommy's house. Insects plopped against the windscreen, already splattered with the innards of others.

'Thomas,' Jock said suddenly, breaking the silence, 'what did your sister mean about a cave in the East Shaft?'

Tommy sat up and looked at him, frowning. '*Ag*, nothing, man, Jock. Just some fairy story she's made up. Cece spends half her time whispering secrets in TJ's ear-hole. She thinks because he sits there with his ear cocked that he understands. She lives in a dream world, man, believes in the Jabberwock, for God's sake. Ask Chris,' he said, turning to me for back-up.

'She reckons that Lulu doll of hers comes alive while she's sleeping, Jock.'

'You can't listen to anything she says, man. Why do you ask?'

'I don't know,' he mused. 'Just that she called it "Aladdin's cave". I mean, it can't be, but still . . . It's an odd coincidence.'

Mr Battersby's doughy face loomed at his bedroom window next door. It's funny how it was us who used to spy on the neighbours when we were real *laities*. I can still picture the lounge: a couch stuffed so your rump wouldn't even dent it, facing three brocaded armchairs, kind of faded but, still, you know, ball and claw legs made of some dark polished wood. There was an old grandfather clock by the door and this gleaming brass pendulum swinging quietly in its glass-fronted cabinet.

When Jock dropped me off last, I wished I could thank him properly. I wanted him to know that I understood what he'd let us see tonight: past the wretched misery of the slum, the mirage of charred dreams, I'd felt the joy and the anger and the yearning brewing with the beer at the Ritz Palais du Danse. I could almost taste it, and I'd glimpsed what was hidden in the shadows – it was hope.

'Thank you, Jock. Damn. Thank you.'

16

The Goofies

Tommy hiccuped the '*uh*', clutching his chest like he was having a heart attack, but he kept on grooving backwards down the path, his threadbare towel slung over his shoulders. Rod's guffaws echoed under the stands, practically drowning Tommy's 'I'm All Shook Up'.

'Hey, Christopher, what the hell is that fool Michaels warbling? A Elvis ruddy Presley number?'

Tommy stopped and grinned. '*Ja*, Mr J. It's the king a rock 'n' roll himself.'

We were behind the stands that lined the long row of plane trees separating the rugby from the cricket pitches. My old man and some of his cronies were sitting on the upper reaches waiting for a pre-season 'friendly' to kick off.

'King a rock 'n' roll, my ruddy arse. Now get your own arse out front where we can see you, boy.'

We clambered through the packed stands and peered up at my dad and Mr O'Flynn sitting beside him. Dad had his sleeves rolled up. He was flushed under the brim of his hat and I could see he was *lekker* loose. Him and Mr O'Flynn must've been at the club.

'They should have that bastard's picture plastered on the front page of the Immorality Act.'

'Arrested for lewd flippin' conduct,' agreed Mr O'Flynn.

'And turn your collar down, boy, you look like a bloody idiot,' Dad said to me.

'*Ag,* come on, Mr Jameson, Elvis has got to beat Pat Boone and that Harry bloody Webb Mrs J's always listening to on *From Crystal With Love,*' said Tommy, making 'Crystal' sound all sugary.

I didn't think my old man knew that Cliff Richard had been feeding the world a bullshit name, but he didn't like backchat, so it was damn lucky for Tommy that the players were running out onto the pitch now. The stand erupted. Mr O'Flynn crossed himself.

'*Jisis,* you ruddy Irish,' my old man tuned Mr O'Flynn disgustedly.

'You get one of these ruddy Leprechauns in the dressing room, got to be seen to be believed. Oke's gaga, man. Spitting on his boots, licking the ball, cracking his skull on the wall, man. Oke plays lousy, he reckons ...'

But we never got to hear what the oke reckons because the whistle blew for the game to begin. We squatted down on our haunches to watch. Fourteen minutes into the game, and the Pirates had scored two tries and a conversion.

'Come on, man, tackle, for Chrissake! Tackle!'

It was the flank who was taking the brunt of it.

'Maybe someone needs to explain to this *poephol* why

they picked him. This isn't the first fuckin' fifteen anymore, my boy!'

Next thing the flank had punched one of the Pirates' players. Right in front of the poles. The hooker joined in, the okes on the stand were burying their faces in their hands and groaning, and the Pirates' kicker kicked the penalty right between the sticks.

'What a cock up.'

It was my old man again.

'In rugby, you want to hit a bloke, you hit him so the ref can't see. Otherwise you wait till the final whistle. That way you can kick him in the balls. I s'pose you *poephol*s are rehearsing for tonight, then, hey? Okes, did you know my *laitie* here is dancing in a rock 'n' roll competition tonight? Helluva proud, I am.'

Mr O'Flynn hosed himself. '*Jisis*, you always had bladdy high hopes for your sons, Jameson.'

'*Ja*, no, I don't even know if I'm going to do it,' I mumbled.

'Hey!' Dad said sharply. 'You made your bed, boy, you got to kip in it.'

My stomach lurched. The three of us climbed back under the stands and headed for the goofies singing about hot lips and chills. It struck me as odd that my dad wanted me to go through with it, though.

Mitch was waiting for us around the side of the post office, diagonally opposite the goofies. He'd chopped his ma's broomstick again for *kennetjie* and she'd clouted him and said he was not to set foot anywhere near the swimming-pool on pain of death, but he'd snuck out anyway.

'Hey, Mitch,' Rod greeted him. 'What you going to do for a face when that baboon wants his bum back?'

It was packed when we came out of the boys' change-house. Most afternoons it was just us *laities*, but on Saturdays, if they hadn't gone joyriding to Lover's Rock or somewhere, Johnny and Mona and their mates from the high school were all there, lounging beneath the palm trees on the lush lawns that flanked the pool.

Sometimes we went swimming in Robinson Lake. It was really a dam, built when they dammed the *vlei* to make a cooling reservoir for the mine's power station. You could always spot when a oke'd been swimming there at the week-end: he pitched up at school on Monday morning with eyes like a bloodhound's from the poisoned water. Mr Erasmus reckoned he was fit for bloody Braille and not much more.

The path to the lake passed by the old Jameson Raid graves. They said that on moonlit nights, lone travellers passing the graves had seen the doomed riders galloping over the rise on their ill-fated quest to wrest the Transvaal back from Kruger. That's what they said. And we only had the one ghost story around these parts.

Still, there was nothing like the rec club goofies. Johnny had his transistor radio tuned to David Davies, who was churning out 'Summertime Blues' from Radio Palace in Lourenço Marques, and it was *lekker* gnawing on strips of marshmallow fish and playing *skaapstert* to the heavy bass.

Jisis, it was turning a bit sadistic, though. It was supposed to be our gang against Errol Terblanche's, but it'd degener-ated into a every-man-for-himself whipping frenzy. It was a bit sickening, the look on Rod's face, as he twisted and dipped his towel before flicking it, and I had a welt across my backside by the time Tommy yelled, 'Geronimo!' and dived into the water. A wave slopped over the side. Me,

Rod, Mitch, Errol and the rest all followed him, but Tommy didn't stop there. He was bombing off the high dive over and over again, the girls were squealing and Cynthia told Tommy she was going to report him to Mr Clack and then he'd be sorry. She stalked off, her ponytail flouncing behind her. It's funny: a year ago I wouldn't have even noticed that ponytail. I watched it, flicking to and fro, thick and glossy, zombied.

'Hey, Cynthia,' Tommy yelled, hauling himself out of the pool. Cynthia glanced back over her shoulder and Tommy curled his lip and sort of groaned, '"I'm all shook up! Uh-huh-huh,"' while thrusting his pelvis at her.

Cynthia stopped. She turned slowly on her heel. She stared coldly at Tommy and then she said, with withering scorn, 'Tommy Michaels, you are such a drip. Elvis would've sooner died than *yodel* like that.'

Johnny and his mates cracked up. Even Mona, stretched out languidly on the lawn, belched smoke and dropped the cigarette she was holding elegantly between her fingers, her huge dark sunglasses slipping off her nose.

That was why Cynthia was rated the hottest chick in our school. Most of the girls looked more like stick insects than chicks, but when she didn't have her arms folded across her chest, you could see Cynthia's buttons just straining to pop loose. When Doc overheard us talking about goosies, he shook his head. '*Ja*, it happens to the best of us,' he said sorrowfully, 'All of a sudden you're more interested in Sarie Marais than the *mampoer* at the bushveld dance. Standing there with the other *kêrels*, like a *poephol*, tugging at the ripped knee on your trousers, wondering how to ask her to dance. Sarie attended the finishing school in Pietersberg and we were all very nervous of her after that. Next thing you're

171

telling her how you nearly died of consumption.' He snorted disgustedly. 'To this day, I don't know why I told her that, except that I thought nearly dying was one way to get her to notice me, and dying of consumption sounded like a very refined way to die, only it was hard to get it in the Potgietersrus district. I told her I'd lain in a ditch on the Government Road to Naboomspruit coughing and sweating, but Sarie didn't take any notice at all. She was swept off to the dance floor by Jan Cruywagen. There were spots of colour high on her cheeks that were very pretty against her dark hair.

'What made matters worse was when Stoffel van der Merwe, who was known the length and breadth of the Potgietersrus district for his lies, winked at me. You know that kind of wink. It was to let me know that there was now a new understanding between us, and that we could speak in the future as one Potgietersrus liar to another,' he finished gloomily.

It wasn't just Cynthia's long dark hair and straining bust that made her so interesting, though: it was her spiteful delight in telling Tommy to stuff off. He instantly stopped his obscene thrusting.

'*Eina!*' he said, recoiling like he'd been slapped and falling back into the pool. I was swallowing gallons of water from laughing and Tommy dunking me at the same time, and we had to get out of there if we were going to make it to Millsite in time.

'How's that, hey? I've got nothing but *kak* in my life,' said Tommy, but he was already pulling himself out.

He was hopping up and down outside the change-house while I towelled myself off. 'Hurry up, man, you okes!'

172

He never entered the change-house alone. None of us did. Not even now.

'You nervous?'

'Nah.' I shrugged. 'You?'

'Shitting myself,' he said, and we grinned at each other, Tommy's eyes glittering like they did when he got razzed.

When we were on our way out of the arched entrance to the pool, Johnny called, 'Hey, Chris?'

I stopped and looked back at him.

'Shoot low, man – they're riding Shetlands, okay?'

I blinked. When I was still a little oke, Johnny used to snatch my dummy and throw it in the toilet. He thought it was funny as all get out when I went in head first to fish for it. After a while, he got to wondering where I'd go if he flushed. He told me he'd chosen me *not* because he didn't want to go down that pipe but for a different reason, which he would've revealed if my mind had been ready to handle it, which it wasn't.

Even when I got a bit smarter, Johnny always found ways of getting me to do stupid stuff for him. He and his friends had this crummy tree-house that I wasn't allowed in because I wasn't a member. I'd beg him to let me in.

'Sure, you can join our gang,' he'd say. 'Oh, wait, you can't because you're not evil enough.'

'I am evil.'

'*Ja*, but you're not like *real* evil.'

And I'd end up trying to prove how evil I was, stealing stuff for them and that. When I whined, 'But, Johnny, Ma said ...' he'd say, 'Oh, please, you don't care about your ma if you're evil.'

Later, when he started boxing, he'd just threaten to

smack my head off. 'You'll do what I tell you, kid – I could take out a welterweight with these hammers, maybe even a light-heavy, except I can't, because you have to be sixteen to be in the weighted divisions, which is bullshit.'

Then he'd chant: 'I am vengeance, I am the night, and these are my hammers of justice.'

I hated him. I'd plan to get caught. I'd lie there, warming up his bed for him, and fantasise about how I'd start crying and then confessing how scared I was of Johnny and his hammers of justice. Bam! He just got sent to reform school.

On the night of Johnny's first fight he came home with lips swollen and lurid. I ran down the steps and out onto the street as soon as I spotted him.

'I lost,' he said thickly, and tears began dripping from his eyes. I was appalled.

As we reached Millsite, I tried to wipe the memory. Jock was standing in the shade of the strangler fig that rose monstrously against the peeling gables of the rec hall, waiting for us.

'Come on, you little buggers, stop dawdling!'

The seed of the strangler fig germinates in the crotch of a branch on a host tree, which is slowly strangled by the roots of the fig as they stealthily encircle its trunk. The Millsite fig was ancient, magnificent, the original host lost beneath the muscular cords grasping down from its upper reaches into the earth and writhing across the ground, but it was dead. Poisoned, Jock suspected, by the noxious chemicals leaching into the ground water from the mine. He refused to cut it down, though.

'There is beauty in its struggle, its sorrow. It stands here on this watershed between the Indian and Atlantic Oceans as a siren for what we have done.'

He and Doc had already loaded all the gear into the pick-up truck and were ready to go. Half the squad had piled into the back. I saw Davie and the O'Flynn brothers had come along too. Tommy hauled himself over the side, using the tyre as a step, Mitch and Rod jumped in the back. I felt a surge of reluctance to get in. Once I did, there was no way out.

In a way, I felt we were ready. I was ready: I didn't need Tommy to get himself between me and the oke I was fighting just so I could get up off my knees. I was ready to fight alone, but still ... A day like today, it left a sweetness in my belly, and I wanted to cling to it. I didn't want to feed Tommy's sickness.

'Hey, Kid Louis,' Rod called down to me, from the pick-up, 'you can run, boy, but you can't hide.'

He didn't stop laughing at his joke even when I told him he had the wit of a burned pork chop. Propped up against one of the grey aerial roots, shaded from the soupy heat, sweat trickling down between my shoulder blades, I squinted up at him sitting beside Tommy and Mitch on the rim of the pick-up; my mates. Flies crawled in the crease of my eye. I swatted them away. Jock had told us that blow flies were scavengers that fed on carrion, excrement or garbage, and that their maggots could heal a festering wound on a human. I climbed in.

17

The Boxing Match

'Okay, boys, listen up. I know the rules says you get knocked down, you have ten seconds to get up, but take a long, hard look at that killjoy over there.' Doc nodded grimly towards the ref bowed over the judges' table. 'You get knocked down, don't bother to get up. So don't get knocked down, do you hear me?' he shouted over the din, only half joking.

We were clustered around him in our corner of the Blesbok Park Hall. I glanced over to the ring rising above the turmoil like gallows. I was hopping up and down in my white singlet stamped 'WRC', my legs sticking out of my shorts like twigs. A bloody *kaffer* chicken would've been embarrassed.

'Listen, you flippin' jitterbug, cut that out,' said Tommy, elbowing me in the ribs. 'You're making me nervous, man.'

'Doc and I will be your seconds,' Jock picked up, 'so we'll be right there with you, okay?' He paused to draw breath.

'Boys, you're ready for this. You've worked hard and I'm proud of you. When you get out there, don't try to get clever. Remember, hit him clean and more times than he hits you. It's as simple as that. If you take a hiding, well, maybe no one should win his first fight. On the other hand, maybe you get a palooka,' he finished, grinning.

I glanced over at the ominous-looking table beside the ring. The judges from the Johannesburg Amateur Boxing Organisation were just taking their seats. I thought I might piss myself.

The preliminary fights for the *laities* started at three o'clock. It was seven minutes to now. The ref was climbing through the ropes, nodding to the time-keeper, who was peering at a large pocket watch. He looked devastatingly elegant in his black tie. Then he was crooking a finger at Jock.

'Right, Christopher, let's go, boy.'

I was going to puke. My gut churned as I followed Jock up to the ring. I climbed through the ropes and perched on my stool. The ref was consulting his clipboard and frowning, and then he was calling Jock over. Doc was on his haunches smearing Vaseline on my temples. I couldn't bring myself to look over at the oke from Durban Deep. They said he was a killer. Since it was the first fight of the day, it was packed ringside. I caught sight of Tommy's in the blur of faces; I could tell he was worried for me. The noise had reached a crescendo.

Jock came back and hunkered down next to Doc. 'Okay, Christopher, the ref's uneasy about the mismatch. He's going to award a TKO if you so much as look winded. I agree.'

177

Jisis, then why'd he agree to the fight in the first place?

'Do you want the fight or not?'

Those were his words, killer's trainer. They echoed in my head. '*No way, man!*' was what I wanted to scream, but Jock hesitated, glancing down at me and then at Doc.

'Give him the fight,' said Doc, and my heart sank. *Jisis*, I'm a wet rag. Jock shrugged resignedly and turned back to the table behind which the JABO official was seated. 'These junior bouts,' he said, shaking his head dubiously.

A bloody dog show was what it was. Boxers from twelve clubs locked up together in the Blesbok Park Hall for three hours and no one had thrown a punch yet; you could feel the fever rising with the heat. The agony of the fight-matching alone was operatic: trainers clutching their sacred box of cards, thronged by edgy boxers shuffling up for the weigh-in, loudly haranguing the almighty JABO, in whose hands our fates lay. And now here I was, about to be slaughtered by a oke who'd had three previous fights.

Jock looked over his shoulder, then turned back. 'You ready?' He sounded tense. 'You know what to do. Keep your hands up and keep them busy.'

The ref beckoned at me and then at the Durban Deep oke. I walked forward on my wobbly *kaffer* chicken twigs.

'What's your name, son?'

'Jameson, sir.'

It came out hoarse. He consulted his clipboard and turned to the other kid.

'Van Blerk, *meneer*, Bokkie.'

Jisis, he looked mean. There was no question I was going to die.

'Boys, I want a clean fight, you hear? No clinches. When

178

I say break, you break. No hitting below the waist or back of the head. You get me?'

We nodded.

He took both our wrists in his hands, then swung my arm into the air.

'On my right, the ungraded contender from West Rand Consolidated Mines, Master Christopher Jameson, "The Tyke".'

There was scattered laughter as he dropped my arm.

'Challenging him on my left,' he boomed, 'with three fights, one knock-out, no losses, Roodepoort Durban Deep's Master Bokkie van Blerk.'

I headed back to my corner. I turned to see Bokkie hunching his huge knotted shoulders and then the bell sounded. My muscles were locked, my whole body rigid. Jock squeezed my own puny shoulders, and suddenly my muscles released me. I was back out there to touch gloves and it was on.

Bokkie circled me for a minute, then he threw a straight left, but he pulled his shoulder back just a fraction too far, allowing me to get my head out of the way and his fist flew over my shoulder past my ear. I nipped in under the arm with a quick uppercut and hit him hard in the ribs. With a thrill, I heard him wince.

Then he caught me with a right on the shoulder, which wrenched me backwards, but I anticipated the left coming at me, ducked and got in another good body blow before his arms wrapped around me and I was in a clinch. I hit him furiously in the ribs but my blows were too short to be effective and I knew he could hold onto me as long as he liked.

'Break!' I heard the ref shout, and his grip loosened.

We moved apart.

'Fight!' he commanded.

I came back with my straight left, but Bokkie parried it and threw his right over the top. As he did so, he dropped his left hand and stepped to the right, perfectly positioning himself for the left hook that rammed under my chin. I gagged.

After that, I let him chase me. I was quicker than him and my footwork was much better, but I wasn't landing either. Just as the bell went, I got inside and clipped him with a short right. When I got back to my stool, Doc and Jock were waiting.

'It's close. I'm not going to lie to you, this kid's good and his experience shows,' said Jock, speaking quickly, in a low voice, 'but he underestimated you, and you're fitter than him, although he's still ahead on points, I reckon. You've got to fight him on the back foot – wait for him to punch first, Chris, *wait*, catch him when he's open.'

'Watch it, man, that kid's got a power jab. And if he finds his range, he's going to hurt you bad,' said Doc. 'Keep your chin tucked in, and drop your shoulder, don't hunch – that way, if he gets one through, you'll take most of it on the ball.'

The bell went for the second round.

'You're doing good, Chris.' Doc pushed me up.

At first I let Bokkie chase me round the ring. He was trying to corner me. He'd work me carefully towards one, but at the last moment, I'd feint left and duck out and his right cross missed by miles.

But then I pulled the same trick once too often. He caught me with a left hook to the side of my head and if it weren't for the ropes behind me I would've gone down. He knew he'd hurt me, though, and in his anxiety to exploit it, he was loading his punches, trying for the big hit. All I could do was block and cover until I could get my feet out of trouble.

When I found my feet again, I stuck to Jock's ploy. I stayed just out of Bokkie's range, waited for him to throw a punch, stepped back while he was still leaning in, set my feet and landed a single shot counter. In the second half, the flurries of punches he'd thrown, most of them landing on my gloves, were starting to sap him. Towards the end of the round, I could detonate my shot bombs at will. A look of desperation had crept onto his face. I wasn't really hurting him, just frustrating him, wearing him down, like a jackal.

When the bell went and I got back to my corner, Jock's eyes were alight.

'Look, Christopher, it's working. I think that round was yours. We're tied up, but you need the third. So get back out there and counter-punch, don't attack. Keep out of trouble!' he urged, but I could hear he thought I had a chance now.

The bell went for the third and final round, and even though I was buggered now, I was buoyed by hope.

I waited for Bokkie to charge, but he was on to me, had sussed out my game, and he hung back, waiting for me too. For a moment we danced around each other. Then I noticed his stance – wide-legged, off-balance – and I threw two jabs as hard as I could. It should have been a left hook or an uppercut, but still Bokkie went down. He fell against the ropes, grabbing at them as his feet slipped. I felt a surge of bloodlust. I'd made it. I'd out-boxed the killer, a three-fight veteran, with no losses on his card, and I'd made it.

But Bokkie pushed himself off the ropes before he hit the canvas, jumped back onto his feet, pivoted and started jabbing wildly. I tried to parry, but missed, and as I leaned forward, Bokkie sprang the trap. His left, the real one, smashed into my nose, followed by his right, and I buckled. I hit the floor just as the bell went.

The ref was kneeling over me, the doctor beside him, shining a light into my eyes. 'Son?' I tried to heave myself up, but he put a hand on my chest. 'It's over, son.'

Jock and Doc were cupping me under my armpits, helping me back to my corner, but I shrugged them off when the ref called us back to the centre of the ring. He took us both by the hand. 'The winner by technical knockout,' he said, raising Bokkie's, and I felt hot tears welling behind my eyes.

But then, suddenly, they subsided, and the funny thing was, I didn't feel so bad. Actually, if I was being truthful, I felt flushed, cocky even. I'd faced down some kind of monster, and I didn't mean Bokkie, and I had survived.

Back in my corner, Doc wrapped his huge calloused hand around the back of my neck. 'You didn't lose your pride, man.'

Then we climbed out of the ring and Tommy and the other okes from the squad were commiserating with me, but it felt more like ... like they were congratulating me.

'You fought like a lion, Chris!' shouted Tommy. 'They'll call you *ingonyama*.'

Jock strode over to us and boomed, 'The glory, Christopher, belongs to the man in the arena, whose face is marred by dust and sweat and blood, who strives valiantly and who, if he fails, at least fails while daring greatly. His place shall never be with those cold and timid souls who neither know victory nor defeat. Theodore Roosevelt would have been proud.'

A cheer went up from the squad.

'That goon's half dead before his next bout.' It was Johnny, and I was grinning like I'd won and I knew I'd never forget this moment, no matter how long I lived.

After that, it was bloody festive, ringside. The okes were getting rowdier, yelling, 'Waltzing Matilda, we're gonna kill ya! We're from Millsite. Fight! Fight! Fight!' louder and louder, but then Tommy went in, and something twisted my entrails viciously again. He was fighting an oke called Billy Fox from Randfontein. He'd had one fight, which he won, he was taller than Tommy by an inch and he outweighed him by half a stone.

From my seat I looked up at Tommy, rolling his shoulders in his corner just above me. His back was to me as he listened to Jock, who was standing squarely in front of him, but as he turned, I could see the raw fear on his face. I knew he was afraid of himself far more than of Billy. I closed my eyes and prayed to the warrior gods; not for glory, but for honour.

The seconds were leaving the ring now and the bell rang for round one. Billy came out swinging, but he couldn't find Tommy: he was nowhere. Tommy was moving side to side or backwards at an angle across the ring and his glancing blows had no effect. He was dancing Billy to death, waiting for his opening.

Then Billy hurled a clumsy right cross and Tommy

ducked under it. The punch was too hard, throwing Billy off balance, and Tommy moved in fast and hit him in the chest with a left and right combo, right under the heart, power shots, plenty of shoulder behind them, and darted away.

Hell. Billy looked thrown, but he fought back, harder and smarter, connecting several times, once nearly knocking Tommy through the ropes, but the same right cross kept coming at Tommy, and Tommy'd move in under it and land two, sometimes four punches to the same spot under the heart. It was blooming on his chest now. By the end of the round, Billy was slowing down a little and Tommy moved in closer to land on the bloom.

'I can't believe this kid's stupidity, man!' Rod bellowed in my ear.

At the start of the second round, Billy came out with a big mouth, trying to provoke Tommy. He was fighting a head game now. I couldn't hear much of what he was saying – he was making sure it was under his breath – but we caught the gist of it in the casual insolence of his stance as he leaned in to needle Tommy, in snatches; 'You learn that from your Daddy Michaels?', and although Tommy just jabbed back with a bland look on his face, I could see his cheek twitch.

'Uh-oh,' murmured Rod, 'here comes trouble.'

'Fucking smart-arse,' Davie Rabinowitz said, from the row behind me.

The problem was that Billy was from Randfontein: he knew who Tommy was, and you could bet your sweet fanny he had a truckload of razor-sharp lip in store.

'You fight like a Bible puncher, Michaels. Maybe your ma's been screwing Pastor Mullins, hey? Maybe he's your daddy?'

'Just stay cool, Tommy, stay cool,' I urged quietly.

'Come on, Fox, is that all you got?' Tommy jeered. 'Show me something, *please*!'

I watched Tommy closely and, sure enough, I could see him slowly getting worked up. He was telegraphing his blows, trying for the big shot, but giving himself away. By the second half of the round, Billy was dominating him. We were doing our best to blow Billy off, screaming stuff about his ma and belting out:

'If I had the wings of an eagle,
And an arse as black as a crow,
I'd fly to the top of the tree
And shit on the fox below!'

But nothing halted Tommy's downward spiral. When the ten-second warning sounded, he charged Billy like an enraged bull, but before he could do any damage, Billy fell against his chest, hugging him tightly.

'Break!' the ref called, and as they moved apart, Tommy lashed out, punching Billy in the face. Blood started gushing out of his nose.

I groaned: that was going to cost Tommy plenty, but the ref just gave him a warning. He rammed his finger right between Tommy's eyes and I could see Tommy blowing heavily as he made his way back to his corner.

'He's lost it!' said Rod, throwing his hands up in despair.

Doc vaulted into the ring and started sponging Tommy down. 'That ref's the *moer in* with you now.'

'*He* ain't my daddy,' Tommy retorted thickly.

I watched helplessly as Jock squatted in front of him,

185

speaking intently. I wished I could hear what he was saying, but the crowd had grown raucous.

At the start of the third round, Billy bounded out of his corner, his nose-bleed plugged with swabs of adrenalin salve, his nose and lips greased, and I braced myself for more, but there wasn't any. Whatever Jock said must have gone in, because Tommy had got a grip on himself. Billy started jibing, but Tommy waited coolly for his opening, then smashed his straight jab right back into Billy's nose. Billy staggered back, his hands over his face, smearing his gloves with fresh blood.

'*Whew!*' Rod whistled. 'Deadly, man!'

'And we're back in the game,' said Davie Rabinowitz, gleefully.

Tommy didn't stop there. He kept hitting Billy on the nose, again and again. It had swollen like a plum on his face and he'd finally shut up, but Tommy was like a machine, his left pursuing its mark with ruthless persistence.

As Tommy's fist pounded into his bloody face once more, Billy's expression contorted. He leaned in close to Tommy, blocking the ref's view with his shoulder, and jabbed his elbow into the side of Tommy's head. The crowd's booing resounded around the hall, but the ref was deaf.

'Hey, ref, come on! Ray Charles could see that one!'

Tommy didn't even flinch, just kept on sticking his jab into Billy's nose. But Billy had had enough. He charged directly into Tommy, jamming his left forearm up under Tommy's chin, forcing him against the ropes. As Tommy struggled to free himself, Billy dropped to a crouch, his legs spread unnaturally wide. I could see it coming; so could the other okes.

'*Oooh!*'

The bastard hit Tommy with two uppercuts below the belt, driving his fist upward into his balls. The ref jumped in and warned Billy, whose face showed no shame. Tommy limped to his corner and sank to his stool.

'You got five minutes,' the ref called to Jock.

'What we need is points deducted for the foul!' Doc snapped.

'I already warned him, like I warned your boy for punching after the break,' the ref said drily.

Not only do low blows hurt, they sap a fighter of his strength, but there was not a damn thing Tommy could do about it now as he gagged over his bucket.

'How do you feel?' asked Jock.

'Sick.'

'Do you want me to stop it?'

'Nah, I can do that.'

Doc watered him and he looked a little revived. At the ten-second warning, the ref came back to check Tommy out. 'You need more time?' he asked.

Tommy shook his head. As he walked back out into the ring on shaky legs, the crowd started drumming. Loads of them had climbed up onto their chairs and were stamping with their boots; the noise was thunderous.

Billy started firing salvos of jabs, rights, hooks and uppercuts, and Tommy was too weak to get out of the way – he could barely move on his failing legs. Billy kept pulling Tommy's head forward and landing shots to the kidneys.

'He's going to be pissing blood tonight,' Rod moaned.

He sagged twice, but his legs held, and my heart was breaking as the stomping became unison, acquiring a frightening, rhythmic power. Then Billy dropped his left hand,

and Tommy spotted his chance; he lifted his left and nailed Billy in the face again so hard that he fell. There was pandemonium in the hall and, over it all, me and Tommy were grinning at each other like we were six years old again.

After the bout, Tommy disappeared out the swing doors to the foyer at the front of the hall where the lavvies were. He returned a few minutes later, holding two bottles of cream soda with straws bobbing in their necks. 'Cheers!' he said, handing me one.

'How'd you pay for these, then?' I asked suspiciously.

Tommy unclenched his fist to reveal two half-crowns.

'Where the hell did you steal those nuggets from?'

Tommy looked smug. 'Davie Rabinowitz. My ma gave me my Saturday shilling for the 'scopes – she forgot about my boxing match. I have to give her the change back from a pound, but I bet the whole lot on you.'

'You bet it on me?' I said in total disbelief. 'On me?'

'*Ja*, pretty stupid, hey? But I figured I'd already seen *The Blob*, and *Old Yeller* is the only other new flick that's showing. Man, you can tell just by looking at the poster that either a kid or a dog isn't going to make it to the end, so I took a punt on you instead.'

I was dumbstruck. Tommy wasn't just rooting for me – hey, you'd expect that of your china – he'd believed I could do it. He had faith. I felt tears stinging my eyes, so I turned quickly to Davie, who was looking pretty sheepish next to Paddy O'Flynn and his brother in the row of chairs behind me.

'Hey, Davie, how the hell can you make odds against your own side? What sort of a Jew are you? I was the bloody underdog, man!'

188

'I'm a special kind of a Jew,' said Davie, grinning.

After a minute, I frowned as it dawned on me. I turned back to Tommy. 'But I lost?'

'*Ja*,' said Tommy, grinning. 'Davie made odds on how long you'd last.'

'What if I'd lost in the first round, then?'

'I knew you wouldn't. Okay, maybe the veteran gorilla from the Deep over there would bring you down in the end, but it wasn't going to be in the first two minutes, Chris – you can dance.'

18

The Jive Contest

The okes had come from miles around. As we pulled into the car lot, I checked pick-ups stamped 'Rand Leases', 'Durban Deep', you name it, packed with jivers. The okes piled out the back, and as I pulled open the door of the cab, Doc said, 'Christ almighty! There's thousands of the greasy little bastards, look at them!'

'Rock 'n' roll,' said Jock. 'The rallying call of the great tribe of war babies. God help the rest of us.'

And the two of them roared with laughter as I clambered out.

'Good luck!' Jock yelled, before reversing out.

Jis, my belly was eely as I jogged up the steps of the banqueting hall with Tommy and the okes. Inside, the place was groaning with Elvises. Everywhere you looked, there was Elvis. The foyer was slick with black boot polish. And the girls, hell, they were out in full force tonight, big posses of giggling petticoats rustling past.

'Hell's teeth.' Rod whistled. 'This place is Antsville, man.'

'Go on.' Tommy nodded at the registration table. 'I believe you've got a date with the chick in skins.'

I eyed Mrs van der Watt in her mink stole and made no move. Tommy gave me a shove and I stumbled.

'Move, you spaz!'

My palms were sweaty as Tommy dragged me over to it. Back in the lavvies of the Blesbok Park Hall, I'd reckoned I looked *lekker* cool in my stovvies and my greased quiff, but now . . . There were more okes here tonight than turned up for Al Debbo.

'*Ag*, man, Tommy, look, maybe we should laugh it off. I mean, check this place, man – it's a shambles. How's a oke going to get it together like this?'

'*Ag*, just shut up, Chris. Evening, Mrs van der Watt,' he said, helluva polite all of a sudden. 'Christopher Jameson here. He's in the Solo,' he added, sounding bloody important and stabbing at Mrs van der Watt's clipboard.

'Ah, yes, Christopher, here you are,' she said, ticking a box. 'Our lone contestant who won't be dancing to Mr Presley this evening.'

I stared at her clipboard. I counted eleven okes on the list. I was reading upside down, but I saw there was even some Elvis from Rustenberg. Hell, I didn't know rock 'n' roll had made it to Rustenberg. Eleven. Apparently I wasn't the only oke who'd spotted that notice; it had been the divine destiny of ten other okes, whom I now had to dance against in front of every bloody *piepie joller* from here to Springs. What the hell was I thinking? I just prayed I'd at least *bliksem* the jiver from Rustenberg.

'Make sure you're backstage promptly by half past seven.'

'No sweat, Mrs van der Watt!' Tommy bared his grin at her.

We made our way back to the other okes, and I could swear that there was a slight parting of the waters for us. They knew who I was. I was not just a wallflower any more, sitting on the sidelines. I was in it. Right up to my bloody neck. I checked Cynthia in a bevy of girls, all dark eyelashes and flouncing ponytail. As they passed, she glanced back over her shoulder and caught my eye.

That's right – she looked back. She actually looked back. I was worthy of a second look. Tommy did an exaggerated bow towards me.

'What?' I asked, with my hands.

'She only ever looks at me like I'm Germsville, man, and she doesn't bother to look twice for that.'

'*Ag,*' I sneered dismissively.

We'd reached the other okes who were hanging around outside the doors to the hall. I slouched with my hands shoved in my pockets, helluva casual, feeling eyes on my back. No need to strut around, like Stu Butler over there. 'Look at him,' I muttered to Tommy, 'preening like a cock.'

'Not cool, man.' He grabbed my wrist and twisted it, squinted at my watch. Stu was laughing too loudly.

'Showtime,' he said, dropping it, and my brief flirtation with brassiness was over.

Tommy manhandled me into the hall and down along the centre aisle to the side door leading to the wings. Rod, Mitch, Davie, even Errol and the O'Flynn brothers had followed; all of them seemed to want to stay near me, but now the time had come for us to part ways.

'*Jisis*, Chris, but I'm only *kak*ing myself for you,' said Mitch, gripping his bowels.

'Hey, what if all the okes have just come here to *lag* at you?' Rod pulled his face into an exaggerated grimace. 'What if every oke you know has turned up just to watch you make a total arse of yourself?'

'Shut up, you arse*hole*!' Tommy said savagely to him. 'Go on, Chris, you're going to blow them off! We'll clap for you anyway.'

I stumbled through the door, looking back forlornly at the gaggle one last time. Rod had that terrified grimace on his face again – not even for my benefit. My legs were jelly – how was I going to dance, man? I could barely climb the steps to the wings. What kind of unholy demon had possessed me to sign up for this?

Backstage had a strange quality to it, and I was briefly distracted by the billowing velvet sails that hung from the shadows far above. They seemed to stifle sound, muffling my steps on the wooden floorboards, and although I could hear the babble and scraping of the audience, it was somehow hushed in the wings.

I spied the other contestants in a huddle around Mrs van der Watt, who was pompously holding a clipboard and lecturing the motley Elvises about their performances.

'Absolutely no vulgarity, gentlemen, this is not Las Vegas.'

From the far side of the stage a man strode from the wings, a bustle in his wake: a harassed-looking older woman clutching a shuffle of papers and a younger one dabbing at the man's shiny face with a flippin' powder puff.

'Mr Finkstein! Good evening,' said Mrs van der Watt, in a la-di-dah voice, hurrying over to him.

193

'That's Eddy to you,' Eddy said, in a loud, jovial voice, winking.

'*Oh!* Eddy!'

'The lads ready?' he asked, nodding at us, but he didn't wait for an answer before he clapped his hands and said, 'Right, best not keep the rabble waiting any longer. I can hear them growing restless.'

He shrugged off the powder-puff girl and walked to the front of the stage. He stood dead centre before the curtains and the clipboard woman whispered something anxiously in his ear before she scurried away. He cleared his throat two or three times, then said, 'Christ, you know it's time to quit when you've sunk to this.'

I think he was talking to himself. He nodded at the roof, and the curtain magically parted for him. He stepped forward into a spotlight and the curtain closed behind him. I heard thunderous applause and the microphone screeched.

'Honourable judges, special guests, ladies and gentlemen ... welcome to tonight's spectacular, the inaugural Krugersdorp Junior Jive Contest. I'm Eddy Finkstein, *the* special guest and your host for this evening.'

There was a cymbal crash, then silence.

'Righty-ho. Before our contestants can take to the stage to show us their hitherto unsuspected talent, a few brief announcements, if you please. First, no jumping up and down and dancing in the aisles. Girls, no screaming, please. Gentlemen, no booing, no foul language, no gesticulation of any kind. That's it. So, how about letting Cliff Rich*aaard* put you in the mood?'

Jesus wept. How was that doo-wop drip going to put anyone in the mood?

194

'Ladies,' he said, in a creepy voice, '*do you wanna dance?*'

The curtain parted once more and Eddy Finkstein, our host for the evening, bounded back, his thumb and forefinger cocked at the crowd.

'Shirley!' he barked, as the curtain closed and Powderpuff Shirley rushed forward to mop his popping brow.

I edged towards the curtain. I knew the okes could probably see the maroon velvet twitching, but I didn't think they could see me peering behind it. I spotted the judges' table right in front. *Jisis*, they looked mean. Mrs Jonker, the tap dancing teacher, looked like she'd stood on dog turd.

The place was crammed, every chair taken, standing room only at the back. I spotted Johnny lounging against the walls with some of his mates. They were definitely here to *lag* at me. Tommy and the okes had a whole row right down in front. I felt a bit better about that. Mrs van der Watt was hissing behind me, trying to boss us into some sort of order.

'Christopher Jameson! You're number seven. Christopher? Get away from that curtain and stand in line.'

I shuffled over to the straggly line and eyed up the competition. To tell the truth, half of them looked in worse shape than I was. For a start, there were only ten of us; one oke had bolted already. Stu looked ill. He was tugging frantically on the seam in his crotch. In the whole scrawny, freckle-faced line-up there wasn't a single dead ringer for Elvis or Buddy Holly or Ritchie Valens or anyone else for that matter.

'Ladies and gentlemen!' The microphone screeched once more.

Yikes. I hadn't even noticed the song ending and the curtain opening again.

'I've checked backstage and the contestants are champing at the bit. I believe the time has come ... to make history. A big hand if you please for the 1958 Krugersdorp Junior Jivers ...'

I was going to run for it. I was looking for a door when ...

Waaaaaaaaaaaaah!

The curtain swept right open.

'Please! Please! *Please!*'

I was craning around the head of the oke in front. Eddy Finkstein was waving his arms like mad.

'Our first contestant, from Rand Leases Mine, performing to "Tutti Frutti",' he said, pronouncing it with clipped *t*s, 'Master Stuart Butler.'

Waaaaaaaaaaaaah!

You couldn't even hear the wop-bop-a-loo-bop-a-wop-bam-boom. I watched in horror as Stu stumbled out onto the stage. The spotlight picked him out, standing there, petrified, moon faced and grinning. Then, suddenly, he let loose: 'Tutti Frutti' was wild, man, and he started jumping frantically round the stage. He didn't have a clue, but at least he was going for it hammer and tongs, and the crowd didn't seem to care. They'd gone gaga.

As 'Tutti Frutti' ended with a cymbal crash on the 'boom', Stu did a wild leap into the wings. He was flushed and grinning like a Cheshire cat. We all stared at him with a mixture of envy and fascination. He was on the other side now.

The next contestant, I didn't even get his name, lurched out and just stood there as Elvis burst into 'You Ain't Nothing But A Hound Dog'. The oke was actually panting. After a few agonising seconds he twitched, then his whole body began to jerk. It took a while before I realised it was his

196

dance. He was shuddering on the spot. He managed a bit of gyrating with the hips, but mostly it was just the juddering.

By numbers five and six, the crowd was getting cocky, and I could hear the woofing and *ow-ow-ow-oooh*'s and fart noises over the thumping music. The okes mostly flopped about; one mimed his song holding a pretend microphone. At one point, he even threw it from one hand to the other.

'And now, contestant number seven, Master Christopher Jameson, who will be dancing, to Little Richard's "Lucille!"'

Crikey! That's me. One last comb of my boot-polished *kuif* with the heel of my palm and I was pushed right up to the edge of the wing by Mrs van der Watt.

'Right, off you go, then!'

But I didn't move. I was supposed to be out on stage when the music started, but I waited for it. The loudspeakers crackled as the needle stroked the groove. There was the gentle rhythmic hiss as the record spun on the turntable, and then, it started.

Low, with just the heavy bass drum, over which the piano tripped giddily. As the tempo climbed, I felt an electric current surge through me and the flesh on my arms pimpled. The piano descended into madness, divine madness, and I ran out onto the stage just as Little Richard screamed '*Lucille!*'

I slid right across it with the groaning sax, like I was back on top of that slimes dump, only with greased soles. Then I glided into my *kwela-kwela* moves, pitching and rolling my hips like a ripple across the stage. My footwork wasn't pretty, but I was churning to the beat, and although I couldn't see the crowd – I was blinded by the spotlight – man, I was sizzling.

I could hear feet thumping on floorboards – the tremors were coursing right through my pelvis – and now I was revving up to *gooi* in some *pata-pata*. As I started grinding lower, I had a vague twinge of doubt, but the music was throbbing and I couldn't help it: I was almost quivering. The thing that had taken hold of Dolly's sax player had me in its grip – I was seething, my hips and shoulders and feet gelling with some secret lubricant. Old Vilikazi would've wept to see me, man.

Then it ended, for a heartbeat complete and utter silence in the hall and then they went gaga. They were on their feet, stomping, jumping up and down in the aisles. I stood there gawping.

'Thank you! Thank you! Please sit down now! *Sit down!*'

But there was nothing Eddy could do. They were screaming the roof off and, for one sweet moment, before I was escorted from the stage by Mrs van der Watt, I *was* rock 'n' roll.

'Heels on fire!' said Stu, reverently, as I reached the wings.

Jislaaik, I was made in the shade, man. There were still three okes to go, but I hardly bothered to watch them. There were three categories – stage presentation, technique and audience appeal – and quite apart from the fact that none of the okes had any stage presentation or technique for that matter, I'd definitely creamed it for audience appeal with my *kwela-kwela* routine. When the last oke was also escorted from the stage, still bowing low and saluting his fans, Mrs van der Watt told us we could go and sit in the audience until the judges announced the winner.

When we shuffled out of the stage door, an actual squeal erupted from the ranks of chairs. I headed for the front row, and as I took a seat next to Tommy, he *klapp*ed me on the back and said, 'Hung like a baboon, man!'

Cynthia had to have the hots for me now.

'You killed them, Chris!' Rod yelped.

He and Mitch had to share a chair to make room for me, but I was a rock 'n' roll sensation now, so what could they do? The judges were leaning in towards one another, conferring urgently. Jeez, what was there to talk about? Then the one in the middle nodded to Eddy's assistant, who was hovering a discreet distance away. She hurried forward and took a folded piece of paper from him and my belly flopped again. She disappeared backstage and I couldn't even pretend to be cool any more.

'Come on, man, what's taking so long?' I said, staring fixedly at the crack in the curtain.

The crowd had begun a slow clap, which gathered momentum until it broke into thunderous applause as Eddy Finkstein emerged from the wings holding the folded scrap of paper between his thumb and index finger. I couldn't tear my eyes from it. It had to have my name on it. I felt faint and black spots mushroomed before my eyes.

'Ladies and gentlemen, after much deliberation from the judges, we at last have a winner!'

My heart stopped. This moment changed everything. It was better than my first taste of booze, better than my first fight, I was born again.

'Cedric Poggenpoel from Consolidated Main Reef.'

I dropped back into my chair like I'd been shot down. Cedric Poggenpoel? The oke did a polka dance to 'My Baby Left Me'. The polka! That's what I'm telling you, man. The crowd didn't clap half as loud for him. What the hell sort of rip-off talent show was this? Tommy was speechless. He was shaking his head mutely, his mouth agape, but I knew when I'd blown it. It was Vilikazi's slightly risqué thrusting move I'd pulled when the delirium hit. Too hot to handle.

'Well you certainly had lots of pizzazz,' said Eddy, gripping my hand with his slippery one when I went up to collect my runner-up prize.

Pizzazz? Clutching my pathetic *Boy's Own* annual – I mean even a *Beano* comic would have redeemed it – I *skeefed* the judges as I walked back past them to my chair. I could see the old *vrots* were pissed off with me. Mrs Jonker glared at me like I *was* the dog turd.

Boy's Own was the worst comic book ever. There was a page for readers' jokes like: 'What can you always wear that never goes out of style? ... A smile.' Who were these okes, man? When I got back to my row, Johnny'd taken my chair.

'It was a fix, man. You whipped that drip's arse.'

'Thanks, Johnny.'

'Foul!' Tommy hollered at the judges' backs. Mrs Jonker turned and peered sourly at our row.

'No heckling, please!' Eddy whined.

Tommy booed loudly when Cedric went up to collect his prize. Rod and Mitch chimed in with some *lekker* catcalls – 'Hey, Cedric, are your parents cousins or what?', 'I'll bet your ma had a bloody loud bark, hey?'. I might not've been the best under-sixteen rock 'n' roller in the West Rand, but *jisee*, I had the best mates.

'What can I tell you?' said Johnny, getting up. 'Some days you're the dog, others you're the lamp-post.' He shrugged helplessly at me and grinned as he headed off with his mates.

I watched him vanish through the foyer doors and felt a rush of love for him. If I thought about it, Johnny was always there. He masked it with a mocking casualness, but I knew he always had one eye out for me.

There was going to be a dance after the contest, and the sound of chairs scraping across the parquet flooring was deafening. Me and Tommy and the okes pushed our way through the crowd milling about the foyer and out onto the steps.

It was a relief to escape the stifling heat of the hall. I felt so acutely alive: my skin tingled in the cool air. The starlight, when I tilted my head to look up at the sky, had a brittle frostiness I'd never noticed before. I was conscious of my breath, the dark, viscous blood pumping through my veins. I felt like anything was possible.

The siren tore the air to shreds. I clapped my hands over my ears, cringing.

19

The Razing

Cece

The women were keening, rivers of tears coursing down their cheeks. My ears hurt and I didn't like seeing them weeping so, those big mamas, with their beefy, no-nonsense arms and huge pillowy bosoms; the whole world tilted dangerously.

They wept for the homes they'd lost. The police came in the night and roped off the whole of Madubulaville and then a convoy of trucks rolled up. The people had to get their stuff and climb in, and then they squashed those sorry little shacks flat. They weren't sanitary, that was why. Vilikazi said it was because they weren't a sanitary distance from the whites, and that was why. Some of the people ran away and others got arrested for throwing themselves on the ground. In the hullabaloo the fat little *spaza* shop owner, who was very rich and drove a Morris Oxford and collected the wickedly high rents for the landlord, got stabbed in the stomach with a glass bottle.

I didn't like the people having their shacks squashed flat

and not having anywhere to live. I watched the little kids playing with TJ over there in the dust and sucked the ends of my pigtails. A girl in a green dress stopped to look at me. She broke away from the pack and took a few steps closer. The ruched bodice was torn and she had roasties on her dusty knees like mine; the blood was shockingly red against her black skin. Then she smiled at me. I smiled back and we looked at each other like that for a moment, until a little boy with a sticky-out belly-button came up and took her hand. She picked him up and turned away. He stared at me over her shoulder with big, calm eyes.

They could've gone to the dormitories in Munsieville, but those mamas reckoned they'd sooner go back to the *kraal* before they lived behind a fence. TJ was dashing about and yelping and I wished the mamas would hush up and I wished they would all go away from my secret hiding-place, but it wasn't mine any more. They said there was fighting in Munsieville now. They said they had set fire to the Location manager's office, and the municipal beer hall. Jeepers, setting fire to the Location manager's office had to be a bad crime – that was the government building! The people knew it too. There were low murmurings under the wailing about the raid that would come, as surely as night would follow this day. They had a dark sound about them, the murmurings, and I was afraid. You did not want to find your name on the list of Stone Throwers or Weapon Brandishers, that was for darn sure. The holy water Ntate Ezekiel was sprinkling around the ground had better keep us safe.

'Nowhere is safe,' said Vilikazi, and I wished *he* would go away. I did not want God to spot me fraternising with the likes of him today.

Ntate Ezekiel was praying as the sun sank and I'd never heard anyone pray so good. He wasn't asking God tonight, but telling Him what He jolly well had to do. He had to look after every one of His flock now in His presence, as He looked after the birds of the air and the beasts of the earth, and not let them perish at the hands of the evil-doers. If He did that, then He'd see *some* worshipping. Then the prophet brought the holy Wrath of God raining down to frizzle and blister upon the heads of the members of the Native Affairs Committee of the city council and especially those who drafted the Insanitary List. Then we sang '*Ke Lella Moya*' – 'I Yearn to Save My Soul'.

Vilikazi sighed. 'In the jail,' he said, 'we sing "*Pasopa Verwoerd*, the Black Man Comes", and the *izinja* are deaf to our words.'

At the gatherings, Vilikazi said, Bioscope Dayimani and the other praise singers raised their voices in song. The *izingoma* were of freedom, and though they were only songs, they flowed into the blood, and it was through them that the people freed their hearts and their minds. 'Then we say, "*Mayibuye iAfrica* – Africa, let it return."'

'What are you talking about, Vilikazi? How was it lost?' I clicked my tongue at him.

Vilikazi started laughing. 'Maybe with all that singing, eh? All those wars with the Boers and the British, every battle, before they would attack, at dawn, the Zulu *impi*, they would sing. Dying on the hills of Isandlwana, they would sing. Even the British soldiers, they'd say, "Hey, maybe we should let him finish his song first, it's a nice song. Then we'll kill him."

'Maybe it's time those *imbongi* think about changing the

words at least, taking out a "prayer" here, putting in a "bullet" there, eh? Next time I hear one of them start singing about Bibles, I'm just going to shout, "*Bopa!*" you know – "Shut the fuck up, this song isn't happening, man!"'

He said I had to go home. I hated Vilikazi. I didn't want to go home. There was something wrong with Daddy: his eyes turned mean. Sometimes I was like an animal – I could sense danger, could smell it. I knew in my gut that me and TJ needed to stay away from him tonight. That was why when I saw Vilikazi washing up for the day under the tap by the outhouse, I crawled out under the coal chute and dragged TJ after me, and why, oh, why did Vilikazi follow me here? I knew we must not go back.

'Come, *ingcosana*,' he said, tugging my hand. I was leaving the holy ground now. TJ bounded over to me, his tail wagging so hard it was going to wag right off. I had a bad feeling inside.

20

The Vanishing

Chris

Jisis! The siren was lacerating my eardrums. The loudhailer was rigged up on the mast on top of the clock tower; at curfew you could hear it wailing across Krugersdorp all the way to the mine, and here we were pinioned right underneath it. Why in God's name had they set it off in the middle of the Krugersdorp Junior Jive Contest? When I looked up I saw two policemen running down the path towards us. They were shouting something, gesticulating, but their words were lost. Then we were being elbowed brusquely aside by Mrs Jonker and another judge bustling down the stairs. They intercepted the policemen just as they reached the first step, and I watched as they leaned in to one another, their mouths working, frowning. I was starting to feel woozy as the siren reverberated inside my head. I was listing to one side.

I heard Eddy Finkstein's voice over the microphone. He

was saying it was over, the junior jivers had to go home. There was unrest in the Location. We had to get off the streets. There was groaning and moaning from the junior jivers. Loads of them were spilling out of the foyer now, milling around the steps. None of them were going home at once, like Mrs van der Watt was ordering them to do, in a stern, panicky voice.

Finally the siren stopped, but the ringing in my skull still went on and on. Through a thick wad of cotton wool I heard the swirling rumours. A riot in the Location. Blacks rampaging through its mean alleys. Some said they'd torched the place. Tommy jerked beside me. 'What the hell is Mr Battersby doing here?'

I followed his gaze to see Mr Battersby hurrying across the lawn towards us. That was odd. Not just that Mr Battersby was headed for the Krugersdorp Junior Jive Contest, but that he was coming across the *lawn*. The footlights that were beamed onto the face of the town hall from below cast only a weak reflection across the lawns, so I couldn't see his face, but there was definitely something unsettling in the way he was trotting stiffly towards us. I got to my feet with Tommy.

'Hey, Mr Battersby, you're too late – they've already picked a winner,' Rod chirped.

As he drew closer, he looked up at us and I saw relief skitter across his face. 'Tommy, boy, there you are. Hell, that's a bit of luck. Come quickly – your ma needs you. There's some trouble.' He touched his hand to his forehead. 'It's Cecelia, Tommy, she's ... gone missing.'

Tommy went rigid for a heartbeat. Then he leaped down the steps, two at a time. I was left teetering there for a second before I vaulted down after him. 'Don't worry,' I called back over my shoulder to Rod and Mitch, 'I'll go with him, make sure everything's all right.' Then I sprinted to catch up with Tommy and Mr Battersby.

'What do you mean she's gone missing?' asked Tommy, and I could hear the edge in his voice.

'Now don't worry, son, she's probably fine, but we don't know where she is right now. Your ma came over to our house, thinking she may have run ...' He caught himself and hesitated before he went on, 'Well, thinking she may be with us. We searched the garden, yours and ours, and have called up and down the street. Your ma thought that maybe she'd gone to find you, or that maybe you'd know where to look.'

He was out of breath by the time we reached his car parked out on Commissioner Street in front of the old magistrates' court.

'I don't know where she is,' said Tommy. 'She didn't come here – we never saw her, hey, Chris?' He turned to me for help. 'I don't know where to look, I don't know.' His voice had risen in pitch.

I couldn't think straight. I shook my head dumbly.

'Well, Mrs Battersby's making a pot of tea for your ma. I think she needs it. Let's go back there, shall we, and put our heads together? No use panicking, is there?'

In the back seat of the car on the way to the mine, Tommy was silent. I stared out of the window as Mr Battersby drove up Kruger Street. When I looked down I saw that I was still clutching my bloody *Boy's Own* in my left hand. No one spoke until we came over the rise and crossed the railway line.

'What happened, Mr Battersby?' Tommy asked bleakly.

Mr Battersby gave a slight shake of his head. A few sparse curls poked out of his collar at the back of his neck. 'I don't know, boy,' he said, staring stubbornly ahead.

'You know what I mean,' said Tommy. 'Why did she run?'

'Really, Tommy,' said Mr Battersby, clearing his throat. 'I wasn't actually there, of course.'

'My six-year-old sister has vanished. Can we stop pretending that our walls aren't paper thin when it comes to this *kak*?'

'Look,' said Mr Battersby, sounding annoyed, 'we heard raised voices, and your father sounded angry, very angry. Cecelia was screaming. We don't often hear her screaming like that any more. The dog was barking its head off, so I don't know what was going on. I didn't want to get involved, not my place, you understand?'

Tommy looked at the back of Mr Battersby's neck. *Ja*, he knew how it was.

'Your ma said it was about the dog. The dog bit him – your father. She said it was a nasty bite too, puncture wounds, lacerated skin. Your father said he was going to kill it, said he was going to wring its neck. Look, fair enough, you can't have a dog that bites its own master. Your ma said Cecelia went hysterical. She says she doesn't know how she did it – your ma was in her own room by then – but Cecelia got the dog away from your father and ran. Your father left for the Union Club, but when Cece didn't come back, your ma started to worry. Anyway, look, that's what she told us. If you want to know anything else, ask your ma when you see her. We're almost there. But

209

listen, Tommy, your ma's a good woman, if a little ... highly strung, so don't start in on her now. She's in a bit of a state.'

I could see Tommy clench his jaw, the small muscle quivering below his ear. His fist was balled on the seat beside him. We rolled slowly down School Road. When we pulled up outside Tommy's house, I could see the front door had been left wide open, light spilling down the front steps. Tommy wrenched the door handle, almost tumbled out of the car and raced up the path into the house. I hurried behind him with Mr Battersby, hoping Cece had come back while Mr Battersby had been gone and that she'd be waiting inside for us.

As Mr Battersby and I reached the door to the lounge, I could see Mrs Michaels sitting on the couch beside old Mrs Battersby. Mrs Battersby was holding one of her hands – it looked like a claw, thin and bony. In her other hand Mrs Michaels was clutching that wretched little hanky of hers and dabbing at her eyes. Tommy was standing right in the centre of the room, glaring at her.

'Oh, Tommy, I'm sorry about all this fuss. It's a bother for you, I know, and I'm probably just being silly.' She gave a shrill little laugh. 'I'm sure she'll come home any minute,' she added brightly. Then she looked down. 'I ... I didn't know what to do quite. You know where to find her, Tommy, don't you?' she said, almost pleading, 'She ran out of here with that vile dog in such a state.' She waved her hanky vaguely and dabbed at her eyes again. They were red-rimmed, watery, anxious.

'He hit her, didn't he?' Tommy accused her starkly.

Mrs Battersby looked away.

'He hit Cece and TJ went for him, didn't he? That's what happened, *isn't it?*'

Mr Battersby stepped into the room and put a restraining hand on Tommy's shoulder. 'Now, now, son, that's not going to help anyone. We've got to find Cecelia, so let's just stay focused on that.'

Tommy's shoulders sagged. Then he shrugged off Mr Battersby's hand and headed out into the passage. I was standing in the doorway as he passed me.

'I'll go with him,' I told them. 'I know you've already searched the garden, but maybe ... maybe she's still hiding,' I finished lamely. 'She'll come out if she hears it's us.'

I was making it worse. Mrs Michaels's eyes were brimming and I dithered awkwardly in the doorway for another moment before I turned to follow Tommy down to the kitchen and out of the back door. We ransacked the whole garden, crawling under every bush, rummaging in the old outhouse, the garage, calling her name over and over.

'This is stupid, Chris,' Tommy said eventually. 'Even if she was still hiding out here, TJ would've given her away long ago.'

I knew that. I would've gone on looking, though, because I didn't know what else to do and didn't want to think about it. I was waiting for Tommy to face it first.

'We'd better go back inside,' I said. 'This is wasting time.' I felt a knot in my gut tighten as I said it.

We headed back in.

'She's not out there,' I said plainly, as we walked back into the parlour.

'How long is it now, Ma? How long has she been missing?'

asked Tommy, with that accusing tone in his voice again. 'How long did you wait?'

There was something terrible in the way he said that.

'He – he left for the Union Club at half past six,' she whispered.

Mr Battersby exchanged a glance with his wife, then looked at his wristwatch. 'Well, it's a quarter to ten now. I think Tommy's right. I think we need to call the police. It would be remiss of us not to at this stage, Rose, now we've exhausted every avenue.'

Mrs Michaels made a small noise at the back of her throat. As she lifted her hand to her mouth, I saw it was trembling. A skin of milk was floating on top of the untouched cup of tea beside her.

'Right. I'll telephone them, then,' said Mr Battersby, going back out into the hallway.

'Hey, Tommy, why don't we go and look down in our cave?' I said suddenly. 'It's not going to help for us to wait around here for the police as well. Mr Battersby can tell them everything. They can start the search, but we still ought to go and look down there, and no one else knows the way.'

Tommy looked at me gratefully. I think we were both desperate to do something.

'*Ja*, you're right, Chris. I didn't think of it, but she might've gone there. We'd better go.'

'It sounds sensible to check,' said Mrs Battersby, nodding at us and then at Mrs Michaels.

I didn't really believe that Cece would have gone there, but going to look seemed better than waiting around here. We retreated from the room and Tommy headed into his bedroom off the passage. Mr Battersby finished his tele-phone call and I explained to him where we were going.

'Someone had better inform Mr Michaels of the situa-tion,' he ventured, 'but perhaps it would be best left to the police.'

I went down to the kitchen to find the torch that Tommy said was in the box under the sink. I was still rummaging around in it when he appeared in the kitchen carrying his BB guns. 'What're those for, man?'

'Don't know.' He shrugged noncommittally. 'Thought we should take them, in case. Catch!'

He tossed me his old No. 1 and we left through the back door and went around the side of the house.

Loping down the deserted streets towards the mine, we were quiet, though I could feel Tommy's fear for Cece leak-ing corrosively out of him. When we reached the dump, we slowed down, picking our way carefully though the quiet canyons, the leaping beam of the torch casting strange shad-ows across the walls. Finally we reached our own chasm and followed it to our cave.

'Cece!' Tommy called, as he lifted the sacking, his voice snuffed out by the thick blanket of compacted sand above us.

I splayed the light across the cave, but we both knew it was empty.

'Damn.'

We stood in silence for a moment. I'd never noticed before how that place seemed to suck sound: footfalls were muffled, even our breathing seemed choked off.

'Tommy?' I said, not even wanting to say it. 'What about the East Shaft?'

213

'What? What are you talking about?'

'Remember, in the compound, that day? She said she had her own cave in the East Shaft.'

'But that was just crap. It's sealed off. It was sealed right after those timbermen died in the last weeks before it was going to be closed for ever. It's impossible. Isn't it?'

The torch sputtered.

'Shit.'

21

The Search

'I know. I know it's impossible, but we've got to check, haven't we?'

Tommy closed his eyes and nodded. He hoisted his gun over his shoulder, and we quickly retraced our steps along our ravine until it opened into the labyrinth of drifts and gullies, lit feebly by the broken torchlight. At length we emerged onto the South Shaft Road and started to run towards the Main Reef. We crossed it at full tilt, not even slowing to check for headlamps. There was something more febrile about our flight now.

We ran through the main gates and down towards the mine police station. When we finally arrived at the tiny red-brick building, breathless and bursting, it was empty, save for a black police boy behind the counter.

Yes, he knew about the missing child, yes, they were assembling a search party; an officer was stationed at the house. He told us to wait and disappeared into the back when Tommy explained that we might have some information.

He returned a few minutes later, accompanied by a young white policeman.

'Constable Bezuidenhout,' he introduced himself. 'What is the information in your possession?'

He was brusque. Suited me. Tommy too, I think.

'My sister, she said something crazy the other day, about a hiding-place, a cave.'

'Where?' he said urgently.

Tommy hesitated. 'In the East Shaft.'

Constable Bezuidenhout looked at him intently.

'I know,' said Tommy. 'It's crazy.'

'Come with me,' Constable Bezuidenhout said, and we followed him behind the counter and down the short, narrow passage leading off the reception area.

To the right was the cell. It was empty, but the thick iron bars winked at me as we passed. Constable Bezuidenhout turned to an office opening off the opposite side of the passage and hesitated in the doorway, as though waiting to get someone's attention. Straining to see past his bulky frame, I could just make out two men inside. One was sitting on a chair with his back to us. It was tilted on its hind legs and his feet were up on the teak desk in front of him. The other man leaned against the window, his legs crossed insolently in front of him.

'If you ask me, it's been a glorious waste of time,' he said to the seated man.

'Just get on with it, Sergeant Fourie,' the other man said irritably.

Sergeant Fourie said no more, but he unbuttoned the flap of his breast pocket, took out a notebook, flipped it open and began to read monotonously: 'Complainant: F. J. du Preez,

216

boiler-maker. Complaint: tool theft. Notes: dog killed. Carcass left at scene of crime.'

'Presumed scene of crime,' the other man interjected. He had a bald spot right at his crown.

Sergeant Fourie didn't acknowledge the interruption. 'Interrogated workshop boys (eighteen). Searched and examined compound, also S of C. No definite clues as to culprit.' Fourie looked up from his notebook. 'The bastards are getting smart,' he said, sounding pleased about it. 'Poisoned the dog – now that's getting *slim*, hey?' He looked intimidatingly smart in his dark blue uniform with the gold buttons and the braid, the gabardine breeches and leather leggings.

'Oldest trick in the book,' said the balding man. 'As for clues, did you look for signs of someone flush with a bit of cash, new shoes, recent meat-eating?'

'*Ja*, Lieutenant, but there was nothing – no bones in the pots, only dried *mielie* meal. Besides, didn't look like any of those boys had been eating meat. You can always tell – they look sleek as cats. You should've let me arrest the whole bloody lot of them. Damn sure I'd have got confessions out of them before dawn.'

The other man sighed wearily. 'I must listen to this crap while they raze Madubulaville and the Location burns,' he said, rubbing his eyes with the thumb and index finger of one hand.

I jolted at that.

'Orright, maybe a trap or something next time, then?' suggested Sergeant Fourie, chirpily.

Constable Bezuidenhout, who had been waiting all this time in the doorway while Sergeant Fourie ignored him, finally cleared his throat loudly to get the balding man's attention. Tommy was smarting beside me at having to wait so long, but it was the police.

He twisted around in his chair. 'Constable, what can I do for you?'

'Lieutenant Ford, sir, this is the brother of the missing girl. He's got some crazy story about the East Shaft, but I thought maybe you'd want to check it out.'

'The East Shaft?' he said, dropping his chair back onto all fours and his legs off the table. The chair grated across the floor. 'Come here, boy.'

Constable Bezuidenhout stood aside, ushering Tommy and me into the office. I breathed in a mixture of stale sweat, mothballs, ink and floor polish. The room was bare except for a green filing cabinet in the corner, a telephone on the desk and a water carafe on the window-sill.

'Lieutenant Ford. And you are?'

'Thomas Michaels, sir.'

'Now what's this about the East Shaft?'

When Tommy explained again, Lieutenant Ford said, 'Christ. Well, I hope not, but we'd better go down there and take a look. Constable, have the patrol officers on duty reported back yet?'

'Yes, sir, they're waiting in the mess to be briefed.'

'Right, then. Escort these *laities* out and we'll rendezvous outside.'

Standing on the steps of the police station, waiting for the van to come around the front to collect us, I shivered in the chill of the night. Tommy dragged our BB guns out from under a hydrangea bush where we'd stashed them, and I shoved mine behind my back and under my shirt, tucking the barrel into the waistband of my pants. He looked at me in the darkness. I couldn't see the features of his face.

'It's my fault, Chris. Jesus. I never came back from the boxing match, just went off on my own *jol*. And I didn't forget. It's worse than that. It's Saturday, man. I know – I know I need to wait for him to leave ...

'She waits for me too now. She doesn't say anything, but she's waiting for me to come home all right, hoping. She's started asking, "Are you coming back, Tommy? After the bio-scope? Are you coming?" And thing is, today, I thought ... I thought, Fuck it. I didn't want to go back. I thought, you know, what a pain, man, why's that little snot-nose my job? That's the truth, Chris ... I left her there.' He groaned.

I felt sick for him. 'Ah, *jisis*, Tommy.'

Then the police van pulled round the corner, the doors at the back flapping open. Sergeant Fourie leaned out of the window and told us to get in with the boys in the back.

I hauled myself up and perched on the edge of the slatted bench that ran along the inside of the van, with Tommy and three black police boys. Constable Bezuidenhout came out of the station last, slammed the doors of the van and we trundled up Loco Road. Tommy was sitting awkwardly with the gun under his shirt – even in the darkness I could see it poking out behind his head, but the police boys said nothing. The van had a grille over the windows, but when it turned and picked up speed, I knew we were on Main Reef.

Rocked by the vibrations from the engine in the disorienting darkness, I kept thinking of the the Ritz Palais de Danse, the slumyard – infested with pimps and *shebeen* queens, *tsotsi*s and fat sewer rats, septic with *bloedvermenging* and shot through with so much life that breathing its fetid air was like a tonic. And now it was gone. The Black Spot was gone from the face of this earth.

The van lurched to the right again and we shuddered over rough ground before jerking to a halt. I heard quick footsteps crunching on gravel, then the doors swung open and the men clambered out with Tommy and me.

The change-house loomed directly in front of us. Two wings jutted from either side of the red-brick body of the building, dark sentinels silhouetted against the sky. We followed the policemen towards the old wooden headgear that stood directly over the shaft. In the moonlight it looked skeletal. Stripped of the pulleys, the machinery that turned the great iron wheels, it was a starkly simple structure: four black masts rising up in a square, two more buttressed against it, sloping down into the ground like tracks. Even as we approached I could see in the powerful beams of the policemen's torches that there was no way in. A huge metal plate had been welded over the mouth of the vertical shaft. Some of the police boys were inspecting its rim, but I could see it was completely sealed.

Two of the men were scouring the area around the shaft and the change-house; another was on the *stoep* rattling the chains on the door, but it was padlocked. The glass panes in some of the windows had been smashed, but they were tiny, studded cavities, and there was no way anyone could have climbed inside.

Lieutenant Ford crunched across the gravel to where I was standing with Tommy under the headgear with Sergeant Fourie in tow.

'Looks like you've fed us a bullshit story,' said the sergeant.

Lieutenant Ford frowned and said matter-of-factly, 'Well, fortunately it does look as if your sister's cave down there was an imaginary one. Funny thing for a little girl to come up with, though.'

He went over to the van, lifted the radio receiver from its cradle and held a crackled conversation with it for a minute or so. Tommy and I stood there uselessly. The men had stopped searching and some were squatting on the *stoep*, smoking quietly. Lieutenant Ford finished and crunched back over to us.

'Thing is, your sister has evidently still not returned home. I've dispatched someone to go and locate your father. Do either of you have any other ideas where she may be?'

Tommy seemed to slump. He'd been chafing before, but now all the urgency had gone out of him. He shook his head at Lieutenant Ford.

Constable Bezuidenhout coughed. 'What about that old incline shaft that bisects the vertical one a few hundred feet down? Wasn't it the original East Shaft? I think it comes out just over there on the ridge,' he said, gesturing towards the east.

We all looked in the direction he was pointing, though, of course, there was nothing to see.

'Good, Constable. Call the boys, let's find it.'

The men fanned out ahead of us as we trudged along the ridge, their search lights flickering dissonantly across the veld. Without one ourselves, Tommy and I stumbled over the rough ground, treacherous with boulders, termite mounds, clods of loose turf, hidden hollows. The gun dug uncomfortably into my spine. One of the men blasted on a whistle.

'*Lapa!*'

He was standing about three hundred yards to the east of the headgear. As we converged on him, I could see what he had found. He was standing on the edge of a trough. It was one of the trenches the old miners had dug before they began to sink shafts. It was a narrow cleft, ten or eleven yards in length, four across, tapering as it dropped down about six yards to no more than two at the bottom. The sides were steep, overgrown with frothy plumed pampas grass, while reeds, rushes, plants that flourish in marshy areas, choked the bottom; even a few trees had rooted in the fractured strata of the rock.

A steep flight of stairs had been carved into the embankment. At the bottom of the gully, on the opposite side to where we now stood, a cavity yawned in the rock. It was the mouth of a tunnel; we had found the original East Shaft. As the beams of the torches danced across it, I could see there was a grille welded across its face, beyond which the torchlight was swallowed.

'This must be it,' said Lieutenant Ford, tersely. 'All right, follow me, slowly now. We don't want any broken ankles to deal with.'

He barked a few instructions in Fanakalo to the police boys. I followed Tommy, who was behind the lieutenant and Sergeant Fourie; Constable Bezuidenhout was behind me. I trod gingerly. The steps were shallow, barely wide enough for a child's foot. At the base of the furrow, just as the steps disappeared into the darkness, there was a platform off to the side, below which I could see the tracks for the cocopans running alongside the stairs down the tunnel. We gathered on the platform.

Even in the torchlight, I could see the conglomerate seam in the shelf of rock that jutted out around the mouth of the tunnel, studded with pebbles, only a few feet in width, dropping down sharply into the earth.

Constable Bezuidenhout was slowly beaming his torch around the rim. Sergeant Fourie grasped the grille and jerked it. It rattled but stayed fast.

'There's no way she got in here either,' he said, over his shoulder.

I was starting to feel hopeless. Constable Bezuidenhout was now beaming right down the shaft, illuminating the corrugated lining of its walls and domed roof. A doorway opened to the right about twenty, maybe thirty yards down, the steeply inclined floor dropping past it. It led into the first of the drives, the horizontal tunnels that branch off the main vertical or inclined one. There must have been openings just like it at regular intervals as the shaft bore downwards, although the beam of Constable Bezuidenhout's torch couldn't penetrate the darkness much beyond this first.

'Come on, let's get out of here,' said Sergeant Fourie, releasing the grille and stepping back on the stairs. Constable Bezuidenhout leaned forward, though, shining his torch right through the bars now. He seemed to be trying to angle it into the drive.

'Just hold on!' he shouted suddenly, and my gut lurched. Tommy gripped my wrist, his nails digging into my flesh.

'What is it, Constable?' said Lieutenant Ford. He stepped up beside him.

'I think I see something, just there. Do you see it? What is that?'

Tommy and I crowded up to the entrance with the two men and pressed up against the grille. I saw what Constable Bezuidenhout had spotted: something pale, lying on the floor just inside the entrance to the drive. I was trying to see what it was – it was hard to make out, only just in our line of vision. I squeezed my eyes shut for an instant, then tried to focus again. Constable Bezuidenhout's torchlight quivered over it.

It almost looked like a tiny human arm.

'Christ,' gasped Lieutenant Ford. 'It's not possible.'

'Cece!' Tommy called, his voice echoing down the shaft.

'Cecelia!' Lieutenant Ford boomed. 'Are you in there? Can you hear us?'

Silence.

'Is anyone down there?' he thundered again.

'Cece?' Tommy called forlornly.

Lieutenant Ford grabbed hold of the grille and wrenched. It didn't budge.

'Fourie, help us here!' he barked.

Sergeant Fourie, Constable Bezuidenhout and the lieutenant all lined up facing the grille. Tommy and I instinctively stepped back.

'All right. On the count of three. One. Two. Three.'

All three men strained against it – Constable Bezuidenhout grunted with the effort – but the grille stayed firmly in place.

'Okay,' said Lieutenant Ford, stepping back. He turned and looked back up at the rim of the trench where the police boys were crowded. 'Hey, Zuma!' he shouted. 'Go fetch those crow-bars in the van! Bring the bolt cutters too. *Hamba!'*

There was a buzz coming from up above. The men, who had been mutely gritty until now, seemed excited.

'Constable, go back up. When Zuma returns, get those boys down here.'

'*Meneer,*' said Bezuidenhout, and ascended briskly. The men started gabbling as he reached the lip. Tommy and I remained below. We strained to see what the thing was, lying there in the darkness, but, of course, light doesn't bend round corners.

At length we heard Zuma return, his pounding feet sending tremors down through the earth to us, and the column of men, led by Constable Bezuidenhout, descended to the platform.

'You boys must get back now, well out of the way.'

Tommy and I reluctantly stepped against the jagged rock face behind us. Constable Bezuidenhout told Zuma and another burly man to wedge the crow-bars under the iron rim of the grille by the rusting bolts. He and Sergeant Fourie and the third man grasped the grille once more. Lieutenant Ford stepped back towards Tommy and me.

'Okay. You ready?'

Constable Bezuidenhout didn't turn but nodded once.

'*Een! Twee! Drie! Magtig!*' he shouted, and the men heaved against the grille. With a terrible noise, it started to tear loose from the walls. Bits of mortar crumbled as the bolts came away.

The men repositioned the crow-bars and Constable Bezuidenhout shouted hoarsely, 'Again!'

With a second huge effort, the bolts screaming in protest, the grille finally tore free and the men staggered backwards.

'Whoa! Whoa!'

The two crow-bar boys rushed to help steady the thing.

'Sweet Jesus!' groaned Fourie.

'Over the side of the platform!' shouted Lieutenant Ford. 'Move!'

The men shuffled to the lip of the platform and hurled the grille over the edge. It clattered to the rocky basin below. In the ringing aftermath, no one said a word.

'Well done, boys.' The lieutenant broke the silence. 'Come on, then, we've no time to lose. Let's get on with it.'

'Thomas, you stay back here, do you hear me? Christopher, you too. I don't want you boys coming in until we've checked what's down there.'

I couldn't see Tommy's expression beside me, but I knew this was agony for him.

'Sergeant, you and Constable Bezuidenhout follow me. The rest of you boys wait here too.'

The lieutenant entered the tunnel with the other two men following. The oldest incline shafts cored out of the rock were low and narrow, and the roof of the tunnel hung only a few feet above their heads as they descended, clinging to the walls for support. Tommy and I inched after them. None of the three black men tried to stop us.

When Lieutenant Ford drew up alongside the hole opening into the drive on the far side of the tunnel, he pushed off gently from the corrugated surface of the wall and inched across the dangerously smooth ramp down which the old narrow-gauge tracks ran, until he reached the doorway. He grabbed hold of the lintel and beamed his torch down onto the floor of the drive.

'*What the hell?*'

Tommy and I reached the same stair, desperate to catch up to the policemen who were now wedged just inside the opening to the drive. I scrambled after Tommy across the slope, glancing down into its yawning depths. It tugged at me: I wanted to let go and fall into it. Then I grabbed hold of Constable Bezuidenhout's belt and hauled myself into the doorway with Tommy, shoving Sergeant Fourie further inside. The policemen barely noticed us.

Lying on the rough floor of the cavern, her body contorted, was Lulu.

22

The Madness

'It's Lulu.' My voice sounded strange to me.

'Who?' asked Lieutenant Ford, still shining the beam on the doll's porcelain face, her painted lips garish in the light.

'It's Cece's doll.' Tommy spoke at last.

Lulu's vivid blue eyes stared up at me with a startling intensity, almost alive.

Sergeant Fourie took a few steps forward and stooped as though to retrieve her from where she lay on the floor.

'Don't touch it!' ordered Lieutenant Ford.

He beamed his torch down the drive. It was surprisingly narrow, the roof so low a man would almost have to stoop. The timber beams propping the roof marched down the tunnel until the light was gnawed away by a darkness that was almost solid.

'Cecelia!' Lieutenant Ford called, but his voice was unexpectedly swallowed.

'Cecelia!'

We all tried, but there was no answer.

'Sergeant, you head down there and see if you can find anything.'

Fourie disappeared into the shadows.

'I thought I told you two to wait!' the lieutenant reprimanded us. 'Now keep out of the way.'

He and Constable Bezuidenhout played their torches around the hanging walls. Skeleton packs of latticed timber had been wedged into the stopes opening up on our right, and the floor was littered with debris from the old miners – bits of rope and plank, an old sledgehammer. A short way from where Lulu was lying there was an upturned candle box. Lying incongruously in the dirt beside it was a Chappies bubblegum wrapper, the creases smoothed to read the joke.

'What's that?' asked Constable Bezuidenhout, shining to the side of the Chappies wrapper. He made his way carefully around and bent down on one knee beside the candle box without actually touching the ground. We followed him and peered over his shoulder. In the soft dust that had settled over the floor of the drive there was a trail of paw prints.

'It's blocked!' called Sergeant Fourie, from further up ahead. 'The way's blocked down here.'

The lieutenant marched off in the direction of the voice and we all followed. Not far down, Constable Bezuidenhout picked him up in the beam of his torch. He raised a hand to shield his eyes. A huge rockfall had completely blocked the way behind him. Lieutenant Ford stopped when we reached him. He sighed heavily.

'Okay, I think we'd better go back and talk to your mother, Tommy. I hope they've found your father. We're going to have to call for volunteers. She was down here it seems. God only knows how she got here, but she's vanished.'

Something in Tommy snapped. His head jerked back and without another word he snatched the torch out of Constable Bezuidenhout's hand, spun on his heel and walked purposefully back down towards the shaft. Sergeant Fourie shouted after him, 'Hey, boy! Where do you think you're going?'

'Just let him go, man,' said the lieutenant.

'I'll go after him,' I said.

I half ran back down the drive, stumbling in the waning light of the torches that beamed down the tunnel from behind me. Tommy was in the shaft by the time I reached him.

'Hey, Tommy, wait!' I called, but he didn't register. He marched up the stairs ahead of me, out into the chasm, and on up to the veld.

Zuma called up after him: 'Hey! What's happening, boy?'

Tommy didn't even look at him. Zuma hawked. His torch flitted over the lather of spittle in the dirt.

I bounded up over the rim of the trench at last and gulped the clean air. I spied Tommy a short way off, dragging his BB gun out from under the clump of pampas grass where we'd flung them.

'What are you doing, man, Tommy?'

He turned to me at last. 'I left her.' He shrugged, almost helplessly, the gun swinging loosely from his right hand.

'TJ ... The bloody dog, man, was all she had. Gutsy little bugger tried ... but now. It was that doll, lying there in the dirt ...' He retched. Then he rounded on me: 'Go home, Chris! This has got nothing to do with you. Just go home.'

I stared at him. I knew what he said was true – as the

230

night had worn on, I'd felt more and more like a voyeur. Everyone else had their part to play, and I was just trespassing, only everyone else was too polite to tell me so. He stared back at me for a minute and then, satisfied by something, he turned and loped off.

I stood there uncertainly. I wasn't wanted here. I was just an intruder. I flushed with shame, and tears pricked my eyes. Then I decided. I was sick of being a coward. Tommy wasn't the only selfish bastard who'd been wanking to forget his treachery. I knew where Tommy was going and I had to stop him.

Having made the choice, I felt better. I gulped another lungful of cleansing night air, retrieved the BB No. 1, and started to run in the direction Tommy had gone, the tears gushing out of my eyes anyway. I broke out of the veld and onto the verge of Main Reef. We'd come down quite far from the mine gateway, and I was almost opposite Monument Street as it came up on the rise flanking the old sand dump to intersect Main Reef.

I crossed over the road and headed down into town. As I jumped over the railway tracks and veered onto Kruger Street below the station, my breath was rasping in my chest, but I couldn't stop. Probably no more than an hour and a half had elapsed since Tommy and I first set off, and the dregs were now roving the streets like packs of feral dogs. I leapfrogged a man collapsed across the pavement in front of me, the vomit pooling under his cheek.

Finally I reached the town square, crossed over Market Street and turned into Joubert Street. The mullioned windows glowed in the mock-Tudor façade of the Union Club. The narrow street was deserted, save for Tommy squatting on the pavement opposite the arched doorway, his gun resting across his knees. He barely turned his head as I approached him.

'Give me the gun, Tommy,' I said calmly.

Tommy ignored me and continued staring at the door.

'Give it to me now.'

Tommy's eyes twitched at the steely edge to my voice, but he didn't surrender the gun.

'Don't be bloody stupid, man. What are you going to do? Pump his *gat* full of pellets?' I snarled.

Tommy flicked his hand dismissively at me.

At that moment, the double doors to the club swung open and Mr Michaels emerged in a halo of light, flanked by two policemen. A movement at the corner of my eye made me turn and, as if everything was happening under water, I saw Tommy aim the gun at his father's head. I turned back to look across the street, my lips trying to form the word 'no', but fear sucked the meat out of it, leaving only its shape in my mouth. The men hadn't seen us as they descended the steps, heads bowed. The click as Tommy pulled the trigger was unnaturally loud in my ears, followed by the crack, and Mr Michaels's right eye exploded.

I watched uncomprehendingly as a gaping hole bloomed in the socket. His hands flew to his face and he fell, cupping the monstrous cavity, his two companions turning on him, their mouths working frantically. Tommy fell forward onto his knees, face down on the tar.

'Cece! Oh, God, Cece!' he moaned.

The noise was visceral, terrible to hear.

Mr Michaels was screaming now, writhing on the pavement. Even from my side of the road I could see his face and hands were slick with blood and mucus. The policemen were stooping over him.

'Tommy, get up,' I said urgently. 'Get up, man.'

He looked up at me, as if astonished by my presence.

'You've got to get out of here, man, Tommy. You've got to run.'

Tommy didn't budge. I was pulling on his arm, trying to get him moving.

'Listen, Tommy, it's done. It's done now, and it's not going to bring Cece back. Just get away from here – we'll figure something out.'

Cece's name got him to hear me at last. He was looking at me now, confused, but he was struggling to his feet.

He stared at me another moment, before I shoved him hard. 'Get moving. For fuck's sake, run!'

And then Tommy was sprinting away into the darkness and one of the police officers looked up as I turned back. He was frowning, striding across the road now, blood and jelly splattered down his shirt front. He stopped as he reached me.

'Son,' he said, looking down at the gun in my hands, 'what have you done?'

I looked back at him, surprised – I'd forgotten the BB No. 1. I felt the hard, smooth contours of the barrel. Instinctively, I uncoiled my fingers like it was scorching hot and stepped back as it clattered onto the tar between us.

PART TWO

23

The Homecoming

The slaughterhouse stood grimly on the hillside above the station. A rusting roof over whitewashed walls stuccoed '1886', there was something gruesome about the place in the gathering dusk, as if the stale blood and fear were seeping out of its shard-rimmed windows that gazed sightlessly down onto the tracks.

The man looked away. Pitching on the lip of the platform in his scuffed brogues, he could see across to the station master's office with its colonial pretensions, the mine dump hulking behind it. He turned back towards the yawning stairwell, his eyes resting briefly on the station bar, with its old Western saloon door. A sign mounted beside it read, '*Moenie Spoeg Nie!* No Spitting!' His lips twitched before he descended the grimy stairs.

As he emerged into the twilight, he leaned against the peeling column of the station's portico in his rumpled suit, surveying the entrance. The ornamental ponds that once cascaded down the main flagstone steps had not been dredged and were now clogged with weeds and rubbish. Shattered glass-strewn dirt had overrun the once manicured lawns. The acrid smell of urine tarnished the air. He felt depressed by the intrusion of this desolate reality on his sepia-tinted memories. Even the feral pigeons that pecked in the dust somehow looked scrawny and wretched. Yet the avenue of poplars that lined the steps still stood, wilted sentinels to the fading glories of long ago, and he admired how the ivy now spilled lushly over the low stone wall. He approved of its uncultivated vigour amid the dereliction.

And the light was still the same. The palette of his memories, and sometimes his dreams, was magnificently resurrected as the sun set over Kruger Street. The relentless dust that sifted down through the air hennaed the light, bathing everything in amber. It was the colour that dominated here, a fierce, pulsating colour. The very earth was soaked with ochre. As the slanting rays lit upon the once swanky Olivana Mansions, Christopher felt a deep pang. He wasn't sorry he'd come back. It was capricious, desperate, really, and futile. He knew Tommy would not be here. Even so, something inside him sang. Christopher loosened his tie and grinned.

He ambled slowly down the hill towards the town square. Not much had changed here: the magistrates' court and the town hall still stood as immaculate guardians of the past. Even the Majestic Hotel remained, tawdry as ever, on the corner of Kruger and Commissioner Streets. The statue of Paul Kruger that had once graced the foreground of the town hall had been toppled, though, and it was with some glee

238

that he passed the old United Party headquarters on the way down, being rocked to its foundations by *kwaito*, washing flapping cheerfully over its wrought-iron balcony.

He walked east along Commissioner Street and then turned south back up the hill where it bisected Market Street, once the frontier of the Indian side of town. Salojee's, which had stood on the corner opposite the Victoria Hotel, was gone, but the Durban Fish & Chip shop was still open for business. In the sixties it had been a sacred part of his Friday-night ritual. The pillars stationed along the shop fronts were pulpy with peeling posters, the shops themselves crammed with cheap, kitschy wares, piquantly offsetting the quaintness of the buildings with their elaborate corner gables.

Two blocks up, he cut across the birch-tree-lined Human Street and felt a twinge at the loss of the Vaudette. A place so sublime should have lasted for ever, as a shrine. Today, planting such thirsty aliens as the river birch in African soil would be regarded as a kind of evil. They cast long shadows in the twilight. Christopher turned left up Kruger Street again towards the crest of the ridge and the vastly shrunken old sand dump. He crossed the tracks and passed the row of railway workers' cottages, avoiding his old shortcut behind the dump.

As he turned west onto the Main Reef Road, he found himself staring directly at the chimney stack of an old ventilation shaft, siren of those dark serpentine tunnels that still twisted down beneath his feet. He did not flinch as he passed the ruins of the East Shaft headgear further along. Finally, he reached the gateway to the mine, and stopped.

He wasn't sure where to go, actually, or what he'd find when he got there. A whole pilgrimage in fulfilment of a promise made over forty years ago by one boy of thirteen to another of twelve and three-quarters was foolish.

The gateway hadn't changed. A sentry box had been built in the middle of it, where before there had been a pair of palms, but that was all. As he entered the mine, though, his memories of the past and what was before him began to unravel.

He wandered the quiet, shady lanes, staring at the red-brick cottages with their green or russet tin roofs. He knew who'd lived behind every door – he passed the McAndrewses' in A Row, old Mr Erasmus's behind the school house – but they had grown worn with the passing of the years. Here and there was an old-fashioned garden, crammed with sweet-peas behind a cotoneaster hedge or morning-gloried fence, geraniums tumbling down from window-boxes and Virginia creeper clinging to the walls and beams shading a veranda, but mostly the little patches in front of the cottages were barren, the tin roofs dulled. The whole place looked shabby, slightly unkempt, but endearing. He peered over the gate of the school and felt a stab at the sight of the summerhouse in the grounds.

It was only as he came down Club Row that the true extent of the desolation became apparent. The fields were ravaged, colonised completely by the tough, wiry high-veld grasses, and the rec club was in ruins. Only the bowling pavilion still stood beside the single men's mess; the club house was gone, burned to a charred foundation marked by three lone palm trees that soared into a sky pricked with evening stars. The goofies. Christopher wanted to weep. It had been back-filled with rubble. Trash and debris clustered at the base of the change-house, which still radiated a kind of menace. A child wailed somewhere. Everything bore witness to heedless, wanton neglect. Christopher felt a wild rage struggling with an underlying despair. What had become of the mine?

As he followed the loco tracks, he came across the old engineering department building. The roof had caved in over the *stoep*, the white pillars stationed along its length buckling under its weight. The sheds, the offices – even the mine manager's – were derelict and abandoned. A few had been commandeered by panel beaters, their dubious credentials spray-painted on the walls outside.

Christopher traipsed back up over the rise to the South Shaft Road, saluting Rod's old house in R Row as he passed it. Below the old slimes dump, the mine had been forsaken entirely. Mostly, he could only tell where a building had once stood by the improbable row of palm trees soaring above the veld. The carcasses of a few still stood: the battery house, where the great tube mills had ground the grist to dust, the boiler house of the power station, the dead power lines still running overhead – all of it stripped bare by vultures, its bones picked clean, like so much carrion.

The veld had also grown back over the workings, tufts of pampas springing up wherever he looked. He saw evidence of *Mad Max*-style scavengers behind the dump, scrap-metal outfits, a truck dumping toxic waste down a shaft, even a couple of blacks panning in one of the gullies. They yanked their shirts over their heads and scarpered when they saw him watching them. Squatters were living in the East Shaft change-house, though the electricity and water must have been turned off long ago. They'd dug open trenches for sewerage outside the old ablutions block and gesticulated angrily at him when they spotted him loitering outside.

He trudged wearily back to the village and squatted on a stone outside the scorched remains of the club. *Jisee*, he felt like a *poephol* now for coming back. Hell, some things a man shouldn't live to see. If some oke had tapped him on the shoulder back then and told him that this was the future, he'd have said, 'You lie, man.' Any oke could see the mines would go on for ever. Even when he was a young buck in the sixties, he'd have said that.

Well, that just showed you, then. He'd been around a long time now, and it was about one of the only things he knew to be true in this life. Everything that has a beginning shall surely end. What in God's name was he thinking? Of course Tommy wouldn't be here, wouldn't even have remembered. And now he'd subjected himself to this grim bloody tour through the wreckage of his past for nothing.

But he'd had to. He hadn't forgotten. When he thought of that night, he always thought of things in a certain order. First he saw the eye explode in Mr Michaels's face. It wasn't so much the blood he saw or anything, just the ragged hole where his eye had been. Then he thought of the skin floating in Mrs Michaels's cup of tea, and that pathetic little hanky of hers, with the embroidered posy, crumpled in her hand. Then he saw the doll, that awful bloody doll, staring at him in the darkness. Sometimes he had dreams about it: he'd see its little china face, its lips a slash across the shiny white porcelain.

After he was taken in for questioning, they'd launched a

manhunt. Sounded the sirens, woken the mine from its slumber. Hundreds of men volunteered, his old man and Johnny among them. They searched all through that night, called for fresh volunteers the next morning; the Krugersdorp police joined the hunt.

Chris knew they'd never find her. He just knew. He paced in the cell, trying to glean information from the officers coming and going, until in the early hours of the morning, he finally admitted it to himself: Cece was dead. He stopped.

Hell, he supposed she must have been clasped to the bosom of mine lore, become one of those ghost stories he and Tommy had loved to tell, living on in small boys teasing out the lurid details of the little girl and her dog who'd slipped down an impenetrable shaft and vanished in those tunnels.

They called off the manhunt before midday, but his mother was only permitted to see him after he'd been taken back to the cell, following his interview with Lieutenant Ford.

She'd begun to fret when he hadn't come home the night before, and after the men were called to join the search for Cecelia, she'd stood for hours out on the veranda, twisting her wedding band and staring into the night, trying to penetrate the darkness with her mind. It had been her grandmother's, her wedding ring, a dainty band of silver glittering with tiny diamond chips. Her grandmother had given it to her before she'd died; she'd been a widow forty years when she pulled it off her gnarled old finger and slipped it onto her newly betrothed granddaughter's. 'May it always bring you happiness,' she'd said.

243

She loved that ring. It had brought her happiness, but the gods claimed a cruel price for the gift of motherhood. Something that clutched so at your heart had to hurt. On the night her child had died, there had been a storm. The light at dusk was tawny; hot gusts of wind tore down from the sky that was swollen and moody with the coming rain. For hours she'd watched it roiling across the horizon, violet lightning flickering through the banks of bruised clouds. She couldn't sleep. Eventually she stole to his cot. She pulled down the sheet, lifted him into her arms, and carried him out into the night garden. He barely woke.

She knelt and watched the sky flaring magenta, indigo; lurid, poisonous colours. She'd folded him against her body, kissed his eyelids, his blue-tinged lips, felt his warmth through the flannel. He whispered, 'Mama,' and his voice was already like a sigh on the wind. He smiled and tried to curl up smaller still against her. After a moment, he drifted back to sleep. She knew she would not be allowed to keep him much longer, not because of what the doctors had said, about his heart murmur, she just knew. She cupped her hand over his soft buttocks, gently squeezed his thighs, held his little foot in her hand, felt the soft fat pad of each toe.

She didn't know when he died. The rain finally fell in heavy, sweeping curtains, but he never woke to the sweet wet morning. She wished now that she had held him when he went; he would've liked that. Now she just died a little with the first summer storm.

As her mind reached out now to her son somewhere in the darkness, she knew she was losing him. He was leaving childhood, shedding it slowly but relentlessly, and though the last of his boyishness still clung, his skin was splitting like a chrysalis to allow the adolescent within to emerge. She'd even, now and then, glimpsed the man he would one day become. Her bruised heart ached for him. At dawn she watched the stars pale, sickly and afraid, retreating with the shadows to await the end of day and its slow, stealthy stealing of the light.

By the time the two police officers arrived at the house, the neighbours twitching behind the lace at their windows, she was frantic. She flew at her son when she saw him in the interview room. 'Christopher! Thank God! Oh, Christopher, what have you done?' she whispered. 'I will thrash the living daylights out of you, do you hear me?' She hugged him tightly. 'God, what will your father say?'

And then Tommy found out. He'd been hiding out in their cave all through the night of the manhunt and all the next day. When he'd fled the scene of the shooting, across from the steps of the Union Club where his father lay bleeding, he'd run right through town and up over the rise onto Main Reef. He'd crossed the strip of tar and headed along the ridge towards the dumps, flinging his gun down the outcrop workings by the old East Shaft, not stopping until he reached the cave. He'd lain in there, sweating, grinding his teeth, the hours chewing up his sanity, until Rod and Mitch turned up late in the afternoon the following day.

But once they'd told him about Christopher's arrest, the tremor in his hands stopped. He got up calmly and left the cave. He walked purposefully along the South Shaft Road, across the Main Reef, and straight down to the mine police station. When he arrived, Lieutenant Ford was out. Zuma, the young policeman who'd accompanied them to the East Shaft, was stationed behind the desk. He informed Tommy that they were waiting for the lieutenant to return from the magistrates' court with Chris's father so that he could be released into his custody pending the arraignment. They were looking for him as well, Zuma told him, for questioning. His father was too sedated in the hospital in Krugersdorp to be seen yet. Then he let Tommy in to see Chris.

As he caught sight of him behind the bars, Tommy's breath snagged in his throat. 'Ah, Jesus, Chris, I'm sorry. I'm sorry, man. I didn't know. I came as soon as the okes told me they'd arrested you. I'm turning myself in. You'll be out of here now – they'll have to let you go. *Ag*, hell, man, I'm sorry.'

Christopher stood there in his cell, holding onto the bars, staring at his knuckles – they were white, bloodless. 'It's too late, Tommy – you're too late.'

'What are you talking about, man? They'll have to drop the charges against you when I confess. I'll make sure they know you didn't have anything to do with it, that you weren't like my accomplice or anything.'

Christopher's lips twitched at the two of them talking like knocked-out jailbirds. 'You're too late because I *already* confessed.'

'No,' said Tommy, in confusion. 'Like I said, I'll clear it all up. You didn't help me or anything.'

'*Uh-uh*. I already confessed to the whole thing. I pulled the trigger. There was no one else there, remember?'

Tommy recoiled. 'What the fuck are you doing, Chris?' He came right up to the bars of the cell, put his hands over his friend's, gripped him by the wrists. 'I'm not going to let you take the fall for this, Chris. I shot him. I'm not sorry. I'm going to tell them.'

Christopher turned on Tommy when he said that. He felt a wave of panic, that time was running out, that Lieutenant Ford could walk through the door at any moment. 'No. You listen to me. It wasn't your fault, Tommy. You didn't hit a six-year-old little kid, man, you didn't do that. And that's it. I'm not sorry you shot him either, but they're going to punish you. You just got to get out of here, Tommy, you got to get away. You got to do that for me, okay? I don't know how, but you got to promise me that. You're going to make it, Tommy. You've got that thing inside of you, I feel it. But you've got to get out of here before your dad poisons it out of you.'

Flecks of spittle flew in Tommy's face. Christopher knew why he'd done it. He couldn't take away all the shitty things that had happened to Tommy and Cece, but he could show Tommy that there was someone on his side, someone who'd stand up for him, someone who believed he was worth something. Tommy didn't have that, and it was the only thing he had to give him.

Tommy stared hard at Chris for a minute. His eyes brimmed with mute regret and he ground the heel of his palm into his eye. 'Sonofabitch was crawling, his eyeball dribbling down his cheek. Did you see that bastard, Chris?'

'I saw him.'

He swallowed. 'Ah, Chris. Thank you.' Then he grinned disarmingly. 'I'm not going to let you do it, though.' And he spun on his heel and headed out into the corridor.

'It'll be my word against yours,' Christopher called after him.

247

Tommy swung back round the door frame. 'Not if I've got proof, it won't. I'm going to find the gun. No one's going to buy your pathetic BB number one story after they've checked my number three, you *poephol*, 'specially if I've got the pellets to match the one in his eyeball. Exhibit A coming up.'

And that was how he found her.

24

The Blacksmith's

Tommy ransacked the old outcrop workings around the East Shaft. He remembered where he'd thrown the gun, or at least he thought he did – his memories of the night were already fractured, strangely hallucinogenic. He saw himself pitching across Main Reef Road and into the camouflage of the veld, turning west and running on the cusp of the ridge, towards the dump below it. He'd slowed as he reached the edge of the embankment leading down into the old East Shaft, stared into its mouth again before he'd stumbled on, but after a few yards, maybe twenty or thirty paces, something overcame him. He'd stopped, and with a surge of rage and horror, he'd hurled the weapon down the crack in the earth where the stopes broke through.

When he reached the place again, he paused to study the terrain. The veld around him looked no different from anywhere else along the ridge, but as he kicked a termite mound with the heel of his shoe, he could clearly see its dark night-time silhouette in his mind's eye, its smooth contours broken by the contorted limbs of the African stink-wood tree that had rooted in its richly fertilised soil. This was the place.

He peered over the edge of the gully, the same one that ran almost unbroken westwards from the old East Shaft, and into the caves that yawned in the rock face at the bottom of the far side. A sill of rock jutted out over the roof of each mouth, but he could still see into them, at least down to where they were jammed with huge skeleton packs. Each section was separated by a wide column of rock, left as a support to prevent the stopes collapsing. The way in to his BB No. 3's tunnel was marked by the termite-mound sentinel. But how to get into it? No flights of steps led down the embankment – it was just a raw shelf of jagged rock. Soldier termites were crawling frantically over his shoe at the site of the cave-in on the mound, desperately trying to repel him.

Jock had once delivered one of his impromptu entomology lectures on the subject of termites, although it had rung more like a sermon. 'Beneath the crust,' Jock had said, piercing the mound with the tip of a stick, 'and continuing deep underground, to the water table, is a labyrinth of tunnels built of saliva and faeces and fine-grained soil particles, on which lovingly tended gardens of fungi grow, cultivated to humidify the mound and provide food for the colony's young. Now crouch down,' he had commanded.

Kneeling, he'd laid a hand at the site of the breach and the termites had swarmed over it.

'The soldiers, boys. Here they come. Just look at them. Huge in relation to their brethren, they have armoured heads and great jaws with which to attack their adversaries. But watch how fearless they are.'

They were attacking Jock's stubby fingers, biting him with serrated jaws that resembled pincers, trying to tear him to pieces. His fingers were wet too, doused in something they were spraying.

'They're using chemical weapons – toxins to kill or paralyse intruders. But their greatest defence, boys, is their bravery, their unfaltering willingness to sacrifice their own lives to save the colony. Some,' he said, and his voice had almost dropped to a whisper, 'are suicide commandos. In mandible to mandible combat, they can contract their stomach muscles, rupturing a special sac that holds a noxious chemical that burns their opponent. The internal organs are fatally damaged, though, and the creature dies.'

Tommy had looked at the grotesquely ugly little insects trying to defend their home against this gratuitous invasion, and felt a pang of pity.

'Once a colony is abandoned, boys, the mound is commandeered by anything from warthog to hyena, monitor lizards and black mamba. Seeds germinate readily in the richly nourished soil and the saplings are afforded protection from fires due to the elevation. In the poetry innate in the circle of life, I have seen the thickets that may ultimately grow on the old mounds claimed by lionesses as ideal lairs for their cubs.'

Tommy felt weak. He couldn't remember when he'd last slept or eaten or even drunk any water, but the memory of Jock's strangely inspiring teachings about so unlikely a creature spurred him over the lip of the embankment. He scrambled down the steep sides, clinging to tufts of bristly grass that sliced his palms open even as he grazed his knees and belly on the rocks. When he reached the bottom, he crawled over to the entrance to the stopes, which dropped away steeply into the darkness, and peered in. He could see an old leather shoe lying in the dust a few feet in, but of his gun there was no trace. 'Damn it!'

He had no choice. Slithering down the steep slope on his backside, the gravelly dirt tearing at his bleeding palms, he made it as far as the skeleton pack, lodged into the tunnel about five yards down. As he hauled himself up on one of the thick struts of timber, he suddenly saw that the pack had partially collapsed at the rear under a rockfall. He inched his way to the wall and, leaning against it, saw that the way down, although completely choked on the right, was still open on the left – a narrow, rock-strewn sliver of tunnel could still be navigated.

He squeezed past the façade of the timber grid and clambered over its broken torso into the tunnel beyond, his heart thudding in his eardrums. He began to climb gingerly down the tunnel, leaving streaks of blood and sweat on the boulders as he crawled over them on all fours, like a baboon. He was moving so slowly that he had descended only a few yards after twenty minutes or more had passed and the light was failing.

'What the hell am I doing?' he shouted into the silence, suddenly giving up at the futility of the quest.

That was when he heard it: the high-pitched, unmistakable sound of a dog barking.

'TJ!' he called down the tunnel, his voice constricted. He tried to take a deep breath, to free the vice-like band that was wringing his chest. It didn't work: he couldn't get air into his lungs. His voice failed him. 'TJ!' he gasped.

That was when he knew he was dreaming, or hallucinating.

The surreal sensation of being under water grew stronger as the barking grew fainter with the ringing in his ears. He struggled to wake up. 'TJ!' His voice found purchase at last, and he knew he wasn't asleep. 'I'm coming!'

The bark hadn't sounded far away, but then the strange acoustics of the tunnels that distorted and echoed or swallowed sound couldn't be trusted. He was desperate, though, to reach it, mangling his ankles and wrists as he struggled down. He was almost blind as he dragged himself up over a huge pile of rubble and found that it completely blocked the way ahead. The tunnel was sealed.

He sank onto the rock, his cheek pressed against its cool, rough face. He noticed that the darkness had deepened, and he looked up. He couldn't see any silvery light filtering down from above any more. How long had it been? How deep had he come? TJ, he knew now, was only haunting his mind. Cece was his baby girl – he loved her, but she was lost.

He had to get out of there. He hadn't found the gun, but he didn't care. He tried to push himself up, but his legs were numb and there was something wrong inside his head: it was spinning, pinpricks of light flickered before his eyes. He lay down, tried to draw breath. He began to whisper slowly, 'One. Two. Three. Four.' At six he lifted his neck, braced his hands against the rock. He pushed with all his strength. 'Seven. Eight.' At the count of nine, he hauled himself up and the rock gave way.

The rocks wedged up against the roof had only been one course deep. He had pushed one loose and a few had avalanched down the far side. He leaned over the edge, trying to look down into the darkness beyond. He closed his eyes.

'Goodbye, Cece,' he whispered, into the silence.

He let her go, as gently as he could, but as he opened his eyes, he had the feeling that it was he who was looking up from deep below. He shook his head, trying to shake off the weird sensation, but TJ's loud bark instantly sharpened his senses.

He crawled through the gap and half fell down into the stope beyond where the rockfall suddenly ended. It felt cavernous even in the darkness after the suffocating confines above. Then TJ was barking again, so loudly he gave a start. 'I'm coming, TJ,' he called, as he crawled forwards.

'Cece?' he dared, but it was only TJ who yipped in answer.

Suddenly he reached the lip of the stope, and as he hung precariously over the edge, he saw TJ on his hind legs looking up at him from just below. He was pawing the wall, his tail wagging crazily. When Tommy lifted his head, he realised where the dim light that had allowed him to see TJ was coming from: Cece lay in a small heap on the floor of the main tunnel, at the base of a rockfall a short way down to the left, a faintly glowing torch in her hand.

'Tommy,' she croaked, 'I knew you'd come. I told you, TJ.'

A sob was wrenched out of Tommy. 'Oh, Cece! Thank God. Are you okay, man?'

'I hurt my leg, Tommy. I think it's broken. I think I'm going to have to go to hospital and the doctor will put it in a plaster-of-paris cast and everyone can write their names over it and I'll have crutches. Tommy? I was scared.'

Tommy reached his hand down to TJ, who licked it with a dry, rasping tongue. At the back of his mind he'd become aware that the tiny prick of light from Cece seemed to be reflecting softly around them. He turned to look down the drive and saw that the stope beside him gaped open. The black walls and floors glittered with a fine web of spun gold.

'*Jisis!*' he said softly, and gave a low whistle.

'It's Aladdin's cave, Tommy, I told you.' Cece began to drag herself on a propped elbow towards Tommy and TJ. She whimpered as she inched forwards.

'Don't move, Cece! I'm coming to help you.' Tommy lowered himself over the rim of the stope and dropped down onto the floor of the main drive. He lifted TJ right into his arms and buried his face in the dusty, matted fur as he crossed to where his sister lay.

Squatting on his haunches, he set TJ down and folded his arms around Cece. She buried her face in his shoulder. 'Cece. I can't believe I've found you. I only came back because ...' When he looked more closely at the dirty little face in his cupped hands, he could see it was streaked with dried tears.

'I'm so thirsty, Tommy, and so is TJ. We tried to lick the walls.'

The shin and ankle on her left leg were painfully swollen. The skin stretched taut over the foot had a waxy sheen.

'God,' said Tommy, looking up at the rock-choked tunnel behind them. 'We must have come down right to the other side of this rockfall. So close.' He shuddered.

'It's far, Tommy, to the other side. We come through our secret tunnel, but last night Daddy, he ...'

'It's all right, Cece,' Tommy said, pressing her to him again.

'I was crying, wasn't being careful enough, I fell and did

255

something bad to my leg, just at the end. Tommy, I dropped Lulu.'

'Don't worry.' He smiled in the dim light. 'We found her.'

Cece gave a little squeak.

'Now let's get the hell out of here.'

Tommy's memories of the climb out of the tunnel were painful even in their peculiar disjointedness. Hauling Cece, who wept from the pain, while pushing TJ, who kept slipping backwards, in virtual darkness, the torch clenched between his teeth, proved harder than he had ever imagined anything could be. His muscles ached from the strain, his limbs quivering as he inched ever more slowly upwards.

Cece had been strangely mysterious about her secret tunnel, when he'd thought to check it to see if it was wide enough for him to fit through. In his adrenalin-marinated exhaustion, he couldn't make sense of her oblique directions to its entrance.

'What in God's name were you doing down here anyway, Cece?'

'Because of you, Tommy. In your dream, remember, you told me you knew I was down here, so I came looking.'

Tommy's desire to get out of there had grown more urgent. Crawling up the steep, hazardous fissure in the stopes, though, he cursed his recklessness. It was impossible.

They ploughed on until starlight-tinged darkness at last penetrated the surly blackness of the tunnel. Buoyed, they reached the skeleton pack, forced their way past it, and Tommy piggy-backed Cece up the last few yards on all fours behind TJ who led the way up the slope.

They rested at the opening of the workings for a few moments, though they were now desperate to get away. Tommy drank in the crisp night air, trying to get his strength back, but it was the thirst, clawing at his throat, that finally drove him off his knees and up the embankment, pulling TJ by his scruff as Cece clung to his back.

When they hauled themselves up onto the ridge, Tommy didn't wait again, but limped on back across the veld towards the Main Reef Road, where he flagged down a passing motorist. 'Please, sir, can you get us to the West Rand Cons police station?' he asked the driver of the pick-up truck.

The man stared at them curiously through the window. He seemed about to say something, when Tommy added, 'Lieutenant Ford will be waiting for us.'

The man shrugged, then leaned over and opened the passenger door. He drove them back to the mine without asking a single question.

Tommy carried Cece into the station, TJ gambolling at his side. He walked straight past the empty reception area and down the corridor to the cell. He sank to his knees as he reached it. The door hung wide open. It was empty.

'Tommy?'

Tommy turned at the sound of his voice. Christopher stood in the doorway behind them, with Lieutenant Ford and Constable Bezuidenhout.

'Cece? Tommy, you found her!'

'Please, Lieutenant, can we have some water?'

Cece smiled at Christopher, her face ghostly pale.

Later, after Tommy and Cece had been taken to the mine hospital and Doc had come to fetch TJ, Christopher went to

257

see Tommy, lying in his metal cot in the children's ward slathered in mercurochrome. Cece slept peacefully beside him, the drip trickling into her arm. He spoke quietly to Tommy, no longer as a boy. After a long time, Tommy agreed.

It was easy after that. Christopher swore he'd shot Mr Michaels. There were no witnesses save Tommy, and it was his word against the unuttered suspicions of Lieutenant Ford, Chris's father, mother and Johnny. He was made a ward of Spackman House until he was sixteen. Tommy and Cece left a week later.

It was Jock who had given them a way out. He quietly approached Mrs Michaels with an offer for Tommy and Cece to go to stay with his brother in Kalulushi in Northern Rhodesia. He said nothing, but most people on the mine had a good idea of what went on in No. 113 Club Row. Mrs Michaels accepted. Christopher never knew if Tommy ever spoke to his father again.

The day before he left, Tommy came to see him. 'So, how they treating you, Chris?' Tommy said, grinning lopsidedly.

'Well, the scoff's bloody disgusting, man – gristly meat, gummy gravy and when they take the lid off the cabbage pots, you're liable to puke, man. You got a lot to answer for, my boy.' He tried to smile.

'Hey, Chris . . .'

Christopher looked at him hopefully. 'Hey, Chris' was always a good start. But Tommy couldn't keep it up. He shoved his hands into his pockets, studied his feet.

'So I'm leaving.'

'*Ja*, I know.'

'Tomorrow.'

258

Christopher nodded, the faint smile fading. 'When d'you reckon we're going to see each other again?'

'Dunno, man.' Tommy shrugged.

'But what if it's never?'

'*Ag, nooit*, man, don't be stupid!'

They were leaning against the fence at the bottom of the grounds. Tommy's eyes slid off into the woods. The leaves were dying, streaming softly from the trees in the twilight. 'Chris, I don't know how I'm ever going to repay you for this. Three years, man, three years. *Jisis*, I feel like *kak*!'

'Tommy, just shuddup. You couldn't leave her again – locked up in that house with him, you locked up in here. We both know that, and that's the end of it. I'm not sorry, not even that you're getting the hell out of here. I'm going to miss you, though, dog breath.'

He'd never come so close to saying he loved him. Tommy turned without saying another word and leaned his head against Christopher's chest. For a long moment they stood like that, the tears trickling slowly down Tommy's cheeks onto the rickety fence that cleaved them from the trees destined to be felled for an eternity in the dark tunnels twisting beneath their feet.

Suddenly Tommy wrenched away. He hurdled the fence and grabbed Christopher's shirt. 'Come on, man, I've got an idea.'

Christopher stared at him for a moment, then started laughing. '*Jisis*, Tommy, why can't I ever just tell you to piss off?'

He glanced back once before he leaped over the fence and fled into the woods behind Tommy. He was stumbling down the steep slope along the banks of a stream that tumbled through a rift. The strip of feral woods that threaded its banks was a dank snarl of roots and vines, tangled creepers trailing down from slick, rotting boughs on which spongy fungus suckled. In the growing darkness, the air was tinged with the raw smell of damp earth churned up by worms and probing shoots searching for the light. As he broke through into the clearing at the bottom, Tommy yanked his shirt from around his waist. He was naked as he plunged into the water, whooping.

Christopher felt a familiar quickening. He went running down the bank, kicking off his shoes and pulling off his shirt. He tugged his shorts and underpants off with his thumbs. On the very edge of the water, he hopped on one leg, then the other, to rip his socks off. Then he dived into the Monument Dam and came up shaking the water from his eyes, his hair plastered to his scalp. 'It's fuckin' fantastic!'

He swam over to Tommy, the cool, clean water silky on his skin. Treading, they grinned into each other's face.

'*Lekker!*' they said at exactly the same moment, then Tommy splashed water at Christopher and somersaulted away.

It didn't seem like much now. Things had changed, but back then ... the recklessness of water, their nakedness, the night, he'd felt a wild abandon. He could see them now, those two boys, goofing off in the water, dunking each other, laughing and swallowing and still laughing. It played like an old movie in his head, grainy, the colours faded, but somehow clearer as the years passed.

Later, floating on their backs in the moonlight, they'd fallen quiet.

'What about the year 2000?' Tommy said suddenly.

'Hey?'

He wiped the back of his hand brusquely across his eyes. 'Shit, seems crying is my new game. You remember, man, that day in these woods, when we checked Spackman, we were talking about where we'd be in the year 2000?'

'Oh, *ja*.'

'So that's it, man. If I don't see you before then, I'll meet you at the goofies at sundown, the first of January 2000.'

'I'll be there, man,' said Christopher.

And here he was, squatting like a bloody *poephol* on a rock as night fell, *dopping* from a can of Castle, waiting for some *tsotsi* to come along with a *panga* and gut him outside the rubble-filled goofies of the husk of the West Rand Consolidated Gold Mining Company on 1 January 2000.

Ag, jisis, he felt bleak. Coming back here, it wasn't just that he hadn't found Tommy, it was like he'd lost the rest too. He was an old bugger now. When he looked in the mirror nowadays, it was his dad he saw looking back at him. He'd even started to listen to that old big-band stuff of his. Old Satchmo – Louis Armstrong. Funny how the past comes back at you.

After he'd got out of Spackman House, he supposed he'd gone a bit *woes*. One night in '63, on the way back from the White Horse Inn, he'd driven Johnny's darling Chevy straight over the edge of Muldersdrift Hill. The car rolled down the cliff and landed upside down at the base of an old Karee tree. After the screaming of buckling metal, there was silence, then a voice, Rod's: 'Hey, you okes orright?'

'*Ja*.'

'*Ja*, I'm okay, hey.'

'*Jisis*, Chris, but you're a *kak* driver after you've been on the wallop. I think I've squashed a goolie.'

It wasn't that it had been so bad in Spackman, really, probably no worse than the boarding-house at Krugersdorp High. He'd taken a lot of thrashings. Jock had come to see him in there, Doc a couple of times. His most regular visitor, apart from his ma and dad, was Johnny. Hell, he even got a royal visit once, right after they'd locked him up: Willie Smith came just to see him.

He said he remembered him from that day with Jock. He wanted Christopher to know that he'd started boxing in the St George's Home for Orphans. After his dad was killed in a mine explosion, his mother had put him and his brother in the orphanage and kept only the babies. Willie said he was twelve years old, a holy bloody terror, two fists and no brain, when George Harris, South Africa's first flyweight champion of 1909, came to teach boxing to the boys twice a week. He said he owed his life to George Harris and Johnny Watson; he said he wanted Christopher to know that.

'There is grit inside of you, Christopher,' were his parting words.

He died less than a year later – heart attack, they said.

Mr Michaels had invoked his lost eye to quit his underground post. He took a job in Witbank, left the mine with Mrs Michaels within months of his children's departure. Christopher never clapped eyes on him again, hadn't since that night. He'd gassed himself in his Datsun Cherry in '72, so he'd heard, in a clump of bluegums outside Witbank. After the thing on Muldersdrift, Christopher left too. He headed up north to Rhodesia. After the war, he spent years on the Lower Zambezi, running the anti-poaching operation

262

in Mana Pools. There were wild nights in Ruckomechi, he and Johnny stumbling down the hippo-studded flood plain at four o'clock in the morning, singing, 'We are the *shumba* drinkers'. Man, the place was buggered now, though.

He wasn't even sorry he'd got slung out this year. It had been Johnny's fault. After the government official had served Johnny with the notice that his concession had been revoked, he'd invited him to remain in a managerial capacity at the camp, which, he was advised, had been appropriated, and was now held in trust for the local community. In retrospect, Johnny could have handled things with a little more tact. It never had been his strong suit. He'd told the man to get stuffed. What? He must sink so low? Out here, with his chop on a block, day in and out, to pad some ZANU PF comrade's numbered account in Switzerland? Johnny always took it too far.

Christopher had hastily stepped into the awkward breach left by the mention of Swiss bank accounts. He magnanimously invited the man to join them for a *dop* around the fire.

As Jobe, Johnny's camp manager-cum-barman, decanted single malt into a tumbler, Christopher apologised for his brother's boorishness. He had been following with keen interest the developments in land reform in Zimbabwe and it was lamentable that Johnny had been unable to grasp the finer points of the party's political philosophy, despite repeated attempts to explain it all to him. 'He just pulls the old snort and head toss, and walks away,' he ended sadly.

Christopher congratulated the man on his minister's decision to grant hunting licences right inside the Hwange national park. 'When I first came up to the Zambezi as a

youngster, I was forced to accompany this arsehole on camp-
ing trips to the Makalolo plains. I look back on those times
with hatred in my heart. It was always bloody hot in the tent,
but you couldn't open the flap an account of those slitty-
eyed hyenas prowling around outside, and once I got stung
by a blister beetle. I remember looking at the bush crawling
with dumb beasts of every kind and thinking, One day,
someone will come along and destroy you. And I will laugh.

'I see in the papers that the bunny-humpers are baying for
your blood. How dare they? I think some of the lentil-
munching faggots have forgotten what it says in the Bible.
Frankly, if the stupid wildebeest still haven't learned to stay
away from pith-helmeted Texans toting Uzis on the back of
Land Rovers, then they deserve to die.

'Your boss is a cabinet minister and does not need
anyone's permission to do anything. You tell him not to
worry about that meddling lawyer and his spurious claims
that the licences are illegal. As he has already pointed out at
a public meeting, the lawyer is white and nothing more
needs to be said.

'As for those Rottweilers in the press, fortunately the new
Ministry of Information will soon gag them. In a place where
the sharpness of political debate is usually reflected in the
glint of machetes at sunrise, there is no need to whip the
unwashed savages into a frenzy with a pack of lies about the
proceeds of the licence auction.'

The government official didn't betray his anger. He
merely reminded Christopher that he, too, was on the government's payroll and that his own tenure was up for
renewal. Christopher demanded to know why the bloated
corps of the civil service was still clogged with Fascists from

the Old Order anyway. Surely the time was ripe for a purge. 'May I remind you, Mr Mboweni, these are not friends of the government. Most of them are slow-moving saboteurs, intent on undermining the regime with idleness.'

By the end, Johnny was spewing Castle through his nostrils and Jobe slopped single malt down the VIP's shirtfront. *Ag*, what the hell? It had been time to move on. Since Jacqui had died, his heart hadn't been in it anyway. He kept seeing her too, standing at the water's edge, shading her eyes. Just a mirage. Still, it hurt. He just couldn't understand how a lifetime had gone by.

You don't think it's going to happen to you, but it does. One day you're a *laitie* grazing a whole box of cornflakes for a Springbok card, and the next thing you're boring the public with stories about you and Johnny playing air guitar to 'Old Time Rock 'n' Roll' pumping across the river at Boet's place on the Chongwe mouth. Hell, he'd had some good times, though.

And through it all, in his mind, it'd been here, West Rand Cons, waiting, as if he could always come home. Seeing it like this ... It made a man wonder what in God's name it was all for. To look at it now, the marrow sucked out of the earth and everything just abandoned, the sheer crazy gluttony slapped you across the face like a bony, gold-encrusted hand. Ah, well, it was a *helluva* thing.

Christopher felt raw and tender. He shivered as night finally fell. The highveld plateau is given to opera; even as the day is so hot it blisters, the tar jammy beneath your feet, so the mercury plunges pitilessly at night. He got up to leave. He walked slowly back down Club Row, to the bend in the road that takes you up past old Ginger Steward's palace to the Main Reef, something sapped from his pith. He was on the corner when he heard it.

It was coming from the old blacksmiths' workshop diagonally opposite. It looked like a condemned building; an old telegraph pole had been borrowed to help prop up a corner of the slate grey tin roof where it was caving in. Slimy Roth's gardens in front of it had given way to weeds and dirt, sticky oil stains; an old wash-stand stood for some reason on the *stoep*.

The sound was coming from inside, the beat unmistakable after forty years. He felt its waves pass right through his chest. He was pulled towards it, yoked. He mounted the step to the *stoep* and stood in the doorway of the one-time blacksmiths' shed and watched about thirty pairs of black dancers jiving across the floor to Little Richard's raw voice bawling, '*Lucille!*'. Then he screamed *Whaooh!* and the pairs of ragged jive cats chicken-legged towards one another. As each pair touched, they shouted, '*Tsaba!*' and jumped back, chiming their twisting and grinding, a patina of pure, sweaty rapture on their brows.

Christopher closed his eyes and opened them again, to see if it was real. I mean, what were the odds, man? Got to be like a million to one. Hell ... It was impossible. You go your whole life thinking you've got the ground beneath your feet, and that's it, and then something happens, and you know there are still some mysteries in this world. It was always the last thing he remembered, when he remembered that night.

Strange that, after everything – Cece lost in the mine, Tommy blowing his old man's eye out, getting locked in the cell – the thing he remembered last was that bloody dance.

The Krugersdorp Junior Jive Contest, and him up there on that stage, Little Richard doing his gravelly thing, and him working it out *kwela-kwela* style, and then he'd start laughing. Sometimes he'd laugh so hard he'd start coughing and he'd be *hoesing* and choking on snot and phlegm and still laughing. In a way, he'd been looking down from that stage all his life.

Christopher gazed up at the stars prickling in the sky above him. The beat broke against his back. It coursed right through his veins, inflicting pain and fierce joy, quickening his pulse, until it harmonised with the music. He hoped Tommy knew that he'd never really been in prison. The strangest damn things can set you free.

Glossary

I am trying to capture the flavour of the South African vernacular and as a result am outside the bounds of the usual grammatical rules, so you may find variations of spelling in this glossary. These discrepancies reflect how language mutates according to region, nationality and date.

Ag – ah, oh (exclamation) [Afrikaans]

Amabele – breasts [Zulu]

Amalaita – organised Northern Sotho/Pedi urban gangs (circa 1900 to WWII); also formed teams of competitive street fighters in urban African locations

Aasvoëls – vultures [Afrikaans]

'Azikwelwa' – 'We shall not ride' by the Alex Casbahs (1957) was a tribute to the so-called Alexandra Bus Boycott, a landmark in the Defiance Campaign of the black liberation struggle

Baas or *Bas* – boss [Fanakalo; from Afrikaans *baas* – master; boss]

Banana Boy – derogatory name for someone from Natal province (now Kwa-Zulu Natal), tropical region, characterised by banana plantations

Bang – afraid, scared [Afrikaans]

Bantu – natives, indigenous people; obsolete official term for black Africans; from the group of languages to which all indigenous Southern African languages belong

Bantustan – obsolete official and colloquial term for black African reserves

Bazalwane – saved or blessed one

Biltong – strips of cured beef or venison, jerked meat

Bliksem – bash, clobber (vulgar slang) [Afrikaans]

Bloedvermenging – blood mingling [Afrikaans] that according to Apartheid ideology, could result in 'throwbacks' and ultimately, in the white race being 'bastardized out' of existence

Boer – farmer, Afrikaner [Afrikaans]

Boet – brother [Afrikaans]

Bopa – tie, fasten [Fanakalo; from Zulu *bopha* – tie; bind]

Brak – mongrel dog [Afrikaans]

Broederbond – secret organization of Afrikaner political intelligentsia, was the nucleus of the Afrikaner Nationalist movement

*Broek*s – pants, trousers (slang) [from Afrikaans *broek* (singular), *broeke* (plural)]

Broekies – girls' underwear, panties

Bult – knoll, hill [Afrikaans]

Burger's Hoop – Citizen's Hope [Afrikaans]

Buya lapa – Come here! [Fanakalo; from Zulu *buya* – to go back; *lapha* – here]

Dagga – marijuana

Dof – stupid [Afrikaans]

Dominee – minister, clergyman [Afrikaans]

Donder – beat up, bash, thrash (slang); bastard, bugger (slang) [Afrikaans]

Dop – drink (alcohol) [Afrikaans, informal]

Dorp – small town [Afrikaans]

'Dr Malan' – by Dorothy Masuka (1956), released by Troubadour Records. The song was critical of the then Prime Minister and was subsequently banned

eGoli – Johannesburg [Zulu]

Eina – sore (slang) [Afrikaans]

Eish! – Gosh! (exclamation) (slang)

Engels – English [Afrikaans]

Fanakalo – South African *lingua franca* used on the mines (also Fanagalô or Fanagalo)

Gat – arse (vulgar slang) [Afrikaans]

269

Gemors – mess, hash, a pig's ear, a dog's breakfast (slang) [Afrikaans]

GMTS – Government Mining Training School

Goofies – swimming pool, swimming baths (slang)

*Gooi*ed – threw (slang) [from Afrikaans *gooi* – to throw] – pronounced with a guttural 'g'

Grils – shivers, the creeps (slang) [from Afrikaans *gril* – to shiver, shudder] – pronounced with a guttural 'g'

Gwebu – froth; home-brewed alcoholic beverage, moonshine

Gyp – cheat (slang)

Hamba! – Go! [Zulu]

'*Hamba Nontsokolo*' – by Dorothy Masuka and the Golden Rhythm Crooners (1953), released by Troubadour Records. Translates approximately as 'End The Suffering', became one of the greatest hits of the Fifties

Hoesing – coughing (slang) [from Afrikaans *hoes* – to cough]

Hoggenheimer – a cartoon character that appeared in Afrikaans newspapers around the Great Depression, obviously Semitic and anti-Afrikaner

Hout kop – wood head (derogatory slang for black Africans) [Afrikaans]

Imbongi – praise singer and composer [Zulu]

Impi – army [Zulu]

'*Indoda Yempandla*' – the lyrics '*Pasopa Indoda Yempandla*' translate from a mixture of *flytaal* – street slang – and Zulu) directly as 'Beware Bald One' which was a reference to the then Prime Minister Verwoerd

Ingcosana – little one [Zulu]

Isigingci – guitar [Zulu]

Izingoma – songs [Zulu]

Izinja – dogs [Zulu]

Ja – Yes [Afrikaans]

Jameson Raid – (29 December 1895 – 2 January 1896) was a botched raid on and coup against Paul Kruger's Transvaal Republic carried out by British colonial statesman Leander Starr Jameson and his Rhodesian and Bechuanaland policemen. It was an inciting factor in the Boer War and the Matabele War in Rhodesia

Jisis / jislaaik – gee whiz, wow, yikes (slang) [Afrikaans] – pronounced 'yus-us' / 'yus-like'

Jol – party (slang) [Afrikaans]

Kaalgat – bare backside (coarse slang) [Afrikaans]

Kafferboetie – nigger lover (derogatory) [Afrikaans]

Kak – shit (vulgar) [Afrikaans]

Kennetjie – (tip)cat (game) [Afrikaans]

Kêrels – fellows, chaps; boyfriends [Afrikaans]

Klap – smack, slap, clout [Afrikaans]

Kraal – traditional rural homestead, incorporating a corral or stockade for livestock

Krul – curl [Afrikaans]

Kuif – fringe; quiff (slang) [Afrikaans]

Kwaito – a contemporary form of urban South African music, a blend of hip-hop with American house music, especially house and techno, and pop, dominated by a pounding bass beat

Kwela (*kwela-kwela*) – a form of urban African music from the 1950s, syncretically composed of traditional, *marabi* and American swing-jazz elements; police van; climb in [from Zulu *kwhela* – to climb in]; get up!

Kyk – look [Afrikaans]

Lag – laugh [Afrikaans]

Laities – lighties, kids [Afrikaans, derived from English *lighties*]. Alternatively spelled *Laaities* and was more commonly pronounced with the Afrikaans '*ai*' or '*aai*'

Langlaagte – Long Valley [Afrikaans]

Lat – switch, stick, cane [Afrikaans]

Lekker – nice, enjoyable, fun [Afrikaans]

Lobola – bride price [Zulu]

Location – obsolete official and colloquial designation for an authorised African residential area

Madala – old [from Zulu – *dala* – aged]

Mahala – free, gratis [Zulu]

Makhulu – grandmother [Zulu]

Malta Bela – sorghum porridge

Mampara – fool [Fanakalo]

Mampoer – home-brewed (peach) brandy, moonshine [Afrikaans]

Maningi tshik – very insolent [Fanakalo; from Zulu – *ningi* – plentiful; English 'cheek' (phonetic spelling)]

Manyano – womens' prayer group

Manzi – water [Fanakalo; from Zulu *amanzi*]

Marabi – a pan-ethnic urban African working-class style of music popular in the 1920s and 1930s

Marashea/MaRussia (corrupted from AmaRussia) – name of the proletarian Sotho urban criminal gangs that began as vigilantes but evolved into violent social predators; suppressed by the police during the 1950s, but existed until the 1990s

Meisietjie – little girl [Afrikaans]

Mfana wam – my boy [from Zulu *umfana* – boy; *wami* – my (poss)]

Mielies – maize

Miggies – midges; gnats (slang) [from Afrikaans *muggie*]

Mlungu ka lo guvment – government official [Fanakalo; from Zulu *umlungu* – a white person; English 'government' (phonetic spelling)]

Moer in – pissed off (with) (vulgar slang) [from Afrikaans *die moer in*]

Moerse – helluva (slang) [Afrikaans]

Mokhukhu – male choir and dance chorus in the Zion Christian Church

Molôi – witch [Northern Sotho]

Morara – potent home-brewed wine

Mpasopi – supervisor [Fanakalo; from Afrikaans *pasop* – watch it/out; beware]

Muti – traditional medicine or cures [from Zulu *umuthi*]

Mynpacht – mining rights

Nats – The National Party

Nederlandse Gereformeerde Kerk (NG Kerk) – Dutch Reformed Church

Nooit – never [Afrikaans]

Ntate – Father

*Ntshontsha*s – thieves [corruption of the Fanakalo/Zulu *ntshontsha* – to steal]

Oom – uncle, respectful form of address for an older man [Afrikaans]

Opfok – fuck-up (coarse military slang for a drill) [Afrikaans]

Ou – old [Afrikaans]

Panga – machete

Passop – Beware; Watch it/out [Afrikaans]

Pata-pata – touch-touch dance [from Zulu *phatha* – hold, touch]

Piepe jollers – teeny-boppers

Pikinin – child (apprentice) [Fanakalo]

Poep – shit (coarse slang); chicken, shit scared (coarse slang) [Afrikaans]

Poephol – arsehole (coarse slang) [Afrikaans]

Rinderpest – cattle plague, an infectious viral disease of cattle, buffalo and other wildlife species

Sangoma – traditional healer, herbalist, diviner, witch-doctor, shaman

Shebeen – speakeasy

Shumba – beer

Sis! – Gross! How revolting! (slang)

Skaam – bashful [Afrikaans]

Skaapstert – sheep's tail [Afrikaans]

Skeef – crooked, askew; to give someone a dirty look (slang) [Afrikaans]

Skelm – a shifty or dodgy person (slang) [Afrikaans]

Skokiaan – home-brewed alcoholic beverage, typically brewed over one day, possibly containing dangerous ingredients, such as methylated spirits, moonshine

Slang – snake [Afrikaans]

Slapgats – slackers, quitters (coarse slang) [Afrikaans]

Slim – clever [Afrikaans]

Sommer – for no particular reason, just, merely; immediately; without further ado, straight off [Afrikaans]

Spaza shop – informal general trader

Stink gat – stink hole; long drop, outhouse [Afrikaans]

Stoep – veranda [Afrikaans]

Stokvel – a working class rotating credit association, principally for women, with social functions

Styf – stiff, tight [Afrikaans]

Tekere – crazy, wild (slang) [from Afrikaans *gaan tekere* – to run riot, run amok]

Tikit – work ticket; certificate (qualification) [Fanakalo]

Tokoloshe – a mythical creature; brown, hairy and dwarflike; largely mischievous, but malevolent under the influence of a witch (note the redundant variant spelling of the musical production 'Tikoloshe')

Tsaba-tsaba – a syncretic style of African urban music blending African melody and rhythm, American swing, and Latin American conga and rumba, used to accompany the *tsaba-tsaba* dance

Tshisa – hot; burn [Fanakalo, from Zulu *shisa* – burn; set alight]

Tshisa lo hol – Fire! (Ignite the charge)

Tshisa stik – slow burning fuse igniter [Fanakalo; from Zulu *shisa* – burn; set alight; English 'stick' (phonetic spelling)]

Tsotsi – gangster [Tsotsitaal; from English 'zoot suits']

Tsotsitaal – black urban dialect; ghetto slang or patois (also *flytaal*; has evolved into *isicamtho*)

Tune – chirp, back chat, cheek (slang)

Utshwala – sorghum beer [Zulu]

Vastrap – quickstep (dance) [Afrikaans]

Velskoene – rawhide shoes (literal: veld shoes) [Afrikaans]

Vlei – marsh [Afrikaans]

Voetsek – bugger off, get lost, sod off, piss off (coarse) [Afrikaans]

Voorhuis – front room (literal: front house) [Afrikaans]

Voortrekker – pioneer [Afrikaans]

Voortrekker Hoogte – Pioneer Heights (monument)

Vrots – old geezers, old gits [from Afrikaans *vrot* – rotten]

*Vry*ed – made out, necked, felt up, groped (slang) [from Afrikaans *vry* – to pet]

Wenela – corruption of the acronym WNLA – Witwatersrand Native Labour Association

Woes – wild, savage; fierce, furious, ferocious [Afrikaans] – pronounced 'vuus'

Zam-Buk – Zambuk Ointment – a local brand of herbal antiseptic balm or salve